This novel will take you on a journey that taps
into information held in the invisible quantum
energy field.

New perspectives thrive here.

Solutions can be found for personal mysteries and
life challenges.

Usually, the 'energy conversations' feel like play.

Sometimes they take unexpected turns.

They always intrigue and pull us into a
dimension often left unexplored.

~ Jeanne

Other Books by Jeanne McElvaney:

Ignite Changes Using Energy
A Guide for Letting Go of Old Thinking

Spirit Unbroken: Abby's Story

Time Slipping

Old Maggie's Spirit Whispers

Light in the Shadows

One ~ Nora

Nora's dream slithered into her sound sleep like a serpent. Arriving as a cozy collage of summer fun with a childhood friend, it gave no indication it was a shapeshifter.

Nora and Julie drank root beer and played Parcheesi.

They rode bikes and walked up the alley dragging sticks behind them to mark the soft dirt with squiggles.

When they got to Nora's bedroom and shut the door, they were in a giggly, wonderful world of their own. This was where secrets were shared while they played with dolls. Sprawled on her bed reading comic books, Nora felt the shift begin.

Playful sunlight dimmed and slipped away.

Julie disappeared.

The bed moved into the corner of the room.

Empty, colorless walls framed an alarmingly bare floor.

Shadows from a solitary, overhead light bulb crawled toward the bed.

Dread took root, and Nora was scooting away from the ominous silence when she saw the rug. Rolled up along the far wall, it sent immobilizing fear through her.

"Nora, Nora! Hey! Wake up, Babe!" Adrenaline exploded, igniting Luke's body as he reached for his wife across the gray flannel sheets. Half asleep and groping in the late night shadows, he found her shoulder. He couldn't tell if he shouted or whispered, "Are you okay?"

Still trapped in the dream that was stealing her soul, Nora heard the question. Her heart pounding, she couldn't respond.

Panic, creeping out of a deep place within, pinned her to the soft mattress. It shut out the moonlight that filtered through the pepper tree and danced on her grandmother's quilt.

Vivid and contained, this dream was a distorted, distant relative of a nightmare. It had branded her and, even now, continued its slow burn.

Irritation covered Luke's lingering fear as he sat up to look at his wife. Her eyes were open. "You made a sound that came out of the bowels of a beast. The hair on my neck is still standing up."

Nora stared at her husband. She started to reply, but the words were trapped in the unnerving silence still seeping from the rolled-up rug she'd seen.

Luke reached out, rubbed her bare arm. This middle of the night invasion was beyond his experience. Relief, like finding water after crossing a desert, had him leaning closer when Nora quietly spoke. "What was the sound?"

Luke tried repeating what had woken him. Shook his head in defeat. "It came from deep in your throat... a high-pitched wail. Strangled and smothered. What happened?"

Nora rubbed her eyes trying to remove the lingering images. "I need to move." She grabbed the edges of the covers, struggling to pull them off.

Concern surging, Luke watched as Nora sat up and gingerly placed her feet on the soft, warm carpet. He tracked her slow, uncertain path around the end of the bed, past the dresser, and into the bathroom. He listened to her turn on the faucet.

Through the doorway, Luke could see her standing over the sink with the water running through her fingers. The only movement was her silky, yellow nightgown, caught by the breeze from the open window.

"What's happening here, Nora? What do you need?"

Nora looked in the mirror above the sink wondering if she looked the same. She wasn't sure. Found she didn't care and reached for the towel to dry her hands. "I had a weird dream. For some reason, I can't shake it off."

Walking back to Luke's side of the bed, she crawled under the covers to find the comfort he gave so easily whenever Nora allowed herself.

He pulled her close. Tucked the quilt around her shoulders. She was shivering from the cool night air... or the dream. He couldn't tell. "Can you remember it?"

"Oh, yes. Every detail. How it moved from a hazy dream, playing with a friend to… I don't know. The first part was like looking at old photos with softened edges. Then it changed."

Nora snuggled in closer. Found the sweet spot in the crook of his neck. "I was playing with Julie, my childhood friend from grade school. We were hanging out, doing the kind of stuff we did back then."

Luke listened as his wife described the entire dream, expecting unspeakable images. None of the details matched her deep distress or the horrifying sound she'd made. He tried logic. "Dreams always bounce around like that. You're in one place and suddenly something else is happening."

Nora pushed away. "This didn't 'bounce around.' It melted. Became darker while everything shifted into a menacing threat. There was no sound."

Luke listened carefully, catching every detail of something he couldn't understand.

"Slow motion," she murmured. "The silence and slow motion…"

He didn't interrupt. Her words hung in the air.

The soft bed, soft light, soft love didn't soothe. Billowing frustration urged tears, but Nora refused to surrender. "The walls, the silence, the shadows. Everything… felt so dark. But the rug was the worst. It turned my bones to ice."

"The rug? Just seeing a rug? Why was that terrifying?"

"I don't know!"

Her hand kneaded his chest, seeking something solid. "It was a big roll on the far side of the room. Something you'd see if someone was getting ready to lay carpet. Nothing happened with the rug. It just sat there, but every time I see it… even now… I feel panicky. Like something's going to happen. I can't shake the feeling."

Nora moved out of his embrace. Sat up. "Talking isn't helping."

"What do you want to do?"

"I have no idea."

That's what she said, but Nora felt like yelling. She wanted a roaring fight. She'd love to be in the courtroom nailing some lying son-of-a-bitch who was trying to get away with something. Or standing up to a bastard who abused his child and then thought he could get custody with his Sunday smile for the judge.

"How about a middle-of-the-night movie?" Luke suggested. "Would that be a good diversion?"

That was her husband's go-to distraction, not hers, but Nora nodded. "As long as it's boring. I don't want any drama."

Nora grabbed her chenille bathrobe. She pulled their pillows and the quilt off the bed, and they headed to the living room.

Four hours later, morning found them back in bed, tangled up in their flannel sheet and blanket. Luke turned off the alarm clock, rolled over, and realized Nora was wide awake, laying on her side, staring out the French doors.

"It's going to be a rough day," he murmured. "Are you in court?"

Nora continued watching the sun delete the nighttime shadows in their backyard. "No, thank god. Mostly prep. A few appointments this afternoon."

Luke began massaging her shoulders. "Do you think you could reschedule them and stay home?"

"I could go in late. Why?"

"Might want to give yourself a break here." Luke knew it was a useless suggestion, but couldn't help himself.

Nora notoriously pushed herself. She filled her calendar, added post-its when something else came up, then embraced spur-of-the-moment requests that just couldn't be ignored. She showed up and got things done.

No matter what.

Tired didn't count.

A bad dream wouldn't even register.

It made her the best divorce attorney you could find if you wanted custody of your children.

Nora crawled out from under the shoulder rub and headed for the bathroom. "You might be right. I feel like an earthquake tossed me into a rift, and I'm still looking for myself."

The mirror confirmed her impression. "Looks like I'm putting up a good struggle."

Luke followed, turning on the shower as she patted the skin around her eyes trying to decide which of her products would work best.

"So what happens now?" He stepped into the warm stream of water. "Does the dream go away? Do we have something more here?"

"Maybe one of my cases is getting to me."

"You have a hotly contested custody battle over a rug?"

Nora felt humor teasing her lips, but the haunting weight of the image of that rug doused it. She plopped on the toilet.

Luke shampooed his hair to the everyday sound of his wife peeing. When he stepped out of the shower to dry off, she still hadn't moved.

"I've been thinking about my uncle."

"Something about the toilet bringing this up?"

"No, I mean he's been on my mind these past few weeks. He was my favorite uncle, you know."

Luke reached over and closed the window. "So you've said."

"Did I tell you he liked to rebuild cars? A side-job when he wasn't working at Dad's garage."

The strange night was turning into a weird morning. What seemed apparent wasn't. What sounded normal felt out of place.

"So you've been thinking about your uncle...?"

"Snippets from the past keep interrupting my thoughts. Catch my attention for no apparent reason."

Wrapping a towel around his waist, Luke rubbed the fog off the mirror with his hand. He did it every morning. And almost as often, Nora told him it would leave smudges, and he should use the hand towel.

Today, she just watched. "The dream is connected. There's something there. My gut's telling me one leads to the other while logic laughs. Pretty sure I'm being overly dramatic."

Luke grabbed the toothpaste and his brush. "You? You're many things my feisty, determined wife, but no one could accuse you of being overly dramatic. Painfully organized. Logical to a fault. Not dramatic."

He put the toothpaste on his brush and opened his mouth, as though he had cleared up that issue.

Nora pulled on the toilet paper, lost in thought. "I'm going to make some espresso."

That, more than anything, told Luke his wife was deeply bothered. Her morning routine never deviated. Before heading to the kitchen, she showered and got dressed. The bathroom was wiped down, the bed made, and her nightgown hung on the hook in the closet, while he was reminded to pick up his clothes.

9

Two ~ Nora

Luke smelled his raisin bagel in the toaster and heard the espresso machine hissing as he came down the hall, wondering if he should cancel his appointments. It would be a mess for his receptionist, but she had a knack for soothing mothers when it came to their kids' appointments. The nice thing about children's dentistry was infrequent emergencies. He could stay home.

Typically, his wife stood at the counter and had two cups of espresso with a series of text messages for breakfast. Today Nora sat at the kitchen table without her favorite cup. Rolling the corner of the placemat in front of her, she stared at the vase their youngest daughter had made in a high school five years ago.

Luke planted his hand on Nora's shoulder, kissed the frown on her forehead. "I thought I might call in and cancel my appointments."

"Why would you do that?"

"As incredible as it might sound, you don't seem your usual self. I thought I'd stick around and see what happens. Be here just in case."

Nora smoothed the corner of the placemat and gave her husband *the look*. She would not be moved on this. "I'm fine. Just thinking about things. You don't need to mess up your day."

"Are you sure? Cause I'd like a good reason to play hooky after last night."

"Really. It's no big deal. I feel more distracted than upset. I'll just take the morning off and get back into the swing of things." Nora shifted in her chair. "Let me put some peanut butter on that bagel, so you won't be late."

"Coffee sounds done. Are you are ready for a cup?"

"Sounds good. Hey, maybe we could start a new morning routine. I schlep out here, plop myself down at the table, and you do the rest." She smiled as her husband moved to the toaster, shaking his head, chuckling.

"I'd like to see the day when you schlep, relax, or let me take charge of the morning."

Nora was finishing her second cup when Luke left for work. She carried her third cup out the French doors off their bedroom where the sun liked to linger. Rarely used, even on the weekends, the deck was everything she needed this morning.

Normally, Nora would have ignored the sunbathing flowers and immediately started a mental list of things she needed to tell the gardener. Today, she looked over the rim of her cup and stared past the colorful serenity.

Her thoughts felt like an over-filled junk drawer: messy, tangled, disorganized.

If you're going to understand what happened, you need to think this through, Nora admonished herself.

Focusing on a yellow rose bud, she sighed, crossed her legs and wished she'd put on her slippers. She pulled up the collar of her bathrobe and reprimanded herself for getting distracted. *You can do this. Start with Uncle Neil.*

Why has he been on my mind lately?

Because someone reminded me of him?

Nora shook her head immediately and moved on.

Because of the client who collected cars and tried to hide them as an asset?

That didn't feel right.

Because Uncle Neil died last June?

But I haven't seen much of him since fifth grade. I didn't even go to his funeral.

A butterfly danced in the air, swooped upward, and slipped away. Nora followed its path and speculated.

I wonder when I stopped feeling close to him. Can't remember when it happened. Or why. That's strange. Isn't it?

Nora shrugged off the shiver that went down her spine.

She wished her dad were alive so she could talk to him about why she and Uncle Neil had grown apart. He'd remember, or they'd have a great conversation trying to figure it out.

Her dad had always been straight-up with her. She'd known where she stood with him and what was going on, even when they butted heads. Nora respected and needed that kind of honesty.

It was so different with her mom.

11

Caroline always said what others wanted to hear. Her opinions were locked up as tight as the Crown Jewels. She was milquetoast with a smile, moving every conversation to neutral. Everyone around her considered her a lovely person.

Nora didn't agree.

She'd been in grade school when she decided her mother wasn't so much nice as she was dishonest. Her withheld thoughts and feelings had the power to hurt. Her evasions gave Nora nothing to lean on as she faced childhood challenges.

Now Nora cut her mom a little slack. She accepted her cop-outs, but didn't like being around it. During their superficial, occasional conversations, she held her temper when her mom didn't give her a straight answer. About anything. Even a question of where they would meet for lunch was irritating.

Nora sometimes imagined saying, "Well, when you decide what you want to eat, give me a call." Instead, she gritted her teeth and arranged their lunch date to fit conveniently into her own schedule. She ignored sporadic feelings that she was riding roughshod like her dad.

In a sudden spurt of determination, Nora stood up and headed back to the kitchen. Her mom was going to get a surprise weekday call from her only daughter. Nora was going to put the witness of her childhood on the stand and question her.

After grabbing her phone off the counter, she went to the cabinet that held snacks. Nora was pretty sure there was a new container of gingersnaps, and they would be a great help during the conversation.

Setting the container on the placemat in front of her, she opened the lid and speed dialed.

"Mom, is this a good time to talk?"

"Nora?" Everything okay? The kids? Are they alright?"

"Yes. We're all doing grand. I just took the morning off and thought I'd give you a call. I had a question about Uncle Neil."

"Neil? I'm sure you know everything about him that I know."

"But you knew him in a different way. I was just a kid who loved her uncle but didn't really know him. For a while there, he was a big part of my life. Remember that?"

"Sure. Remember the year I got sick, and he took you to see Santa?

"He was around a lot, wasn't he?"

"Oh, yes. He and your dad were thick as thieves. From their childhood, I think, probably because their mom died when they were so young."

"Did you like Uncle Neil?"

"What?"

"Did you like him? Uncle Neil?"

"He was my brother-in-law."

"Mom, I'm wondering if I would have liked him if I had met him now and he wasn't my uncle. Was he the kind of person I would have enjoyed?"

Nora's mother didn't hesitate. "Oh, you like just about everyone."

"I don't like everyone. Being pleasant or friendly doesn't mean you especially like someone." Nora's patience was already starting to slip. She tried another tack. "When I was a kid, I liked him coming over to the house. Did you?"

"He was family."

Nora didn't know what she wanted to hear from her mom, but she knew she wanted to reach through the phone and shake her. Ask her to have a damned opinion. Say he was a saint or an asshole. A dolt. Did he donate to Greenpeace? Anything!

She felt the familiar band tightening across her forehead and struggled to keep her voice even. "Did he stop coming around when he married Susan? I don't remember her being around a lot."

"She was a quiet one."

"Did you like her?"

"You know she's offering beginners belly dancing at the senior center. The poster says it's for exercise."

"You going to sign up?" Nora knew the answer but wanted to hear her mother's excuse.

"No. It's not for me." Nora heard aversion ooze off every word. Something shriveled between them. The band tightened. Expecting honest thoughts was like trying to see the wings of a hummingbird in flight. You knew the wings were there, but you were never going to actually see them.

Nora grabbed a gingersnap, popped it into her mouth, chewed twice before swallowing. "Mom, I was close to Uncle Neil when I was in grade school. Then he dropped out of my life. Do you think he got busy... racing cars? Did he have a fight with dad? What do you think happened?"

13

"Things change. It's part of life."

Nora gave up. "Yeah. Well, thank you, Mom. You have a nice day. I have to get off the phone and call my office."

"Oh. Okay. Give the girls a hug for me the next time you see them."

Nora tapped her phone to hang up. Reaching into the tub of cookies, she took a handful. Shaking her head, she gulped back the unexpected… the *unacceptable* emotion roaring through her.

Feeling alone made no sense.

Five gingersnaps without taking a breath didn't stop the threatening tears. Brushing them away, Nora reached behind her to grab a kleenex. *There's no reason for this. Nothing happened. I had a dream. I was thinking about Uncle Neil. So what?*

So what if my clueless mother didn't have any insights?

What the hell. It doesn't even matter.

I just need a shower.

Snapping the lid shut on the cookies, Nora dialed her office.

"Nora Ruben's office. This is Sally. Please leave your name and phone number, and we'll get right back to you."

The answering machine had more personality than her mom. It was a voice and attitude that made the office a safe haven for clients in the throes of divorce. Nora made sure the legal system served her clients, but her compassionate receptionist was equally effective in getting them through rough choices and challenging changes.

Leaving a short message about staying home to get some work done, she told Sally not to call unless it was critical. She'd be in for the one o'clock appointment.

Now, it's time for that shower. Time to get this day back on track.

Setting out her clothes and turning on the water, Nora made a mental list of what she could accomplish on her iPad before she went into work. If she could get the Swanson case lined up, she'd hit the weekend without that particular mess hanging over her head.

Stepping into the warm water, Nora wondered if the Swanson home-study had given her the ammunition she needed. She was determined to protect the two daughters who were being abused.

Scrubbing shampoo into a thick lather, she was lining up her arguments like soldiers when tears broke through. They hesitated only a moment… and then took charge.

14

All thoughts about the young Swanson girls washed away with the shampoo as Nora stuck her head under the water. She stiffened against the emotions assailing her... swarming fear... billowing vulnerability. And most of all, appalling loss of control.

She reached for the bar of soap and turned away from the stream of water that seemed to be melting her core of strength. Slowly, it pushed her to the floor of the shower, and she submitted. Tears rained on the tiles. They washed down the drain as Nora grabbed her usual life raft: angry resolve.

Three ~ Nora

Nora's one o'clock client was new and probably wouldn't notice her tear-wounded eyes, but Nora was sure Sally had a dozen questions. She also knew her receptionist would never ask. They had worked together for years and, while Sally chatted easily about her own private life, both women knew Nora did not.

With gentle grace, Sally followed Nora into her office and moved the afternoon into their usual routine.

iPads in hand, they settled into chairs that were a mix-and-match of different floral patterns.

Sally got the ball rolling. "Looks like Sophie Carmine is a good fit for the Amanda Fund."

"We've got room?"

"She'll push us to our pro bono limit, but she's a mouse ready to roar. You'll like working with her." Aware that her arrow of enthusiasm hadn't found a target, Sally continued. "I think she felt reassured when I asked her to bring her sons. She's definitely overwhelmed right now."

Sally looked down at her notes, instinctively giving Nora privacy when she saw her boss's eyes tear up.

Taking a deep breath, raising her chin, Nora looked around her office and felt comforted. She loved the purple sofa piled with pillows that clients often hugged. "We'll do whatever we can to ease her burden."

From the moment Sally returned to her desk, Nora didn't have a moment to spare. Calls came in. Back-to-back clients needed her full attention. Emails had to be answered.

But Nora made her last client wait while she placed an important phone call.

After her morning shower, while she paced, resisted, ranted, and then accepted her feelings, she kept thinking about Carly Pedersen.

When Nora had worked with this client, she had deemed her a bit strange. Carly, herself, laughed about being 100% "woo woo."

Nora thought that also described the energy detective Carly had used during her divorce proceedings. With the unorthodox Ivy Clemens, Carly had discovered her husband was a bigamist. Further research confirmed his activities, and he was forced to sign the divorce agreement Nora had drawn up.

By the time Nora was dressed for work, she had decided to call Ms. Clemens. It wasn't practical. Didn't even seem reasonable. But it offered hope.

Four ~ Nora

Luke was drinking a glass of wine, scanning the *Press Democrat,* when Nora flew through the door. She was beyond hungry. Lunch had bowed to her roller coaster emotions. "Let's beat the Friday crowd at Antonia's."

"I'm ready. The wine can wait for dessert."

Nora laid her briefcase on the end of the counter. "We'll have them box up a couple of pieces of cake to-go."

"Chocolate cake it is." Luke grabbed his fleece vest off the hook next to the door.

During the short drive to Antonia's, neither of them mentioned the dream or how Nora's day had gone. Both knew it best to let her take the lead, even if Luke was burning with questions.

He focused on the traffic, glancing now and then at his wife for clues.

Nora gazed at the purple hair on the teenager at the crosswalk, the apple blossoms more profuse than earlier in the day, and the rhythm of her community as it reached for the weekend.

Antonia's had been a family favorite when she was a child. It still commanded the corner next to the music shop, and Nora could feel her dad's presence every time she walked through the heavy double-doors. Tonight, nostalgia mingled with sounds and smells she could taste.

While waiting for their favorites, carbonara for Nora and seafood linguine for Luke, a plate of garlic-soaked, buttery bread captured their attention. Nora savored each bite as Luke spun a story about his dental patient, Tommy Smith. The eight-year old could not be cajoled to open his mouth until Luke bribed him with another story about the mystery-solving rabbit, J.P. Wigglybop, and his horse, Straight Away.

Nora was pleasantly distracted by Luke's story until the waiter poured their wine and the waitress had served their meals. Then the dark wood paneling and low-hanging stained-glass lamps wrapped around her. As Dean Martin sang, "That's Amore," Nora leaned forward to tell Luke about her day.

"This morning didn't go well. I shouldn't have called my mom."

"You called your mom?"

"About Uncle Neil."

Luke had expected a trail of logic, an outline of thoughts. A call to her mother was going completely off-script. "How do your dream and your mom fit together?"

"I told you this morning. Uncle Neil's in there somewhere. But I got nothing from mom. Zip. Zilch."

She massaged her left temple. Laughter erupted several tables away. "I cried."

Nora looked at her husband, knowing those two words gave him more information than any conversation. "Went to the shower to put that crappy dream aside and ended up sobbing on top of the drain."

Luke reached across the table to take her hand.

Nora reached for her wine glass, dodging his concern, avoiding his sun shining on her shade-seeking self. "It wasn't the kind of morning I wanted. My paperwork on the Swanson case went down the tube, so I'll have to work on that this weekend."

Luke watched his wife sip her wine. "That's it? All done with the dream?"

It was a challenging question… the kind Nora liked.

She set her glass down and reached for her fork. Played with the pasta. "No. Not done." She met her husband's stare. "Definitely not done."

Luke raised his brow. Tipped his head. Waited.

"There's no way in hell I'm going to let this dream run my life. I'm going to find some answers."

"How does that work?" Luke glanced down at his food to start eating, but his wife had his complete attention.

"Remember the Pedersen case from a few months ago? That client worked with a woman right here in town to find information. "I made a call this afternoon, and I'm going to be seeing Ivy Clemens Wednesday morning. Sally cleared my calendar."

"A private eye?"

"Sort of. She's an energy detective." Nora's voice was determined. Shaky.

Luke set his fork down and reached for his wine. Taking a slow drink, he focused on his wife's flushed face. Nora didn't do things lightly. "I think this is going to get interesting."

Five ~ Paul

Petting her dog's curly, blonde head, Ivy let Spirit know when she was leaving the house. "Going to work."

With *Princess Di eyes* fixed on Ivy, Spirit's ears flattened. She turned right, heading for the comfort of her bed.

Ivy stepped out the kitchen door. The sound of the latch signaled a complete shift in her thoughts as she focused on her upcoming appointment. Geraniums along the short path to the barn failed to grab her attention. Earlier in the day, they had stopped her in her tracks.

At the barn, Ivy stepped through the leaded-glass door, bringing the sunshine with her. She turned off her cell phone and laid it on the wide windowsill. Anyone calling would have to leave a message. For the next hour and a half, Paul Bascom would have her complete attention.

Flipping the light switch, Ivy stepped out of time and stood in front of the picture window overlooking the small meadow. She looked past sun-drenched wildflowers and into the gathering storm of feelings and insights she was exploring with Paul. She let their past sessions flow through her.

When she heard the door open behind her, Ivy was ready.

Paul pulled off his hoodie and hung it on the rack. "Hey."

"Hey… isn't Mother Nature giving us a nice day?"

They walked toward each other for a hug. His long, athletic legs no match for Ivy's quick, enthusiastic stride.

"She sure is. Spent a little time riding my bike this morning."

Both smiled, nodded. He had proven the surgeons wrong. When remnants of college football injuries had ambushed his life with back pain, they'd declared surgery the only answer. Paul had walked out of that consultation determined to find another path. Work with Ivy was part of his answer.

Riding his bike was testimony to his daring journey into the energy field to find answers. So was getting back to his drums. Now he wanted to continue exploring. Paul wanted his life to express his authentic self.

It was the kind of journey Ivy had traveled with many others. Since learning everything is energy, she had been on a personal quest to understand just how that affected everyday life. Gathering information felt like a treasure hunt. Creating practical tools and sharing was the treasure.

"How is your back?" Ivy wasn't being simply conversational. She knew physical symptoms were messengers, arriving to enable and encourage personal growth. Paul's back was telegraphing empowering information.

Both sat down on the two leather chairs in front of the fireplace. Paul perched at the front edge, leaning forward, clasping his hands on his thighs. "This morning, I could've ridden my bike all over the place. But, yesterday, my back complained like my mother in one of her piss-and-moan days."

Ivy pulled her footstool closer and put her feet up. "Did you wake up with it hurting?"

"No. It came on after breakfast. Like a nosy neighbor with bad news."

"Tell me about your morning. From the time you got up until your back started bothering you."

Paul settled back in his chair. It was the same one that had felt like a life raft during his first sessions with Ivy. "Nothing much to tell. Picked some berries. Had a call from my mom. Checked my emails."

"Then we've got three clues to check out with energy dialogues. One of those events is very likely connected to your back pain.

"I have a pretty good idea where this is going."

Ivy nodded. "Your family keeps coming up when your back flares."

Paul wasn't ready to go there yet. His silence was the sentinel, holding the conversation at bay.

It wasn't an unusual response. Nearly every client, at one time or another, avoided an issue. Not knowing what would come from finding answers and fearing it would make things worse, they weren't ready to venture out of the shadows and into the light.

Knowing Paul was at the tipping point for exploring the mystery around his mother, Ivy anticipated the rewards he would experience when he dared to go there.

Paul changed the subject. "I got a call last night from a dad who wants his autistic son to start drumming with me."

Ivy moved seamlessly with the change in direction. "Seems you're getting quite a reputation. Parents of special needs kids must be talking about the life-changing experience you offer."

Paul's blush was as endearing as the exaggerated swagger he managed while still sitting in his chair.

Ivy reached out for a high five. Their hands met with a snap, acknowledging his courageous journey to believe he could make money by honoring his spirit and embracing his passion.

"How are you going to celebrate?"

"Pay one of those bills on my counter?"

Ivy slipped her shoes off and pulled her feet up on the chair. "Oh my gosh. We've got to do better than that! Chocolate chip cookies, at least. You want to let the energy field know how much you appreciate what's happening. That's how it knows you want more." Her excitement radiated. "Come on. What can you do to mark this moment?"

"Replace my computer before it dies on me."

"Is that feasible? You want something that's pretty immediate. Something to make you feel on top of the world. That way, it keeps the energy flowing, the wonderful ignited."

Ivy knew he'd take the idea and grow it into something that would serve him. She loved working with him for that very reason. It took one kind of courage to seek life-shifting insights. A very different kind of bravery had to be summoned to weave a tapestry of change.

"Okay. I'm ready. Let's focus on family stuff."

"Sure." Ivy knew he was choosing to explore the most challenging piece of his journey. So far, he knew his back pain was connected to anger. Today she would nudge and see if he was ready to take another bold step. And she would honor the beautiful way his inner wisdom protected him until he was ready.

The young man, who'd been seeing her for three months, couldn't hug when they met. His back throbbed in the good moments, screamed when he dared to bend.

Together, they had begun a gentle, firefly dance of illumination. Each time he followed his inner wisdom, the anger held in his back eased. The pain lessened. Flexibility emerged. Out of dark days, he had made stunning shifts in his life.

Ivy got up and moved around the footstool. "Something just hit me."

Since starting with Ivy, Paul had become adept at *talking to energy*. Anyone could do it, beginning the first time they tried, but confidence came with practice.

He joined her, anticipating the answers they were sure to find. He no longer paid attention to hesitations that occasionally arose. Paul had learned he was safe with Ivy, no matter what they discovered.

"I'm going to set you with two similar energies. By 'set' I mean I'm going to totally focus on one thing, so you can pick up on the energy communication." Ivy settled into place about two feet in front of him. "I want you to see how each one feels, so you'll have a comparison."

Paul nodded. He faced Ivy, closed his eyes, and imagined his usual chatter flowing out of the top of his head. Shrugging his shoulders, he tried to become as neutral as possible.

Paul stayed detached until he felt Ivy approach. He was ready to receive whatever images or feelings came to him. In a familiar pattern, she gently placed her hands on his upper arms. Without speaking a word, her eyes closed, Ivy completely focused on what she wanted Paul to explore at a subconscious level.

She saw him drumming with abandon. No distractions. No clocks. No back pain. She silently thought, *"Paul, his drums, his love for drumming."*

When Ivy felt this energy pouring out of her fingertips and into him, she stepped back and opened her eyes.

Paul's head was nodding up and down. A soft smile spread across his face.

"I was playing," he blurted out as he opened his eyes. "I was a kid on the monkey bars and knew all the moves. I was flying".

Paul couldn't stand still. He pulled off his flannel shirt and tossed it onto his chair. Ignoring the way his faded Fleetwood Mac t-shirt was left askew, he paced, his joy flowed. "That was a great set, whatever it was."

Ivy laughed. "I could see that before you opened your eyes."

"It hit me like a bolt."

"I wanted you to experience different kinds of love." Ivy saw the light go on in Paul's eyes. You just experienced *love and drumming.*

"I gotta say… it's a great kind of love." Using imaginary drum sticks, he gave Ivy an air performance. Head bobbing, torso gyrating, he glowed.

Ivy could almost hear his music. She saw notes bubbling up around him. "Okay, shake it off. I want to set you with another love energy."

Both of them cleared their thoughts and feelings.

Paul closed his eyes and went back to his Zen state of mind.

Ivy moved forward, placed her hands on his arms, and completely focused on love and his mother.

When he opened his eyes, they were bleak. "I saw creatures crawling out of a swamp."

"What did you feel?"

Paul looked over her head, going back to the image. "It was like a sci-fi movie. They're creepy, but you still feel compelled to see what will happen next."

Because he was still staring into space, Ivy waited to see if there was more. There was. "I felt like the creatures would grab me and pull me into the swamp."

Paul didn't like the sensation, but he loved the strength and clarity of energy messages. It was always fascinating to experience the images and sensations that seemed to pop out of nowhere. "What was that love connection?"

"That was how you experience your mother's love."

Paul shook his head. In heaving silence, emotions flashed, a neon sign of pain was recognized and squelched.

Ivy watched him heading toward denial. "You now know two kinds of love and how they feel to you. We often think love is one thing... that we experience the same feeling no matter what we're loving. But it comes in different colors, textures, and sensations. We experience all kinds of love, every day."

"So what do we do now?" Paul wanted to know.

"We have more conversations with energy. Explore. Find more answers. Do you have any direction you want to follow?"

"Not really."

"Then let's do a couple about the different ways you feel about yourself."

"I'm pretty sure I could describe everything that makes me such a great guy."

"And yet," Ivy countered, "talking to energy will take you deeper. You'll get to tap into information beyond your awareness."

"That's what I'm paying you for." Paul's humor matched his curly hair. Both were unpredictable. Appealing.

Amused, Ivy kept focused. "Before we get going, I had an image come through when I was setting you with love and your mother. Something with thick-walls like an airbed. There was a slow leak so it couldn't fully inflate."

Paul tipped his head. Waited.

Sometimes Ivy felt he tipped his head when he was saying, "Show me." or "Prove it to me." Other times, like now, she was sure that expression said, "I'm open. Go for it."

"Like all of us, you have an energy relationship with everything… whether it's a fight with your brother when you were five-years old or something as tangible as a baseball bat." You're constantly sending energy out that connects to every aspect of your life. You're also receiving energy. Everyone has energy going out and coming in, all the time.

"Sometimes it becomes lopsided. So the leak could mean you're consistently giving away your energy to someone or something. It makes it impossible to fill yourself up and feel complete."

Paul didn't like the implication. "So some of my energy is pouring down a drain. That's the shits."

"Not pouring. A slow leak."

Paul growled. "And it's connected to love, this slow leak."

"Let's look for the leak. Do you want to set or should I?

"I'll set. I've got a couple of ideas coming up."

"Okay. Shake off this conversation and let's get started."

One-by-one, Paul set Ivy with possible energy leaks in his life. He explored his finances, procrastination, and spirituality. While each set was interesting to witness, ten minutes went by without finding the leak.

"Your turn," he said to Ivy. "You always come up with good ones."

"I do have some ideas but don't discount what you just set. Finding the answer you're looking for isn't more valuable than the other insights you discover along the way. All of it gives you a new way of looking at what's going on."

"Yeah, I get that, but I want the answer before I leave."

Ivy wanted to hug his volcanic exuberance. "But no pressure, right?" With a quiet giggle, she got them back on track. "Okay, shake off your thoughts, and let's get this ball rolling."

Paul shrugged his shoulders and saw the top of his head opening up to release his thoughts, feelings, and beliefs.

Ivy stepped forward, put her hands on his upper arms and set him with a connection between the energy leak and the young woman he'd dated in college.

He opened his eyes. "Felt like I was on a merry-go-round. It wasn't fun like when I was a kid. More like having a conversation with your grandmother while you wait for the Thanksgiving turkey to get done."

"That was connected to Denise. We've had several conversations about your college sweetheart, and I wanted to see if she was the source. She isn't, but you might want to notice you haven't disconnected that energy and you broke up years ago. You're spending energy on a relationship that's over."

Paul had never thought about it that way.

"And," Ivy added, "if you only have so many hours in the day and only so much energy to give, is that the way you want to use them?"

She watched his face. "There's no right answer. It's about choices. In every moment, whatever you're thinking, feeling, and believing is sending energy forward. Those thoughts, feelings, and beliefs are creating an energy pattern that is making a blueprint for your future. This insight can help you decide if you want your thoughts about Denise shaping your future."

Paul sighed. "Pretty obvious but easier said than done."

"Of course. Insight is always easier than action. If you want to work on it together, let me know, but you're pretty good at finding ways to make changes once you've seen what's not working for you."

Ivy rolled her shoulders. Felt the smooth flow of energy coursing through her body, a current of intuition nudging her. "I have another one when you're ready. We're looking for an energy leak."

"Let's go." Once Ivy set Paul, he closed his eyes and experienced eating a lemon while everyone around him insisted it was lemonade.

"That was your childhood family," Ivy said.

"A no-brainer."

After the next set, Paul exclaimed, "This time, it was pouring rain, flooding my kitchen. I was racing around trying to stop the water. We found the leak, big time. What is it?"

Ivy moved forward as she spoke. "That was your relationship with your mother."

"Shit. Shit! "Wouldn't you know it!"

Paul went to his footstool and sat down.

Ivy sat in her chair.

"Does it surprise you?" she asked.

"No."

"It's a big one, isn't it?"

Paul nodded his agreement and went to the quiet place inside where he consulted with his feelings. He wished he still smoked.

Ivy let the moment float. She knew he was his own Sherlock Holmes when given a clue.

Checking in, Ivy offered a boost. "Information is power."

"You always say that, but I thought everything was settled with mom, when I started establishing those new boundaries with her."

Ivy gave Paul's declaration time to be acknowledged... felt.

The room darkened as a cloud passed over the sun, and she watched him take deep breaths.

She waded in gently. "Big issues are revealed in layers. You discover the first layer and peel it off with awareness, acceptance, and action. And yes, for a while, you feel done. You are done... until you're ready to peel another layer and expand your life again. You must be at the edge of new growth."

"My gut says this is about making money from my creativity. Mom was nagging me about that again when she called yesterday morning."

"Because you're supposed to have a real job?"

Paul's sarcasm oozed, releasing puss of a deep wound. "Something nine-to-five that sucks the life out of you. If you don't bleed, it doesn't count."

"The good news is..." Ivy waited to see if Paul was ready for her optimism.

"Hit me with it. See if it sticks."

"The good news is... we found the leak. Something in your relationship with your mother is creating an energy drain for you.

Paul rubbed the back of his neck. Defeat hovered, offering a cloak of avoidance. He stood up and shook it off. "Another layer, huh? How do we peel this one?"

Ivy mined her instincts, sifting through nuggets of information she knew about Paul. "I'd love to see you write a song that expresses your feelings. It might be a good way for you to explore this leak. Would that work for you?"

His eyes lit up. "Yeah, I'll do that. I can feel it coming already…."

"This isn't about defending yourself. It's not even about your mom. Write something that celebrates you making money celebrating your spirit."

They looked at each other. Both knew celebrating one's spirit was like a first date. It asked you to believe in yourself enough to show up.

Ivy was sure Paul was ready. "Think you can share your song with me next time?"

"You got it. But don't expect an acapella moment."

"Lyrics will be perfect."

Standing up to bring their session to an end, she added, "I look forward to it."

Paul gave his muse a hug. "I love this stuff. Blows me away every time."

"Another love relationship," Ivy murmured. "One that we share."

As Paul walked out the door, Ivy moved to the window and let the vivid insights, images, and feelings from the dialogues settle into a corner of her mind. It was like watching a bouncing ball slowly coming to rest on the floor.

Personal mysteries were uncovered in spurts and starts. Through surprises and serendipity. There were no maps, but Ivy never doubted answers could be found. She knew Paul was on the verge of a personal breakthrough that would ignite his potential.

The people who came to work with her were *explorers*. Some, like Paul, had exceptional courage to slay the dragons hatched in old wounds. Others moved tentatively through the landscape of their subconscious world. All of them learned a new language so they could hear their inner wisdom and the whispers of the energy field.

Ivy was constantly thrilled to be a traveling companion where feelings hid in shadows, yet had so much power to fill lives with light.

Picking up her cell phone, she quickly jotted down a few highlights from the session and headed for her house.

Spirit would be at the back door. The sound of the closing barn door was always her signal.

Tail-wagging, love-infused enthusiasm greeted Ivy. Rubbing, petting, massaging, and cooing, Ivy bumped the door shut with her hip and gave Spirit her complete attention.

"So much happy! Oh my goodness. What can we do with all that joy? Shall we go find Sam?"

Spirit immediately led the way to the front door. Ivy opened the screen and followed her dog down the path of smooth beach glass set in cement. They crossed the driveway and walked toward the small orchard of fruit trees.

Sam looked up from his work when he heard the sharp bark. "Done already?"

"Done and hungry. I was thinking about a Redwood veggie burger. Sound good to you?"

"Great. Just let me finish pulling the nails out of these last boards."

Ivy nodded.

Spirit moved closer to Sam and nudged his hand with her nose.

"Hey there, girl. Want to see what I'm doing?"

Ivy smiled as her husband explained the details of removing the joists on the old shed and saving the wood so he could use it another time. Spirit sniffed the tools, listening to every word.

"Be about fifteen minutes," Sam guessed as he went back to work.

"Sounds good. I'll take Spirit for a short walk while we wait."

Ivy knew she would have to double that estimated time but thought she could make it without getting cranky.

Working with energy burns calories as easily as a Nordictrack, she mused as she headed into the half acre of young trees.

In the past month, blossoms had filled their orchard with colorful fragrance and then been gone as quickly as watermelon at a picnic. This could be the year for a good crop, if the weather continued to be kind.

And that would take Ivy to the precipice of cooking-guilt. She could feel it building already. She imagined the trees gossiping about the terrible waste if no one took time to pick, can, freeze, and use their bounty.

Spirit circled around and sat directly in front of Ivy, requesting more petting. Ivy responded, as her thoughts turned to the new client she would be seeing the following morning.

She had never met Nora Ruben but remembered Carly Pedersen and the mystery they had unraveled some months ago. She did know Ms. Ruben by reputation: smart, dedicated to her work, passionate about protecting women and their children. Ivy was amazed the attorney would be interested in working with energy.

30

Six ~ Nora

Though the country lanes were beautiful, nothing could ease Nora's anxiety as she drove to her appointment with Ivy Clemens. Her dream still held her hostage. Confidence had fled. Dread kept her company.

It'd been a few years since she'd come out this way, but she remembered the sculpture Ivy mentioned when giving directions. The six-foot fairy was memorable. Made of painted junkyard treasures, she had been captured in a moment of wide-eyed anticipation as she dropped a coin into a wishing well.

The fairy announced the turn-off for her appointment. As Nora turned on to the long driveway, the gravel road led her forward like an usher. She wondered what the hell she was doing.

Ivy stood on the path that led from the barn. She liked being visible when clients arrived for their first session. It was an uneasy moment for every one of them. Each, in their own way, was leaping without a net. All came seeking insights but were afraid of the answers.

Ivy knew that getting out of the car sometimes took *Tarzan courage* in a jungle of emotions. If they saw her as they drove up, clients didn't need to wonder if they had the right place or if they were coming to the right building.

As Nora opened the car door, Ivy imagined a shimmering, purple vortex surrounding her new client. She knew the color represented power and believed it made a difference. "You found our driveway."

Nora pulled the strap of her purse over her shoulder. "Your fairy does a good job of pointing the way."

Ivy's smile widened. "It's so much more fun to give directions when you can tell people to turn at the fairy."

Nora didn't respond as they walked together toward the open, barn door, but she was feeling calmer. Ivy's lavender jeans and pink T-shirt soothed her doubts. It was unassuming and ordinary, not the gypsy look she'd expected.

The barn helped too. It was a pleasing mix of open space and old wood. Simplicity was the theme. With a bouquet of white irises on the table by the large window, Nora didn't feel as far from her own reality as she had imagined she might.

Ivy pointed to the hooks and sideboard in the entryway. "You can leave your blazer and purse here or bring them over to the chair. Whatever feels best for you."

Leaving her things at the door, Nora followed Ivy to the chairs in front of the fireplace. "I know your neighbors down the road. Our daughters were best friends."

Ivy didn't have to think about that. "You mean the Johnsons? Both daughters are in college now, if I can trust my sense of time. Mazie use to come over now and then, but I haven't seen her for a while." Ivy settled into her chair. "How's she doing?"

"She's studying psychology. Going for her doctorate."

Ivy's chair hugged her. "I'm not surprised. I'll have to make sure I connect with her the next time she's home."

Though Nora's soft chair didn't embrace her, she was feeling more at ease as she sat down. The connection between the Johnsons and Ivy was further confirmation she hadn't done something completely, over-the-top strange. This was going to be okay. And, surely, getting to the bottom of her dream couldn't take more than one appointment.

"When you called, you said a dream was bothering you. Would you be comfortable sharing it with me?" Ivy asked.

Nora responded with an automatic nod, but her body didn't agree. Her heart beat faster. She felt light-headed. Without realizing it, she put her hand on her chest and gently massaged.

Ivy noticed the distress and knew talking would make Nora feel better. "You can start anywhere. We'll put the pieces together later."

"I'm surprised it bothers me so much. It's just a damn dream."

Ivy put her feet on the footstool in front of her. "It might make you feel better to know there are different kinds of dreams. Those connected to a strong emotion come from an experience trapped in your unconscious.

"Your body's reacting because that's where the intense feelings from your dream are stored. Take a deep breath and tell me what you remember. It'll help you release what you're holding."

The gentle insistence was offered like extra whipped cream on strawberries, but Nora reacted to Ivy's statement. "Emotions are stored in my body?" That was just the kind of woo woo stuff she'd expected.

"Yes. And you'll get more comfortable as you talk about them."

Nora took a deep breath, firmly pushing her misgivings aside. She outlined her dream like she was reading a grocery list… her voice flat, revealing tightly wound emotions to Ivy.

"The dream started out feeling very ordinary. I was young, playing with a friend. Then everything started changing. My bedroom became a different room. My friend disappeared. That's when it got spooky and deadly silent. I felt scared but panic didn't come until I saw the rolled up rug."

Ivy nodded. "It can be incredibly unsettling when everyday images become a haunting presence. It turns our world upside-down."

The hand massaging Nora's heart stilled. "You know what I mean?"

"Yes. I do. Your dream is unique, but you aren't alone in having this kind of experience.

"We get used to having daytime insights about ourselves that nudge us. With nighttime message-dreams, we don't have our emotional guards in place. Our minds are free to create unwanted and impactful images to get our attention.

"To release these message-dreams, you have to intentionally explore the emotions that were ignited. And… you have to find words to describe the images."

"I told my husband about the dream that night, but it's still with me. It didn't help." Nora was very clear on this.

Ivy challenged her assumption. "It did make a difference or you wouldn't be sitting here with me. Sharing your dream with him opened the door."

She watched Nora slowly nod her head. "The next step… what I'm talking about now… is actively, consciously walking back into the dream and looking for details. It goes beyond describing what you experienced."

Ivy leaned forward, gently breaching the protective space Nora was creating between them. "I'm glad you chose to share this journey with me. Very often, instead of releasing the effects of a dream like this, people find ways to manage them. They take the stark images and jolting emotions into the future and continue being affected by them."

Nora pulled her hand from her chest. "My heart isn't beating as fast."

"Good. Would you be comfortable if I asked a few questions? Sometimes we know more than we realize. For instance, where was the rug?"

"On the other side of the room, against the wall." Nora rubbed her hands along her thighs. "Go ahead. You can ask more. I'm ready."

"Good. The more we know, the faster we'll get to your answers."

For the next half hour, the two women worked together to glean as much information as possible.

Nora became increasingly confident as they lined up the facts. She described the sights and sounds, discovering two elements she hadn't noticed before. A single light bulb was hanging from the ceiling... not in a fixture. The bare floor was cement. She wondered if those were significant.

When Ivy began prodding Nora about her feelings during the dream, her confidence melted. She became subdued. Her answers were agitated. Any discussion around the rug and the eerie silence etched Nora's face with deep lines and uneasy eyes.

Ivy noted the changes but didn't point them out or respond. She saw them as powerful clues to be explored at another time, when Nora was ready to investigate using energy.

As much as Ivy was seeking information to help Nora find answers, she also knew her client became increasingly empowered as she scoured the dream for the details. It put her in charge. Instead of feeling attacked, she was declaring her intent to know what was still hiding.

When Ivy felt the dream had been fully explored, she summarized the physical details of the dream to make sure she had them right.

"We have your childhood bedroom shifting from summer fun with a friend into a completely different room. There's a light bulb hanging from the ceiling. A cement floor. Scary silence. A tan, rolled-up rug that creates panic. Bare floor and walls. "Does that cover it?"

Nora nodded.

Ivy rolled her shoulders and shifted in her chair. It was time to talk.

"You mentioned several times that your experience was only a dream. I know you would prefer to dismiss it, but dreams like yours don't just go away. Actually, they come with a message, and they only leave when you understand their significance."

Ivy recognized Nora's complete resistance. Her tension spoke volumes and would make it hard for Nora to hear, but Ivy continued. She knew some of the information would get through.

"This kind of dream isn't common, but it can be identified by specific characteristics you're experiencing.

"It's significant that the dread and panic you felt at the time is still affecting you. The intensity of those fears is holding you captive even now.

"Also, there was lots going on in your dream, but the rolled-up rug stood out with stark clarity. That's a key."

A quick shiver passed through Nora as she remembered it. "What about the silence? That seemed significant to me. It haunts me. I can be standing in line at Oliver's and feel that unnatural stillness crawling up my spine."

Ivy was encouraged by her active participation. "That's part of the dread and panic, I mentioned. In message-dreams, sensations are deeply embedded rather than noted. You can't shake them. The chill you experienced when you saw the rug stays with you. The silence you heard continues to resonate."

Ivy paused a moment. "Did you smell anything?"

Nora immediately shook her head, but her eyes made it clear she was searching her memory. "I feel like there was a smell, but I can't place it."

Ivy waited.

The barn soothed.

As Nora closed her eyes and tried to pick up on the smell, the studio echoed quiet encouragement, but she gave up. Defeated. "It keeps slipping away."

"It's okay. We'll find it. When we start talking to energy, we can track it down. Meanwhile, tell yourself the smell will come when you're ready. Struggling to remember never works."

"What do you mean, 'talking to energy'? Explain that." Nora, the attorney, had just shown up in full force.

"My work is based on quantum physics. On information Einstein set in motion."

Ivy's voice changed. Nora recognized the energy detective was in her element. She wasn't trying to convince or assure. She was simply drawing a map with words.

"Most of us have grown up believing logic, learning, and experience are the only sources of valid facts. Quantum physics has confirmed the energy field is a vibrating, omniscient source of information. And, by its very nature, it's constantly communicating with us. I work with that amazing resource."

"You'll have to explain that." Nora didn't try to temper the sharp demand.

Ivy dove in without hesitation. "We now know that everything is energy. Everything. The chair you're sitting on. Your body. Your beliefs, feelings, and thoughts.

"So, as you sit with me today, you probably see the world through an old lens where some things are solid, like your chair. Other things are abstract, like your feelings. In fact, they are both vibrating molecules of energy."

Ivy brushed her curly, blonde hair away from her face. "We live in an ocean of energy and that drives the way you and I will be finding answers.

"Energy exists outside time so the past, present, and future are all happening in this moment.

"Energy communicates… and that communication is independent of both time and distance."

Ivy knew all of this was a lot to take-in, let alone accept. She just hoped to plant seeds that could blossom into new awareness.

Nora tapped the arm of the chair, struggling with her skepticism. "So I'm not a solid person. I'm vibrating energy, and, not only that, my feelings are also energy."

Ivy nodded and took the conversation to a place Nora might recognize. "You've probably experienced some of this energy communication when you've had déjà vu or felt an immediate connection to someone you just met. Or, as an attorney, I would bet that you sometimes *know* things for no apparent reason. You might have called it instincts or a gut-feeling."

Nora was nodding.

"Have you experienced coincidences that have brought a case together in ways you couldn't have logically figured out?"

Again, Nora nodded.

"Quantum energy explains all of that.

"In my own work, I have found ways to tap into this energy field whenever I choose. I can ask for answers rather than waiting for occasional and unpredictable insights. I call it *talking to energy*."

Ivy leaned forward. "As you work with me, you'll be talking to energy. You'll be learning how to ask questions and recognize the answers. It's like learning a new language, but the techniques can be used by anyone."

Ivy's animation and explanation cut through Nora's hesitation. It was giving her an anchor. "So that's how you think we'll find the significance of the rug in my dream. How can you be so sure?"

"Because the information is stored in your body and your subconscious. It's just a matter of finding the best way to access it."

"With energy," Nora murmured.

Ivy's answering smile had encouraged others as they took this leap into a new view of possibilities. "Yes, by talking to energy."

There was more than a hint of doubt in Nora's voice, but it also carried a note of hope. "Then let's talk to energy."

Ivy was comfortable with her client's misgivings. Though it was a new world for this controlled, compelling woman, it was a landscape Ivy knew intimately. She knew how to cross raging rivers of fear and swim through the ponds of doubt. She knew how to find her way out of the shadows and into the light.

"Before we begin, it's important for you to know that you are ultimately in control. I'm not the one who has your answers. Those are held inside you… in your body and subconscious… as well as in the collective knowledge of the energy field. I know how to help you find your answers, but you'll be pointing the way."

Ivy's conviction animated her words as she continued. "Einstein believed there was just one brain, and all of us were extensions. That's another way of saying there is a pool of limitless knowledge available to everyone. You and I will be going to that pool."

Nora glanced out the window and caught sight of a soaring eagle. She wished for its sharp focus and ability to see with accurate perception. "So the answers will be coming from within me or from an all-knowing source outside me."

"Yes," said Ivy. "I'll be referring to them as your *inner wisdom* and the *energy field*."

Nora felt like she was being led through a maze, blind-folded. It was darkly daunting but also brightly intriguing. "If I'm understanding this, finding the answers will depend a lot on how much I want them. How willing I am to go the whole nine yards."

"That's absolutely true," Ivy confirmed. "I have clients who are sitting on the edge of their chairs, ready to jump into this way of gleaning information. Others sit back, hoping I'll pull them out of the chair. Guess who finds their answers more quickly, clearly, and fully?"

"I'm going to be the client who's off the chair and in your face." Nora's penetrating brown eyes declared war on the last minions of her own doubt. "If I'm going to do this, I'm going to give it my all. And I *am* going to do it. I refuse to have a lurking dream hijack my life. I need to know I can count on my steady emotions."

"Then you and I are going on an adventure," Ivy responded. "We're going to explore your inner world and navigate the ocean of knowledge held in the energy field."

Ivy wanted to jump up and hug the bold woman sitting across from her. Instead, she gave her a promising smile and added, "While we work together, I'll be referring to your *spirit*. By that, I mean what makes you beautifully, wonderfully unique. Your spirit is your undiluted self before you learned to manage life's challenges."

"I like that." Nora sighed and nodded her head.

"I do too." For the first time since meeting Nora, Ivy saw her vulnerable softness.

"Although we often lose track of this burning ember of spirit because of busy lives and challenging events, I believe it holds the blueprint of our potential and life purpose. And, our spirit is in direct communication with our inner wisdom and the energy field. The three of them work together, and we'll be tapping into it."

"I'm ready to go," Nora declared.

"Okay. But first I want to emphasize something important. Your spirit is always, always *for* you. It's your best friend. An ally. When we're working with energy, it's giving you insights and answers that will serve and empower you. Always."

Nora loved Ivy's passion. Here was a woman who could talk about a completely foreign world with clarity and zeal. A woman who didn't apologize or soft-pedal to win her trust. Nora was sure she didn't understand everything about spirit, but she got it enough to move forward.

"We're ready to step into some work. Do you need to use the bathroom before we get started? I do," Ivy said.

"You go first." Nora was glad to have a moment to gather her thoughts.

As the quietude gently wrapped around her, Nora realized she not only liked Ivy, but they were much alike. She used the rigid framework of law while Ivy dipped into realms like spirit, inner wisdom, and the energy field. Both of them avidly believed in what they offered. They were both self-confident, articulate. And their passion was helping others through troubled times.

Now, for the first time in her life, Nora was the one needing help rather than giving it. It wasn't comfortable, but she was 100% sure she'd found the right person.

After the bathroom break, Ivy asked Nora to join her in the middle of the room. "We're going to be moving around now as we have conversations with energy."

As Nora walked away from her chair, she had the sensation of being in two places at one time. She was completely aware of Ivy stepping in front of her, but also felt herself standing on the asphalt of her grade school playground. Nora shook her head against the slapping sound of the long jump rope being turned by two friends.

Ivy's voice interrupted the unexpected image. "Earlier, we talked about those things you *just know,* even though you don't understand why."

"I remember." Nora pushed away the odd sensation that had flashed by.

"I want you to experience that *knowing* in a very conscious way. I'm going to make a series of statements, and I want you to respond to them. For instance, I might say, "Chocolate cake is better than carrot cake.""

"Okay," Nora said.

"But you aren't going to respond verbally. You're going to use movement."

Ivy backed further away from Nora so there was about five feet between them.

"When I make a statement, you'll move toward me if you agree. You'll move backward if you disagree. Let your movement be instinctive.

"Don't think about what I say. Just respond. And respond in a way that honors the strength of your feeling. So if you like chocolate cake more than carrot cake, you might take a step toward me. If you love,

love, love chocolate cake, you might want to sit on my shoulder. I invite you to get right in my face if the statement feels 110% true.

"If you really disagree with my statement, back all the way into the corner. As much as you can, let your body guide your movements. Does this make sense?"

"Don't think about it, just react," Nora confirmed.

"Yes. Perfect. But before we begin, it's important to clear all the thoughts and feelings you're having right now. For instance, you might see yourself as a computer, and you hit the delete button. Some people feel like water washes through their head, taking their thoughts down a stream. One of my friends imagines a gigantic, pink eraser doing the job. I like to shake off my thoughts and feelings… like a dog shaking off water. Anything will work as long as it has meaning to you."

Ivy supported with a smile. "I'll give you a few minutes to think of something that might work for you. When you do find something, clear your thoughts and feelings and let me know by nodding your head. Don't worry if it doesn't work the first time. This is all about learning and practicing."

Nora quickly nodded her head. "I'm ready."

"Okay. Christmas is the best holiday."

Nora took a couple of steps forward.

"Perfect." Ivy assured her. "As I go through these next statements, just let your body move without wondering why or evaluating your response."

Ivy put more space between herself and Nora and said, "Apples are better than oranges."

Nora took one step back.

"Cell phones cause cancer."

She took another step back.

"I can't live without my computer."

Nora laughed as she walked up to Ivy and stood toe-to-toe. "I think this is where I would climb on your shoulders."

Ivy laughed with her. "You're doing great. Are you feeling it in your body, or is your mind still trying to be in control?"

"No. I feel it. I start thinking about it as I take the steps, but my gut-feelings are leading the way."

"Good. You're a natural." Ivy reached out and gently squeezed Nora's arms. "Move back a little, and let's do a few more."

Nora responded to several more statements. Learning the language of energy felt like play, a hopscotch break from emotions. "I'm getting pretty good at this."

Ivy agreed. "I love that you have no hesitation. That means you aren't thinking about it."

Nora liked the sincere praise. She felt surprisingly comfortable as Ivy continued talking. "In the past, you might have described your responses as gut-feelings. I'd like to do a few more of these exercises, but this time, I want you to be aware that we are actually working with energy."

Nora's brow rose in question.

Ivy gently touched her forearm. "Remember, every thought, belief, and feeling is energy. And energy is always communicating.

"This time, I'm going to cup my hands and *hold* the energy. I'll focus on something rather than making a statement. Instead of saying, "Tulips are beautiful," I'm going to hold my hands in front of me, palms up, consciously holding the energy of beautiful tulips." Cupping her hands, Ivy showed Nora what she meant.

"How do you hold energy?" Nora wanted to know.

"Holding energy is another way of saying I'm focusing on something. So I would be completely focused on tulips. I'd think of tulips I've seen. See their colors. I'd feel myself walking in a garden filled with tulips… anything that comes to me that is related to tulips. I might concentrate on the word, tulips."

"When you do that, are you planting thoughts in my head?" Nora had to be sure.

"No. I've cleared out my personal beliefs, feelings, and thoughts. I'm not trying to convince you of anything. My job is to simply hold the energy in the most neutral way possible. Your spirit and inner wisdom will respond to that energy in a way that honors your truth."

Ivy paused, giving space for any other questions, then added, "This will become more clear and solid for you as you experience the information. The pure authenticity becomes evident pretty quickly."

Ivy glanced at the clock. They still had some time. "Let's expand what we've been doing here. This time, I'm going to silently hold the energy rather than using my voice."

"I'm finding that I trust you." They both laughed at Nora's blatant surprise. "Let's go ahead and see what happens."

"You'll do great," Ivy encouraged.

Nora's expression held a good dose of doubt. "So we're doing the same thing. I'm still instinctively responding, but this time, it's nonverbal. I'm aware your cupped hands hold the energy, and I'm either drawn to it or repelled by it."

"Exactly."

Nora gave her shoulders a quick shrug. "I can do this."

"I know you can. Clear your thoughts and feelings, and give me a nod when you're ready."

Eyes closed, Nora imagined looking at a folder on her computer screen labeled Thoughts-Feelings-Beliefs. Then she highlighted it and hit the delete button. Pleased by how well this was working, she nodded.

Ivy responded. "I'm holding the energy"

Nora immediately stepped backward. Then took two more steps back. "That was interesting. My body was completely committed to moving away from that energy, like I was pushed. What did you hold?"

"Women are weak."

Nora's laughter exploded.

Ivy's heart swelled as their amusement mingled.

Each time Nora tried to talk, giggling took charge.

This often happened during sessions, and Ivy treasured it. Exhilaration was the natural extension of connecting to personal truth and feeling free to express it.

They were sharing the soft aftermath when Ivy asked, "Did it feel different that time?"

"It really did. More like an interaction." Nora stared ahead, completely still. "This time it went beyond thought. Became more physical."

Ivy was delighted. "That's a good explanation. And it's true. Your spirit and inner wisdom were interacting with the energy I held. When we use our voice, it's harder to recognize what's happening."

Ivy moved back a step. "Clear your thoughts, and I'll hold another energy."

Cupping her hands and holding the energy she had in mind, she watched Nora close her eyes.

Nora immediately moved back. Her eyes popped open. She was animated. "This is so curious. I felt compelled to move."

"That's because your answer is coming from your inner wisdom. You're standing in your personal truth without logic or past experiences taking charge of your response."

Nora let that sink in. "It feels good. Empowering. I see why it's hard to explain. You almost have to experience it. So what were you holding?"

"Everyone should have children."

"I can see why I stepped back." Nodding, Nora asked for another set.

She backed up again. Turned around and walked toward the bathroom, calling over her shoulder, "Is there a back door?"

"Lots of clarity there," Ivy responded as Nora walked back to the middle of the room to join her.

"What was that about?" Nora's curiosity was on fire. "There was not a shred of doubt in my body. None."

"Children are inclined to lie."

Annoyance chased away all evidence of the laughter Nora had expressed on the previous set. "It's the parents who lie. They might get the children to go along with them, but the child's coerced by their need for love."

Both women stood in the passionate energy of Nora's response. Ivy knew her client had just found a clue to something deeply and personally troubling, but Nora focused on the present. "So often, the children are just along for the ride, trying to survive the mess created by their parents. I see it all the time in my practice."

Ivy reached out and gently squeezed Nora's arm. "I'm glad those kids have you on their side."

Praise felt like a weight Nora refused to accept. "So where do we go from here?"

"It's getting close to 11:30, so we're going to be stopping for the day. Let's take a moment to talk about whether or not you want to come back."

"I'm definitely coming back. I still have that dream hanging over me. And besides..." Nora hesitated but then charged ahead. "You're going to think I'm bonkers, but I saw something during the last set. I want to know what it meant."

Ivy's response encouraged Nora. "It's not at all strange for you to see images when you're working with me. It means you're doing a fantastic job of opening up to the communication. Are you comfortable telling me what you saw?"

Nora rubbed her forehead, drawing a path with her middle finger. "It was just swirling colors of different greens. But the thing is... I felt like it was looking at me."

"Did that scare you?" Ivy's instincts told her Nora was scared, but she wanted to see if her client had noticed.

"A little bit."

"Nora, don't think about the question I'm going to ask you right now. Just respond. Let your answer come from the knowing place you've been using. Was that green presence part of the reason you reacted with such a strong desire to find the back door?"

"Oh." Nora hated it. She wanted to deny it. But the truth was clear. "Definitely a part of it."

"Then your inner wisdom, spirit, and the energy field have given you a clue. In our next session, we can explore why the idea that children lie evoked such an extreme reaction."

"Why did that happen?" Nora wanted to know now, not later.

"You have just experienced the magic that can unfold in energy conversations. I didn't decide to ask you about children and lies. It just came to me, and I trusted it was the right path to follow. That path took us to this insight. You could say we're being guided to find the answers you seek."

Nora shook her head but paid close attention. Old thinking was at war with new understanding.

Ivy wanted to hug her courage. "The energy field is always fully engaged. It listens. It knows what's happening. What you're thinking. What you're feeling. This rich source of communication nudges us with clues when we pay attention. We can explore or ignore the messages that come up."

Ivy's confidence resonated. Nora felt the heart beat of the detective's passion and competence.

"Remember when I said your inner wisdom and spirit are always *for* you? This is one of those moments. The thoughts, feelings, and beliefs of old thinking will no doubt come forward and warn you to stay away from the clue. But it's there to serve you. To enrich your life. To release you. Free you. If you can let yourself follow the path to your personal truth, you will find it's like emerging from a cocoon to experience your beautiful, butterfly self.

Nora chewed on her lower lip and sighed. "When you're talking, it feels so real and logical, but I'm pretty sure I'm going to get in my car and think you're from another planet."

"More like an unexplored universe," Ivy responded. "Today you opened up to a whole new realm of possibilities. You've tapped into a new way to find answers. Celebrate how it works. Encourage yourself to explore it. Say something like, *My spirit has always served me, and it's with me now.*

"Or talk to your old feelings, beliefs, and thoughts when they try to pull you back to what's no longer serving you. Say something like, *Thank you for trying to protect me, but I'm safe. I'm learning new tools. Learning to trust my inner wisdom. I've got an ally to guide me through this journey.*

"If your dream starts to haunt you or the rug scares you, say similar things." Ivy reached out for Nora's hands. Held them in a warm embrace. "And though it might seem strange, I encourage you to start thanking the dream for coming to you. See it as a messenger. A messenger bringing you compelling information to honor your truly delightful, determined personal spirit."

Seven ~ Susie

Ivy's body was buzzing with anticipation. The energy detectives were gathering, and they were getting very close to solving Susie King's mystery. The day promised, at least, a major breakthrough. And who knew where that might lead?

Cleaning strawberries for breakfast, Ivy thought about the other four women and the skills they'd developed since their first days together. Each of them had come to her for personal sessions. All had wanted to share and expand the success and fascination they'd experienced using energy. A circle, dedicated to helping others, blossomed. They'd been working together for fifteen years, and it still felt amazing every single time.

Ivy sliced more berries, thinking about the women. They didn't socialize. They weren't everyday friends. But when they gathered in the barn to help someone find answers, a deep bond flowed effortlessly. Their diversity fed their work. Their dissimilar lifestyles and experiences created an almost magical force.

Ivy finished the berries, smiling. It was Jill who had started calling the group "energy detectives". The description tickled all of them, though they seldom shared it with others. They believed their work needed to be discovered rather than broadcasted.

Vanessa still didn't feel comfortable sharing their work with her husband and kids. Today, she was trying to slip away from family plans and thought she might be a bit late, but Ivy was sure she would be walking through the door right on time. Vanessa wouldn't want to miss anything. As Kendra had pointed out several years ago, working together was better than chocolate and most sex.

The back door opened, bringing Sam, Spirit, and cool morning air into the kitchen.

Ivy reached over and started the toast.

Opening the cupboard that held an eclectic array of cups, Sam asked, "You want some coffee this morning?"

"Thanks. And a possible favor?" Ivy grabbed the butter dish. "We're bringing food for lunch, but if our work runs into the evening, could you order pizza and deliver to us?"

"Sure. Glad to do my part."

"I'll text if that happens, so be ready for a message as early as 4:00. You know how we get."

"I do. You've been known to devour a bucket of cookies during one day's work, leaving no leftovers for me." Sam settled into his chair. Spirit sat beside him, ready for the nibbles she was sure to get.

Ivy sat down and buttered the toast. Shook her head with a smile. "You're not going to let that one go, are you?"

"Nope."

"Well it might happen again. We got so close last time... I'm hoping Susie's able to open up today. She's at that volcanic place in her healing where her dissociated memory is ready to erupt." Ivy handed Sam his toast.

"I'll make popcorn if you run into the evening." In his typical way, Sam's encouragement came with action and perception.

"That would be perfect."

Ivy nibbled on her toast. She piled strawberries on top to see if that would ignite her appetite. It was still a bland appetizer when she had a feast of energy insights waiting.

Susie was learning about what had happened in her dad's office over twenty years ago. The team's detective work had already shed light and provided some release from the trauma, but there were still gaps to be filled. Their job was to go into the black hole in Susie's childhood and find the answers. Having those insights would allow her new life choices.

As Sam stood up, Spirit moved to Ivy. "I think she knows you're going to the Place-Of-No-Time."

It was the name Sam had given the barn when they remodeled it. As far as he was concerned, that's where Ivy took her clients. He saw them traveling where time didn't exist to release past events that held current possibilities captive.

Ivy gently pushed Spirit away. "You get to spend the day with Sam," she said as she walked to the bathroom.

Ten minutes later, her husband was at his computer with Spirit sitting beside him.

Grabbing a chocolate chip cookie and holding a large plate filled with six dozen more, Ivy took a bite and walked over to say goodbye.

"There's more cookies in the freezer."

Sam looked up from the screen. "We'll meet you on the other side of your mystery, whenever you get back."

"I know, and that means everything to me." Ivy held her cookie up in the air and bent over for a quick kiss. Spirit kept her eye on the cookie as Ivy moved in closer.

"Okay then, I'll leave you two. I need to get going. Ivy gave their dog a heads up. "Going to the barn, Spirit. Going to work."

After placing her cookies in the barn kitchen, Ivy turned off her phone and stood before the large window to center herself.

Miriam walked through the door ten minutes later. "I'm shivering with the energy that is already building," the tall, slim woman announced as she walked into the room. A ballerina couldn't make an entrance with more natural grace. "I haven't gotten any hits these past two weeks, but I can feel answers hovering around me constantly. It's been hard waiting for this day."

Holding a pot of soup didn't stop Miriam from leaning in for a hug from Ivy before heading into the kitchen. "Have you been feeling it?"

"I told Sam it might be a long day," Ivy answered as the door opened again.

"Three bags of chips and some trail mix." Kendra's deep voice trailed off into laughter. "Gotta have the salt, but I'm being a good girl with the nuts and healthy shit. I'm sure Jill's got us covered on the fruits and veggies." Kendra gave Ivy a quick kiss on the cheek and headed for the kitchen.

"Yep, the tree-hugger has her usual raw delights." Jill walked through the door and set her canvas bags on the floor. She moved toward Ivy like mist coming off the ocean. They hugged, and Ivy was pulled into a bubble of unhurried time. "How are you doing, Little Butterfly?"

"Butterfly?" Ivy giggled.

"Look at you… all yellow with pink wings in that flowing pajama thing."

"Oh, the sleeves." Ivy looked down at her silky top. "Butterfly feels good. Thank you."

Jill picked up her bags. "You know, butterflies are considered messengers between heaven and earth."

"I like that."

Laughter filtered out of the kitchen. Jill walked toward the echo of joy. "It's going to be a good day."

The door opened again and Ivy moved forward. "Here, let me help you," she said to Susie. "What do you have here?"

Ivy's client was hesitant. "It's some hummus, falafel, and pita chips. I know you said I didn't need to bring anything, but I wanted to contribute. You're all so kind, and I didn't bring anything the last two times we met."

"If you didn't have such an armful, I'd give you a huge hug." Ivy knew bringing food was an empowering step for this tentative young woman. She was like a rabbit coming out of its burrow. With her food offering, she was daring to engage the connection the detectives offered.

"I'm pretty sure your food elevates you from guest sleuth to a full-fledged detective," Ivy said as they walked into the kitchen.

Miriam, Kendra, and Jill turned to greet the young woman who was determined to find answers that would help her understand why her life felt so bumpy. Unhappy.

Jill stepped forward and reached for the bowl of hummus Susie was holding. "I love this stuff. I thought about bringing it myself but ran out of time. Thank you!"

Kendra gave Susie a hug. Then a high five.

Magic often happened in the barn kitchen. It was happening now. Instead of lingering in the doorway, Susie was standing in the middle of the cosmic bustle.

When Ivy and Sam had remodeled the barn, a small kitchen made sense. But logic had been set aside. They knew a large kitchen with an old, round table would invite the magic of conversation and companionship.

Vanessa walked in, all regal in commanding black slacks and white tunic. "I could hear the chatter and feel the energy the minute I opened the door. You sound like children at a birthday party."

"Holy crap, what did you bring?" Kendra moved around the table to help Vanessa with her bag-filled arms.

Ivy reached out to help. "We've pretty much established that no one needs to bring food when Vanessa's around. She doesn't know how to leave anything at home."

Eyes snapping, laugh lines emerging, the newest arrival defended herself. "Now girls, you never know what we might want."

"Or how long we'll be here." Miriam gave the dynamic woman a warm hug.

Jill added her support. "Exactly. I think we might be surprised today."

"Nothing will surprise me today," Miriam said. "I've got that feeling."

"Me too. I have something I want to try." Susie's quiet statement was heard above the chatter. The feminine pandemonium became still in an instant. Every woman turned to Susie and supported her with their full attention.

Jill held her bag of raw, organic carrots and turnips suspended in motion. "That's awesome. What a way to start the day."

Without direction or a leader, the food was instantaneously put in the refrigerator and organized on the counter. The soup was placed on a burner and turned to simmer. The sun-splashed room buzzed with intention.

Moving into the studio, the women flowed. They were a steady stream working as one as they prepared the space to begin the day's adventure.

Four chairs and two footstools from the other side of the room joined the two leather chairs by the fireplace. Notepads and pens were scattered on the end tables that sat between chairs. No coffee, juice, tea, or water came to this anticipated moment. Excitement and curiosity were the sustenance.

Everyone dropped into a convenient chair, but Vanessa immediately jumped up. "Don't start. Don't say anything until I get back. My last cup of coffee just caught up with me."

Miriam grabbed the notepad next to her. "Anyone else?"

Everyone but Ivy and Miriam decided they should take their turn in the bathroom.

Meanwhile, the conversation turned to the unseasonably warm weather. It was a safe topic that didn't let them slip into revelations or ideas everyone would want to hear. But the moment everyone was back together, Miriam jumped in with an observation. "Susie, you seem different today. In our other sessions, you were certainly willing, but now you're more open."

Kendra wiggled further back in her chair. "More confident."

Susie usually stared at her lap or the floor. Now she looked directly at Ivy. Whenever she became the center of attention, a thief seemed to steal her voice. This time, Susie was neither robbed of breath nor silenced. "I think it's the memory Ivy and I worked on last week."

She didn't take her eyes off Ivy. They pleaded. "You tell them what happened."

Ivy settled back into her chair, consciously leaning away from being in charge. She encouraged Susie. "Remember how we talked about sharing your experience with the right people? You have a great opportunity here. You're safe. Everyone cares."

Looking around the circle of energy detectives, Ivy knew each one wanted to jump in and help Susie find her voice.

Kendra was stone-still, a sure sign she was holding an explosion of support. "Every time you speak your truth, you bring the memory out of the *secret room* of your subconscious. It can't hide there any more. Trust yourself. Give it a try."

Vanessa, sitting next to Susie, reached out to touch her arm. "Another thing to consider. Ivy can tell us what she experienced during your session, but that's different than you telling your story. If *you* tell us what happened, we will hear what is important to you, what you noticed, and what stayed with you."

Susie tried to breathe deeper. Her eyes dropped, seeking the comfort of her well-chewed, ragged fingernails.

Miriam folded her hands in her lap. "Maybe it would help if we did a little meditation. We can't expect Susie to jump into the thick of things like we do."

"Oh… good idea." Jill wiggled in her chair, slumping into the soft leather so she could lay her head back.

Miriam focused on Susie while the others made themselves comfortable. "We did this last time we were together. Do you remember how I took all of you to a quiet state of mind to focus on feeling grounded and relaxed? Now I'm thinking you might need to visualize a path that helps you feel empowered to speak out."

Susie nodded, looked around, and copied the laid-back postures.

Miriam lowered her voice to a soft murmur and invited everyone to close their eyes. She asked them to be aware of their personal spirits. Encouraged them to imagine their spirits as wisps of color and energy gently floating around the group.

"Let your spirit move from person to person… connecting, embracing, loving, and fully accepting this moment together.

"Feel Susie's courage. Surround her with energy that helps her remember her personal power.

"Feel our oneness as we continue seeking answers for her.

"As you open your eyes, let this day begin with limitless possibilities in our Place-Of-No-Time."

Eyes opened when each woman felt ready. Jill was the first to speak. "I saw your spirit join us, Susie. What did you feel?"

Her voice a whisper, Susie's eyes shouted as she described what she saw. "It was a bright yellow ball that started bouncing in the air."

Miriam was just as excited as Susie. "I think that means you're feeling safe with us."

Murmurs of agreement came from every chair.

Susie looked around the gathering of women. "It's true. I feel different. Do you know what I mean?"

Vanessa answered for everyone. "We do. We're all survivors of some kind of trauma. We know going into memories and understanding how they affected us, both then and now, transforms lives. In this case, it's about feeling safe enough to share your personal spirit. To see it. To know it's there for you."

Vanessa wasn't about encouraging smiles like Ivy, but her eyes cared, her posture was protective. "It's why we're here today. Feeling safe is huge. It might start with us, but you'll find it expands outside these walls as you heal."

Miriam jumped in. "The first time I knew I was totally, completely safe, I felt exposed. Like I was turned inside out." She remembered that moment in her healing journey. "A tortoise in a shell. That's where I use to live."

Vanessa brought the focus back to Susie. "Do you feel safe enough to tell us what happened last week? I promise you'll be happy you did."

Happy was on another planet for Susie. In an unknown galaxy. It definitely had no place in her thoughts as the faces surrounding her started becoming distorted. Picasso-like images were replacing their familiar visages.

It always happened when people put Susie in the spotlight.

52

It was happening now.

In previous sessions, they'd let her hide in the corners of the conversations. Sit mutely at the edges of their work. Today, they were all looking intently at her.

All of them.

Susie tried to blink away the facial distortions. She knew blinking would bring her back to the moment. That and moving her head until she caught a glimpse of a normal face.

Jill's face came into focus. It was the lifeline Susie needed. She remembered Jill teaching her how to tap her collarbone when she was distressed and losing contact with the present moment.

Moving her right hand through air that felt as thick as mud, Susie made contact with her upper chest and tapped. She tapped again. Slowly, she found a rhythm until the distortions cleared.

Everyone was tapping with her.

In that cohesive moment, Susie remembered that using her voice was her true power. She desperately wanted that potential. And so she tried. In a vaporous voice she began. "During deep relaxation, Ivy took me back to my dad's office."

No one moved. The silence was absolute. From their last session with Susie, everyone recognized that cold cavern of fear.

Her voice becoming stronger, louder, Susie recapped. "Remember the chair from last time? How my dad made me stand in front of him while he was tutoring me?"

There were nods all around.

Susie started flicking the nails of her thumb and middle finger. In the past, that sound had soothed her through much worse than this moment.

"The chair was there. He was sitting on it, but it wasn't just me standing in front of him."

Ragged breath seeped out. A haunted mumble followed. "My older sister, Crissy, was there too."

No one tried to stop the silent tears that followed. They knew crying had great power to release old pain and current heartache.

"You didn't know your dad brought your sister into his office?" Kendra commiserated.

Susie shook her head. "I thought I protected her. I thought... I thought it was only me."

Jill handed her a kleenex.

"But that's not why I'm crying." Susie turned to Ivy. "It gets all messy and confusing when I try to tell it."

Ivy's voice was a gentle massage. "You're doing a beautiful job. It doesn't have to be nice and tidy. Your emotions are part of the story."

Miriam spoke softly. "I think it's only feeling messy in your head, Susie. You're making it very clear."

Vanessa reached out, gently putting her hand on Susie's shoulder. "What happened to your sister in this memory?"

Remembering that moment, Susie felt the weight of remorse pulling her under. A sigh tumbled out. She used words to paddle to the surface of her sea of shame. "What I felt is really awful. Really, really awful. And humiliating."

She sighed again. This one flowing from the place she held her courage. "I was relieved when I saw her there."

The words got caught in her throat, barely escaping. She covered her face with her hands and slowly shook her head. "I felt better because I wasn't the only one."

Susie looked around. Not knowing what she expected, she wasn't surprised to find understanding and acceptance.

Resolution stood toe-to-toe with her churning stomach. It urged her to continue talking. "In an energy set, Ivy held the feeling I had in that moment. It was bone-deep relief."

Jill watched closely. Susie's aura was robust, though she looked more fragile than usual as she continued, "At first I hated knowing that."

"At first?" Miriam wanted clarity.

Susie started flicking her nails again.

Kendra's voice was clear and steady. "Susie, you were a child when this happened. That child is still part of you, and she gets to have any emotions, *any* emotions at all. Without shame.

"When you were a child, you were powerless. That child did the best she could while her world was falling into pieces. Honor her relief. We do."

Kendra's words, her conviction, mopped up the last of Susie's tears. Color found its way into her cheeks. "That's what Ivy said, but I needed to hear it again."

Ivy leaned forward. "Would you be comfortable telling everyone what you told me last week?"

"What?" Susie searched through her tumbling thoughts. Sat up straighter, took a deep breath. "Oh. When my dad took me into his office."

Susie looked around the circle and saw everyone looking, waiting for her answer. None of the faces started morphing. It gave her confidence. "I believed what happened to me was my fault. "Now I know it wasn't about me being stupid or incompetent because it happened to my sister too. Crissy was smart, on top of it. She obeyed every rule. She…"

Every woman in the room felt Susie's timeless grief. Their investigations into childhood trauma often took them to strong emotions. It never got any easier, but the detectives went willingly. They knew truth was often found in the bleak foreboding of children's lives.

Susie turned to Ivy once again. "This is where it really starts getting tangled up for me."

Ivy blinked away her own tears and nodded. "It's like finding your way through a maze, but you are doing it, Susie. You're doing it."

Glad she never wore mascara to these sessions, Ivy rubbed away the moisture gathering along her eyelashes. "Take your time. Maybe share how your sister's suicide fits into your insight."

Jill took off her shoes and tucked her feet into the chair. The vibrant colors of her tattoo peaked over the edge of her forest green socks.

Miriam slipped her shoes off, pulled a footstool closer, and prompted: "Your sister died when you were teenagers…"

Susie clasped her hands together, looking past Ivy and into the tunnel that led to her past. "I was fourteen. She was seventeen, and I've spent the past twenty years believing it should have been me." Susie's anguish squeezed out in a high pitch. "I was the one who was bad. The one Dad needed to take in the office."

Shaking her head, Susie was lost in the numbness that surrounded memories of her sister. "Now I know it wasn't about being good… or bad."

"Hooray!" Kendra shot her fist into the air. "I'm so glad you see that. Hooray. Hooray." She pumped the air, pulling all of them out of the sorrow. "No wonder you came today with your hummus and a smile in your eyes."

Vanessa was more reserved, but she was just as pleased. "That's a huge breakthrough, Susie. Neither you nor your sister were responsible for what happened in the office. Neither of you deserved to be wounded."

"And neither of you could have stopped it," Jill added.

Miriam followed without skipping a beat, "And you couldn't stop your sister's choice."

"I'm starting to see that now." Susie's diluted smile was beautiful to see. "Ivy says healing is like finding your way out of a maze of old beliefs. Then you can start embracing the good things about yourself."

Kendra added an exclamation point to Susie's quiet statement. "I already know a shitload of things that make you special. You're not going to have to look very far before you start bumping into your awesomeness."

Miriam jumped out of her chair. "We need to check some energies before we get into the dialogue Susie wants to set." She looked around the circle. "Ready?"

No one needed to hear what Miriam had in mind. They trusted each other and believed in the way spontaneous insights guided their epiphanies.

Miriam turned to Susie as everyone else stood up. "This is where you leave the room and then come back and feel the different energies each of us is holding for you. Do you remember how you do it?"

"Yes… where you guys stand in a big circle, and I go from one person to the next feeling the energy each is holding."

Jill sat down on Susie's footstool. "Just remember to clear the energy you experience with one person before moving on to the next."

"I remember now. I'll wait in the kitchen."

"Grab me a cookie." Kendra was ready to graze.

All five women moved out onto the open floor and huddled to hear Miriam's idea. "I want Susie to feel the energy of the different ways she's special."

"Oh cool." Jill knew immediately she wanted to hold Susie's *sweetness.*

Kendra didn't have to think about it either. "I'll do her *courage.*"

She looked at Miriam. "Did you have something in mind?"

"I want to do her *loving heart.*"

Vanessa shook her head. "That's too much like Jill's *sweetness.*"

56

"You're right. It's important to show her five distinct qualities that we've noticed and admired." Miriam thought back over the last two sessions and what she'd learned about Susie. "*Smart.* I want to do *smart.*"

"I love that." Ivy was delighted. "Her dad made her feel so stupid. Okay, we've got Jill/*sweet,* Kendra/*courage, and* Miriam/*smart..* What other two qualities would give her a good sense of herself?"

Vanessa knew the energy she wanted to hold for Susie but was struggling to find the right words. "I want to do something that helps her experience her potential. She's felt so beaten down, and yet, she's created a thriving business doing medical billings. She came to Ivy because she was trying to hold her marriage together. There's something there that is strong."

"You just said it," Kendra said. "Her *strength.* It would be wonderful for her to feel that."

Everyone agreed and turned to see if Ivy had come up with something.

"What do you think about me holding *beauty*?"

"Is that too close to Jill's *sweet* energy?" Miriam glanced around the loose circle.

"Actually, I'm thinking about her physical beauty. She can barely stand to look in the mirror. All she sees is skinny, but she has a lovely, sprite-like beauty. I'd like her to feel it."

"That's good. Personal beauty's an important energy to experience." Vanessa pulled a large hair clip out of her pocket and secured her long, brown hair at the top of her head. "I think she's still wearing the awful shame we accept during our abuse. It's hard to feel attractive with that slime on us."

Ivy agreed. She looked forward to the *beauty* energy Susie would experience.

"Are we good to go?" Vanessa never let a moment dangle unused.

"Wait a minute." Miriam's eyes sparkled as she laughed. "What was I?"

Four voices answered. "*Smart.*"

Jill laughed and summarized.

"I said I was going to hold *sweet,* but I'm going to make that her *love* energy.

"Kendra is *courage.*

"Miriam is *smart.*

"Vanessa is *strength*.

"Ivy is *beauty*."

Jill was beyond enthused about Susie feeling the energies they would be holding for her. "I'll tell her we're ready. We're ready, right?"

Everyone nodded and moved away from each other to form a large circle so their energies wouldn't intermingle. This Saturday session had just been set on fire.

Eight ~ Susie

As Susie walked back to the studio with Jill, she was told about the upcoming dialogue. "We want you to experience different qualities about yourself that we think are wonderful. Things you might not recognize."

Susie blushed. Started chewing her nails.

Jill encouraged her with a hug. "Do it. It'll give you some empowering insights.

"Stand in the middle of the circle and give me a moment so I can take my place. Then all of us can clear our thoughts and feelings. When you feel ready, approach each of us, one at a time, and feel the energy."

Closing her eyes, Susie took a deep breath and tried not to resist what they were offering her.

Remembering how to clear made her feel confident. She liked to imagine her inner chatter flowing into a basket at her feet until there was complete silence. This time, it happened within moments, and she opened her eyes. Eyes that had learned not to look but now wanted to see.

The five detectives looked like relaxed statues as they focused on the energies they wanted to share with Susie: *beauty, smart, love, courage, strength.*

Susie started with Ivy who was focusing on her physical *beauty.* Ivy pictured Susie's light blue eyes, clear skin, eyelashes that needed no mascara, graceful fingers. She saw Susie's slender build and shiny straight, blonde hair. As she saw these in her mind's eye, she silently repeated, *your beauty, your body's beauty, your physical beauty.*

Susie felt the energy around Ivy. She saw a bowl of ice cream with chocolate syrup pouring over it and didn't like the feeling. The syrup kept coming. It flowed until the ice cream disappeared. Her stomach started aching.

She stepped back. "What were you holding, Ivy? It didn't feel good. When I walked up to you, I saw a bowl of ice cream. I think *I was* the ice cream, and that was pretty cool because I was being bathed in chocolate syrup."

The rippling laughter was sweet enough to be served as dessert.

"But then the syrup kept coming, and I felt smothered. Good turned into something that could hurt me."

Ivy leaned forward. "I was holding the energy of your physical *beauty*."

Susie's hand massaged her midriff. Her heart started beating faster. "So ice cream and chocolate syrup seem great, but they are too much?'

"You didn't say it was too much, you said it turned into something that could hurt you." Jill knew the distinction was significant.

Kendra nodded. "It looks like your beauty distresses you."

"I don't even like talking about it. Do we have to discuss it? Can we move on?"

Susie looked to Ivy for an answer. "This is one of those red flags we've talked about during your personal session. Your strong reaction is telling you there is an empowering insight waiting for you. The question is… do you want to explore why beauty feels like such an issue? We're here to nudge you, but you get to set your pace."

Knowing how past insights had been key to changing her life, Susie overcame her hesitation. "I want to keep going."

Ivy's nod was encouraging. "You've been massaging your stomach. It's talking to you. What does it want you to know?"

"It's saying, 'Stop.'"

"Stop what?" Miriam's voice was a soft hug.

"Stop looking at me. Everyone thinks it's so nice to be pretty, but I don't like it."

The detectives knew they'd uncovered an important clue, but it was hitting too close to home for Susie to process in the moment. Ivy suggested they move on. "Shake off the discomfort, Susie. Release the energy so you can get rid of your stomach ache."

Susie closed her eyes and rolled her shoulders and head. She breathed deeply. Exhaled completely.

She felt no hesitation as her instincts moved her toward Miriam who was holding *smart*. Standing almost toe-to-toe, she immediately saw an Erector set with pieces snapping together. Each piece fit perfectly.

Susie stayed with Miriam's energy to see what else might happen and realized the structure was just going to become larger and more complex. She shared her impression. "Erector set."

Miriam was sure Susie would like the energy she'd held. "I was how smart you are."

"The Erector set kept getting more complex," Susie recalled. "It kept building without any effort. That makes sense."

She seemed indifferent and that intrigued Miriam. "It doesn't sound like that pleases you."

"I really don't care about being smart. I'm surprised that energy felt calm."

"Is this because your dad was a teacher? Is it about expectations?" Miriam asked.

"My dad was always tutoring me. Always! I dreaded it. No matter how well I did in school, he'd take me into his home office, lock the door, and make me stand in front of him for my lessons."

"You had to stand during your lessons?" Kendra's radar was on high alert. "He locked the door? What was that about?"

Susie shook her head. "I don't know. Guess he didn't want to be interrupted."

Vanessa was trying to keep track of Susie's responses. "So far, you don't like being smart or pretty."

Susie nodded. She felt as lost as Hansel and Gretel.

Stepping back a few feet, she cleared and moved on to Jill who was holding *love*.

The energy around Jill felt immediately teary but not sad or upset. Nostalgic images of Christmas caroling, Santa, and decorating cookies with Crissy came to her.

Susie didn't touch Jill, but she leaned closer and kept moving her hands through the energy that was present. She wanted to bathe in it. It felt safe. Tender. It was a giving energy.

With a deep sigh and big smile, she said, "Christmas."

Jill opened her eyes as Susie expanded on her experience. "I wanted to crawl into that energy and stay there. It felt like the best parts of Christmas." Her smile was soft, dreamy. "We really did have some nice times, Crissy and I. That energy felt tender and safe. Generous."

"That's how you love. It's your heart energy… the way you care." Sharing this was pure joy for Jill. "I loved holding that energy. Even if you don't like being pretty, I hope you feel beautiful inside."

"I do. It doesn't disturb me at all."

Susie was all smiles as she emptied the energy she'd just experienced. She moved on to Kendra who held *courage.*

The energy was so vivid, Susie stayed only a moment to feel it. "You felt like a big rock. It didn't feel good or bad. Just very strong. Solid."

"I was holding your *courage.*"

Susie's eyes widened in surprise. Wonder followed. "Ivy and I have talked about courage. She told me it isn't always standing up against the bad stuff in your life. Sometimes it's just surviving. Sometimes it's making a phone call and asking for help."

"And sometimes it's bringing hummus and falafel," Miriam added.

Susie thought about that. "That's true. I'm finding I do have courage, but I wouldn't have guessed it was like a big, immovable rock. I like that."

Kendra rolled her shoulders, releasing the stiffness of being so intent and focused. "I think you're beautifully unique in having Christmas kind of love and rock-solid courage. What a combination."

Susie's stomach didn't ache. She felt raw but not vulnerable. It showed up in her eyes. "You guys make it seem okay."

"It's more than okay. It's fantastic." Kendra was all over this. "Own it. Grab it. Embrace it… that combination of being sweet and soft and courageous."

Susie had no idea what to do with all the encouragement and turned to Vanessa to feel the last set.

Standing within inches of Vanessa, who was deeply focused on *strength*, Susie moved her hands close. She tilted her head to the right, tuning into the energy. A drop of water quickly turned into a stream and then a wide river. It rushed around boulders, fell over a waterfall, and flowed into a lush, green valley. "Am I nurturing?"

"Your strength is nurturing," Vanessa said. "I was holding your strength."

Susie looked around at the five women and smiled. "I really love that."

"So, *strength, courage,* and *love* feel good, and we want to do some more energy work with *beauty* and being *smart.* You never know where this stuff is going to take you," Vanessa mused. "And that reminds me... when we were in the kitchen, you said you had something you wanted to set, Susie. Do you want to create a dialogue now?"

"Yes. It's the kind where you guys move around, sort of like interactive charades."

"Sounds great." Miriam especially liked these sets. They were as spontaneous and uninhibited as child's play.

Knowing the detectives had no idea what she had in mind, Susie intuitively picked Miriam for the first energy. They walked into the space away from the chairs.

Standing face-to-face, Miriam closed her eyes and cleared her thoughts and feelings. Susie gently held Miriam's upper arms and focused on the energy she wanted this detective to experience: *young Susie*

She set Jill as *Crissy*.

Vanessa as her *dad*.

Ivy and Kendra smiled encouragingly as Susie sat down with them to watch what would happen.

Miriam and Jill were in obvious distress. They seemed fragile and didn't interact.

Vanessa began moving around them with heavy strides. She circled Miriam/*young Susie* and Jill/*Crissy* and moved their arms in various positions. It was a show of control. Annoyance and power were palpable. When nothing further developed, all three broke out of the interaction but remained standing.

"Wow! Susie, what did you set?" Vanessa shook off the strident energy she'd held.

Reaching for a kleenex, Susie waited for Vanessa, Miriam, and Jill to sit down. "Miriam was *young Susie* in the office with my dad... from the memory work I did with Ivy last week. Jill was *Crissy*. And you, Vanessa, were my *dad*."

Looking at Susie, Jill spoke up first. "The moment you set me, I was anxious. I couldn't move. Shit might happen if I stayed there, but moving wasn't an option." She shook off the feeling. "I hated Vanessa touching my arm and chin. Her energy was creepy. I felt terrorized and there was nothing I could do to stop it."

Susie asked, "Did you notice Miriam standing next to you?"

63

"I knew she was there, but it didn't make any difference. I felt alone. Her energy was more like a shadow than a person."

"What did you experience? Susie asked Miriam."

"I felt a lot like Jill…. anxious, couldn't move. She couldn't help me, and I knew I was safer if I didn't move." Miriam continued, "When Vanessa bumped me, I knew she wanted me to react, but I felt strong because I ignored her."

Jill agreed. "Utter stillness was my protection, too."

As Susie became increasingly distraught, Ivy moved them forward. "Vanessa you were Susie's dad. You seemed to be all about power and satisfaction."

"Yes. Powerful. Arrogant." Pointing to Miriam and Jill, she added, "Those little twits irritated me with their meekness, but I liked it. I liked being the bully. I liked how their cowering justified anything I wanted to do. That's why I moved their arms and posed them. Because I could." Vanessa shivered. "Creepy."

Thinking about her different feelings during the set, Vanessa turned to Susie. "What part of this upsets you?"

"Seeing Crissy and me standing beside each other, both of us feeling powerless and not able to help each other. It seems sad."

Vanessa was emphatic. "You can't protect someone when you're feeling powerless. By the time you got to this traumatic moment, your dad had stripped your capacity to take care of yourself, let alone your sister. You were two little girls doing the best you could.

"The man who should have protected you was using his power to make you feel helpless."

Vanessa shook her head, thinking about the dynamics of the dialogue. "He taught you to submit as surely as he taught you to ride a bike or proper table manners. Little-by-little, you learned his rules for surviving. That included making sure you felt isolated."

Ivy smiled at Vanessa. Their everyday lives looked as different as summer and winter, but when it came to energy work, they seamlessly shared insights. "I have another set."

The mood of the detectives instantly switched gears, and Susie was pulled into their anticipation.

One-by-one, intuitively choosing each woman as she went along, Ivy set three different energies:

Miriam/*young Susie*,
 Susie/*beauty*,

Jill/*dad*.

Returning to her chair, she watched as they began silently interacting.

Miriam stood quietly. Self contained.

With swan-like grace, Susie flowed around her while sprinkling something over her head.

When approached by Jill, a domineering and menacing energy, Miriam cowered, but Susie was unaffected. She continued sprinkling.

Ivy watched, fascinated, until everyone stopped moving and Kendra asked, "What was that about?"

"I wanted to see the interaction between *young Susie, dad,* and *beauty.* Miriam, what did you experience?"

She listed what had come to her:

"I was indifferent to Susie's energy, with her sprinkling fingers.

"I couldn't bear Jill's overbearing energy.

"I felt unable to move or do anything to help myself."

Ivy looked at Jill. "What did you feel?"

Jill sat down next to Ivy. "Did we use the word slimy today? That was my energy. I was a big, slithering snake and nothing could stop me. Miriam was like a mouse. Susie felt like my ally... we were in it together."

"I didn't feel that way at all," Susie protested. "I felt completely separate from Jill's energy. I felt like I was scattering fairy dust, and I knew it was for Miriam and not Jill." Recalling how she felt in the set, Susie smiled. "Yeah. I felt like a fairy spreading magic."

Ivy turned to Jill. "What did you feel when you were adjusting Miriam's arms."

Jill scratched the back of her neck as she thought about what she'd experienced. "Power. Nothing could stop me. Sort of... I COULD do it, so I did."

"E-yew. You better shake that off," Miriam suggested.

Jill got off the footstool, brushed off her clothes, hair, and face. "Okay, I'm clear, tell us what you set, Ivy."

"This was about the office again. Miriam was *young Susie.* Jill was *dad.* And Susie, you were *beauty.*"

Everyone was silent as they thought about what they'd witnessed.

Jill spoke first. "As *dad-energy*, I was pretty much the same as last time. And we have Miriam cowed and immobilized."

Ivy nodded. "Those dynamics are definitely becoming clear."

She turned to Susie. "What did you think about experiencing the energy of *beauty*?"

"It's a huge 'aha' for me. *Beauty* was a positive force not a predator. I'll never forget the feeling of being a fairy with magic dust." Susie looked over at Jill. "I didn't feel any connection to you... to my *dad's energy. Beauty* was a non-factor to him."

Jill nodded. "That's very cool. Now you know you can have a relationship with beauty that is completely separate from your dad. You can nurture it. Appreciate it."

Vanessa knew they could discuss this particular energy set to death, but she'd had a hit and was ready. "I have the next dialogue."

"Okay, but, after this one, I'm going to grab some of Ivy's cookies." Everyone agreed with Miriam's sentiment. A late morning snack was needed.

After setting the other five women with energies, Vanessa sat down to observe. She thought she might have something that would help unravel the mystery. It only took her a moment to see a new insight emerging, but she sat quietly and let the dialogue unfold.

Kendra, set as *dad*, was the only one who moved out of the line. The other four women never looked around, interacted, or showed any expressions. They stood in a mixture of timid postures while Kendra strutted around them and glared. *Dad* manipulated their arms, legs, and heads. Compliance and acceptance were the unanimous responses.

Kendra turned to Vanessa. "I think we're done here."

Everyone fell out of line. Each one shared similar feelings: they couldn't move, they were under the control of Kendra's energy, and they felt no connection or unity with each other.

Vanessa said, "In the words of Alice in Wonderland, 'things are getting curiouser and curiouser.' We just discovered there were more children involved."

"What!" Susie walked away, then turned back and looked at Vanessa. "What did you set?"

"During the previous dialogue, it occurred to me that we keep working with your family. But your dad tutored other children, so I wanted to see if his controlling behavior extended beyond you and Crissy.

"Strutting, glaring Kendra was your dad, of course. We've got him responding in the same way over and over. The rest of you were different tutoring students who came to his office."

Feeling like Jell-O, Susie listened to the detectives hash over this new clue. Her memory supported this new information. Her dad locked his door for every one of his students. No one was allowed to interrupt the sessions for any reason.

Joining the others as they moved back to the chairs, Susie sat down on Ivy's footstool and shared it with her pink, leather ballet slippers. "I'm having flashes of different students as they came out of the office. I always wondered why they kept coming back. They looked like their time with him was too much. It wasn't the lessons, was it?"

"That's what we need to find out for you." Ivy's expression was a mix of encouragement, understanding, and confidence.

"This was an important insight, but not the root of your dissociated memory," Ivy said. "If it were, you would be feeling relieved right now. Knowing your truth is like warm, bright sun breaking through heavy fog."

Miriam leaned over the arm of her chair and joined the conversation. "I think getting to the root feels like someone has handed you a coat, and it fits perfectly. You know it's yours even though you don't remember wearing it."

Susie looked over at Miriam. "So we're closer but not there."

"Exactly, and I think we need nourishment before we continue. Are you guys hungry? I'm thinking... forget the cookies, I want lunch. What time is it, anyway?"

Jill stood up. "In the Place-Of-No-Time, the clock doesn't matter." She headed for the kitchen. The others followed her like ducklings trailing their mother.

The conversation among the women was music at its best. Bread was cut, the pot of soup was placed in the middle of the table. Plates, bowls, silverware, and glasses created a rhythm as they were gathered. Chairs moved across the floor and laughter was a steady beat. The chatter of what they'd learned felt like a harmonizing choir.

While the detectives ate, they marveled, as they always did, at the way the energy field and inner wisdom guided their exploration.

Susie wanted to hear, once more, how Vanessa decided to set the last dialogue that included the other children. She was assured it wasn't a decision. It was Vanessa trusting her intuition and the process.

Everyone agreed there was a strong resonance of truth in what they were witnessing. Each set supported the previous set. They were following the right thread.

"How do you feel about other children being involved?" Jill dipped a celery stick in the hummus and turned to Susie. "And, by the way, this is excellent."

"Thank you. I feel the same as when I realized Crissy had also been taken into his office. I don't like thinking my dad upset those other kids, but I feel better knowing it wasn't just me."

"We need to know why all of you were so silent and still." With her eyes on the butter, Kendra cut a thick slice of bread. "Tell us more about your dad and his tutoring."

Susie stopped eating. "He tutored at home to make extra money. Since he taught at the grade school, everyone was an elementary student."

"Oh my god." Everyone turned to Jill. "I just got a hit."

Vanessa raised her brow as only she could do. "Then we better put the food away and take the cookies out to the studio."

That's the way it worked...sometimes you walked around and around a question and suddenly a possible answer appeared. Now the challenge was how to use energy to look deeper into what happened behind Mr. Cassidy's closed office door.

Nine ~ Susie

Conversation and curiosity were carried back to the studio. Miriam led the way with the plate of cookies. Ivy turned off the kitchen lights and picked up some napkins as she followed the trail of excitement.

Sunlight didn't join them. It was caught behind darkening clouds after playing hide-and-go-seek while they were eating.

Miriam set the cookies and her coffee on the nearest end table.

"Don't start on the cookies. I've got a dialogue that needs three people." Jill paced the floor in front of them, shaking her head and laughing as Kendra snagged a cookie.

"A girl needs her comfort food when investigating." Kendra's sentiment was met with agreement as the others gathered around the plate.

Tracking down the specter from Susie's past was serious stuff... they knew that. But the promising tickle of an insight felt like the last day of school for these women.

Leaving Susie and Kendra eating cookies, Jill waved Miriam, Vanessa, and Ivy on to the floor.

"Okay, Jill, we're ready." Miriam winked at her friend as she spoke around a mouthful of chocolate chip pleasure.

Jill moved toward Ivy, and the room became still. Each detective, in her own way, cleared the mood and chatter around them. Buzz became serenity. Connections dissolved. They became open receptacles for Jill as she began setting the energies.

After setting Ivy as *young Susie* and Vanessa as *dad,* Jill tapped Miriam and they stepped off to the side to watch the dialogue unfold.

Ivy's energy was serious but lively. Silently, she mouthed a conversation into open space. She drew squiggles in the air.

Vanessa knew she was male energy from the moment she was set. Her body aligned in a way that was not familiar. She felt in charge of the situation in a way that was missing soft curves.

"Okay," Jill said. "I want each of you to stay in the energy you are holding while I add another entity into the mix."

She set Miriam between Vanessa/*dad* and Ivy/*young Susie*.

Miriam stood still, feeling nothing. Wondering if she hadn't gotten the set accurately, she closed her eyes and opened them again, checking to see what came up. There was no connection. No feelings.

Vanessa/*dad* immediately found Miriam's energy compelling. She walked behind her and turned Miriam toward Ivy/*young Susie*. Ivy froze in place.

She was the first one to break out of the dialogue. Jill asked, "What did you experience, Ivy?"

"I felt like I was giving a speech or explaining something. Everything changed when Miriam's energy was added to the mix. Whatever I was doing didn't feel important anymore."

Jill nodded. "What was your emotional reaction?'

Ivy closed her eyes and went back to the dialogue. "I hated it when Vanessa/*dad* turned Miriam toward me."

"Were you afraid?" Jill asked.

Shaking her head, Ivy was sure it wasn't fear. "More like I hate being splashed at the lake, but I'm not afraid the water's going to hurt me."

Jill continued unraveling the experience. "How about you, Vanessa?"

Holding her arms up in a body-builder pose, she laughed. "It made me feel like my muscles were big. I knew I was in charge of this entire dialogue, and I felt complete control over Miriam's energy."

Miriam responded. "That felt fine with me. I had no will. No needs. Sort of creepy, isn't it?"

Jill laughed. "It's actually perfect. Vanessa, did you notice that Ivy froze when you connected with Miriam?"

"I was aware, but expected it, so it didn't feel like a big deal. It was part of the muscle-thing."

"What have we got here?" Kendra asked as she grabbed another cookie and held the plate up to see if anyone else wanted to join her. No one responded.

Jill moved back to her chair.

Vanessa, Miriam, and Ivy followed.

Picking up her coffee cup, Jill turned to Ivy. "You were *little Susie* being tutored in her dad's office."

"I was talking, writing, and felt it was important until Miriam was added to the set."

"Vanessa, you were *dad*."

She nodded. It made sense.

Jill rubbed the bottom of her cup. "I set Miriam as a *camera*."

Kendra laid her head on the back of the chair and stared at the ceiling. Their ghost now had a name. On its own, the *camera* was inanimate and disconnected. But it had caught Mr. Cassidy's attention and made him feel like he had muscles.

In the stunned silence, each detective recalled pieces of previous dialogues. A memory was shaping into a story, and it had the same thread consistently found when working with survivors of abuse. Innocence was caught in a web of distorted power.

"God damn him." Kendra's hushed voice shattered the silent musings. Three simple words released her outrage. They stirred a voice in Susie's vault of secrets.

Shaken, she turned to Jill. "How did you know? Why didn't I see it?! The camera sat on the shelf behind his desk, but I've never... not once did I think about it.

"Now I see it sitting there, a boogie man on the shelf. Not in a cupboard or drawer, even though dad hardly used it." Her words began wobbling. "Maybe Christmas morning. Some family photos now and then."

Susie's arms wrapped around her waist as the tears started flowing. "His camera was a soul-robber. Every click, every flash, took another piece of me."

The child within Susie, feeling safe for the first time, crumbled, taking the young woman with her. Susie instinctively covered her face with her hands to hide shuddering tears.

Each sleuth found the courage to remain still so Susie could begin releasing the shock and pain. The past was bridging with the present. She was reclaiming some of the pieces she thought she had lost in front of the camera.

The moody clouds had settled low over the valley and were shedding their own tears. What had started as a gentle, warm rain was now a storm with no care for Saturday plans or fragile blossoms.

When Susie came back from the timeless portal of salty, soothing release, she wiped her eyes with wet fingers. She looked up when a cluster of tissues was pressed into her hands. Gentle touches and caring faces greeted her.

Blowing her nose a second time, she shook her head. "He killed Crissy. It might have been a camera instead of a gun but that's even worse." She didn't hold back. "He sucked the life out of Crissy every time he pulled the camera off the shelf."

Turning to Ivy, Susie asked, "What am I going to do? I have to do something." She looked around at the women who had helped her solve her mystery. "I can't know this and not do something."

Susie felt distress revving up. A buzzing chainsaw stripping branches from her childhood.

"The first thing you do is gather more information." Jill kneeled in front of Susie to get her attention. "Information is power. Whatever you choose to do about the camera and your dad, you want to have the power of knowledge behind you."

Vanessa sat on the floor next to Jill. "You want to give this some time. When you take action, you want to feel centered, calm. Not raw and stunned."

Susie nodded. Their words muted the ricocheting clamor of her mind. Appealed to her logic. And felt like hope on the horizon.

Ivy placed her hand on Susie's knee. "It's important that any choice you make feels empowering to you. Once you decide what you want to do, we can check it out with some energy work. We want to be sure your inner child and your adult self come away from the experience with your spirit soaring. It's important any actions leave you feeling confident, that they move your life forward in a positive way."

Kendra sat forward in her chair. "I'm glad you feel moved toward action. It says a lot about what's happening in this stew of insights and feelings."

Susie turned her attention to the ever-practical, outspoken detective. She needed clarity.

"You could be feeling helpless or filled with shame. And that would be okay too, but I like that you have a warrior showing up. It might be one of those pieces that disappeared under the onslaught of the camera."

"Warrior." Susie breathed deeply.

"Warrior with a heart." Miriam cleared her throat. "You immediately thought about your sister. To me, that says you're seeing this beyond your own experience."

"Just think of the lives he hurt!" Susie exclaimed.

Everyone did.

Susie broke into the silent thoughts of dreadful possibilities. "I can't stand it." Her tears flowed once again.

It was time to end this session. No discussion was needed. Every detective had traveled to this moment of stark revelation when solitude was needed. A warm bath. A foot massage. A favorite walk. These were the tools that would help Susie process the inconceivable.

As the kleenex piled up next to the footstool, the barn filled with comforting quietude. Outside, the storm had passed. Jill noticed it first. "Look. We have a rainbow."

Susie looked up. Everyone turned to the picture window. The band of color met them like a lover's hug.

Miriam broke the loud silence with a quiet suggestion. "Let's do a quick circle and get Susie heading home."

Jill was the first to move out of the stillness. "While the rainbow shines its light on us."

Susie followed the detectives as they moved into the open space and formed a ring, taking each others' hands. All turned to Miriam to see what she had in mind.

"A lot has happened here today. Susie's been on a roller coaster of emotions. She's claimed her truth. She's leaving us with powerful insights. I know she'll remember everything that will serve her journey of healing, but I wanted each of us to tell her the one thing we want her to take from this session."

As quick as a kitten can melt your heart, Jill spoke up. "I'd like you to remember your courage is like a rock."

Miriam looked across the circle at Susie. "Don't forget you didn't have the power to stop what happened in your dad's office."

Squeezing Susie's right hand, Vanessa added. "Claiming your truth is giving you back those pieces you thought the camera stole."

Ivy, on the other side of Susie, squeezed her left hand. "Remember how beauty felt like spreading fairy dust."

Kendra added her reminder. "Susie, you came here today and kicked-ass!"

The young woman, who had come to Ivy to get help with her floundering marriage, had found so much more. She was the mouse who dared leave her nest and discovered she could roar.

"Is this it?" Susie asked as the circle broke apart and flowed forward to give her hugs.

Ivy answered. "You and I have another personal session scheduled. We'll talk about where you want to go from here."

Kendra, standing next to Ivy, added. "Personally, I feel like there are still answers to find, but you're the one who will determine if we continue exploring. It's not my curiosity that needs to be satisfied. It's your personal empowerment."

Vanessa glanced at the clock above the kitchen door. Maybe she wouldn't miss her family's entire Saturday get-together. Draping her arm around Kendra's shoulder, she had a warning. "Don't let our ever-curious Kendra get you going. She's a mystery buff, a wizard of undetected details. Once you're satisfied, it's done."

Susie accepted the observation with a smile and was quickly on her way. She was exhausted and wanted to be home.

Everyone, satisfied Susie was in a good head-space, quickly cleaned up the studio. This decompression was the part of their time together Miriam especially enjoyed. After traveling through a myriad of emotions, insights begged to become center stage. Each perception was part of the cast in an unfolding play, and they awaited their review. By tradition, it happened in the kitchen.

Heating tea in the microwave, Miriam broke into the chatter praising Susie's intrepid perseverance. "I keep thinking about the sets that revealed her dad's connection to his camera. It makes me think about addiction."

"What do you mean by that?" Jill nibbled on a carrot she'd grabbed from the refrigerator.

"At its core, addiction is an indescribable craving that takes over good intentions."

Responding to the ongoing microwave beep, Miriam opened the door and carefully removed her hot cup. "I think that's what we saw in the dialogues."

Vanessa listened. Found it interesting. And didn't want to pursue it. "The idea of addiction definitely resonates with me, but we don't want to wander into logic and personal experience to find possible answers."

Sitting down, Miriam grabbed a cookie. "You're right. It's so easy to slip into observation."

Kendra was working on a bag of potato chips. "I love how energy work consistently solves mysteries by walking in the back door...

"Susie comes to Ivy to shore up her marriage and ends up tracking down a dissociated memory.

"In choosing to veer off her intended course, she finds her inner wisdom.

"That journey increases her self-esteem, and I have no doubt it will help her marriage.

"In the back door!"

"You, my friend, have a brilliant mind." Jill was sincere.

"Right." Kendra struggled to hear the observation. Her brother's "You're dumb as a door nail," still shouted from the past.

"So. What did we do right today? How could we do better next time?" Vanessa felt the day slipping away and hoped to soothe some feathers if she got home in time to help with dinner.

A potato chip crunched. A carrot snapped. Another cookie left the dwindling plate. And Miriam sipped her tea.

Jill volunteered. "I think we did a good job of balancing. We definitely pushed Susie, but also gave her the time and space to honor her feelings."

"Don't you think it would've helped if we'd taken notes so she could look at them later?" Miriam thought it worthwhile to bring this idea up again.

The same arguments she'd heard before won the day. Notes would take the note-taker out of the moment, and everyone else believed the sleuths would remember everything they needed to know.

Kendra closed the potato chip bag. "Personally, I think we're fantastic. And each person we work with creates completely unique dynamics."

"Number one rule of working with energy?" Jill asked as she stood up.

All five laughed and repeated what they knew so well. "Trust what you know!"

They packed up and left as smoothly as they'd arrived. Heading back to their scattered lives, they didn't know when they'd get back together again, but they knew they would rock the world when they did.

Ten ~ Nora

Nora turned at the six-foot fairy and headed down Ivy's driveway. The past week had felt like a rubber band stretched to the point of breaking. Each long day had challenged.

The image of the rug had clouded her thoughts when she needed to be clear.

The dream's petrifying silence had surfaced and captured her attention during meetings with clients.

Luke's solicitous presence had made Nora feel like she was being pulled under while she tried to navigate unknown waters. He made her *feel* when she wanted *logic* at the helm.

Nora was glad Ivy wasn't waiting at the driveway today. It gave her time to check her hair. Turn off her phone. Chastise herself for being nervous.

When she entered the barn, Ivy was standing at the window looking out at the meadow, and Nora wondered if there was such a thing as pastel energy. If it existed, she knew it would feel like Ivy… a force of soft strength. The kind of energy that would encourage you to jump, knowing you would land safely.

Ivy turned to greet her client and noticed Nora remained standing just inside the door. *She's not quite ready to step further into the unknown,* Ivy surmised. "I was thinking about making some tea. How does that sound to you?"

"Okay. Sure."

"I'm partial to licorice tea, but we've got quite a collection if you have a favorite," Ivy encouraged.

"Licorice is fine."

"Make yourself comfortable, and I'll be back in a flash."

With the instant, hot water spigot on the kitchen sink, Ivy was as good as her word. They settled into the two chairs by the fireplace, the mugs at home on the end table between them.

"How has this week treated you?" Ivy recognized that Nora might be feeling hesitant or overwhelmed. She could just as easily be bursting at the seams wanting more information.

She was bursting at the seams. "It's clear to me we need to focus on three things: that damned rug, the unearthly silence, and Luke."

"Luke? Is he uncomfortable with what you are doing here?"

"Quite the opposite. He's fascinated. That's not the problem." Nora picked up her mug and held it close to her face, breathing in the spicy licorice. "Even though we're close, we've never hovered. If one of us is working out a problem, we give each other space, but he's different now. He's become a mother hen, and it's driving me crazy."

Ivy watched as Nora instinctively hid her feelings with a sip of tea. "Would you like to start with Luke since he's triggering a strong response?"

"Whatever you think is best. You're the expert."

Ivy smiled at that description. "I don't know about that, but I'm inclined to start with Luke so you can understand what's going on there."

"You are the expert, aren't you?" Nora's challenge was clear. She wanted the very best for this upheaval in her life.

"When it comes to energy work, I think different people respond to different techniques and perspectives. If you want to be very proactive, then I can promise you I know how to get to the answers you want. I'm a strong ally."

Nora's agitation eased. She liked that she didn't have to pussyfoot around Ivy. That Ivy didn't try to coddle her. "You're the expert."

They laughed.

"Let's move right into a dialogue." Ivy stood, inviting Nora to do the same. They moved away from the chairs. "I've got three energies I'd like you to experience. Clear your inner chatter and nod when you're ready."

It took a moment, but Nora was able to get to a thought-free state of mind. She nodded.

"Okay. I'm focusing on an energy. Go ahead and approach me like you learned in our last session. Trust whatever you feel, sense, or see."

Stepping forward, Nora reached out to hold Ivy's upper arms, and felt herself become part of an image that popped into her mind's eye. She was relieved. She hadn't forgotten how to read energy.

Discomfort shaped Nora's lips as she described what she'd experienced. "I was standing at the edge of a large park. People were coming together, and I knew I would only be a witness. Not be a part of what was going on."

"I was holding the way your mother loves you." Ivy waited for Nora's response.

"That's a good description." Nora wasn't surprised or bothered by the insight. "She observed my life more than taking part in it. Would you call that love?"

"Yes, it's one kind of love... if you grew up aware that she was watching out for you even though she didn't get involved."

Nora shook her head. "I wouldn't say she watched out for me. It was more like I was a wildflower growing in her yard, and she noticed but didn't nurture. Didn't weed and water... or fertilize.

"So she didn't feed you or make a home for you."

That caught Nora's attention. "Yes. She did." Her rapid blinking told Ivy that Nora was looking back on the mother/daughter relationship. "We have a distinction here. She was a homemaker. She took care of the home, not me. Is your premise that she showed her love for me by simply being a homemaker during my childhood?"

"What do you think?"

Nora nodded as she considered this possibility. She was shifting old impressions. "I'll give you the point. She may have thought clean floors and dinner at 6:00 sharp were loving gestures, though I thought it was nothing more than wanting others to think well of her."

"Maybe it was the only way she knew how to express love." Ivy planted the seed.

Nora rubbed her forearm. Sighed. She knew her mother would say she loved her daughter, but Nora hadn't felt it. Was it possible love was there, but she hadn't recognized it? Nora found herself in territory she'd never explored and turned to Ivy. "Do you think we can be loved without knowing it?"

"I do. Love is an energy of connection. We tend to think it doesn't exist unless it's strong, a tornado that makes a big difference. But love can be like a gentle breeze... only discernible when we pause and focus on it."

"Love is an energy." Nora picked up her tea and thoughtfully massaged the colorful, dancing lady embossed on the side. "That blows me away."

"It's possible your mother's homemaking was an expression of her love. She made life comfortable, convenient, and predictable while you were exploring your childhood world. What do you think about that possibility?"

Nora tipped her head. There was more than a dose of doubt, but she shrugged. "I'm willing to consider she loved me that way."

"Let your feelings around this unfold in the days ahead. See if it resonates as your truth." Ivy's smile was encouraging. "And remember, any conclusion is simply an insight. It's not a call for action. You don't have to change anything.

"But, if you do find yourself having a different perspective, you may start noticing shifts in your relationship with your mom. It happens automatically when you have a new view."

Nora was relieved. This wasn't the right time to switch things up with her mother. Not while she was consumed with the nightmare.

Ivy and Nora moved into a second dialogue and then sat together to explore the insights.

A strong, clear image had come to Nora. "In that dialogue, I saw a block. Some of the sides were black. Other sides were white."

"How big was the block?" Ivy was sensing something quite large.

"Like an elephant."

"How did it feel?"

Nora had to think about that. "A bit confusing, really. The block was very distinct but, for some reason, I sensed there was something that wasn't being revealed to me."

Ivy noticed Nora had become very serious. "That was the way your dad showed his love."

"Oh my goodness." Nora massaged her mug again. Glanced down at the design her fingers were tracing. "Not sure what that's about, except Dad did see the world as very black-and-white. Things were wrong or right. Good or bad. But... in the way he loved me, I don't know how that fits."

Ivy spoke up. "I'm getting something. As I describe it, tap into your inner wisdom and see if it rings true. It's okay if it doesn't."

"All right."

"Whereas your mom's way of expressing love felt detached, the way your dad loved felt very clear to you. Black and white."

"That's it." Nora felt it to the core of her being. "He was big hugs. The one who talked me through tough times. I admired the way he

79

took charge, got things done. But then he'd make time to take me out for ice cream." She quietly added, "It made me feel special. I still miss him."

Nora gazed into her mug as though the tea held a hug. A flicker of sadness was quickly replaced by a chin raised in determination. "What about the feeling of something there that I wasn't seeing?"

Nodding, Ivy responded. "That's definitely intriguing. Let me hold something so you can investigate it."

Standing face-to-face, they both cleared and closed their eyes. Ivy held an energy. Nora slowly began moving her hands in the space between them. The air didn't feel different, but Nora felt different about the empty space. It helped her focus on the energy Ivy was holding.

When Nora felt there was no more to see, she said, "I saw the black-and-white block again. This time, there was a combination padlock on it. I felt confident that I knew how to unlock it."

Ivy could see Nora was trying to understand what she'd experienced even as she described it. "Were you able to open it?"

Nora nodded. "I don't like this one."

"What don't you like?"

"All I saw inside the block was a maze, but it's making me uncomfortable."

"Do you want to explore the cause of your discomfort?"

Nora shook her head. "No. Not now. I have the feeling I'm going to find something I don't want to know... like he had an affair or cheated on his taxes. We can look into that later, but it's nothing I need to bring into the mix right now."

"Hooray for you... for paying attention to your inner wisdom. First, your inner wisdom pointed out there was something more to your dad's love. Then it triggered your curiosity. It gave you a clue.

"You can be sure that clue will weave into your healing journey in a way that empowers you. With energy, you never have to push through when it doesn't feel right. It's about allowing. Not conquering."

Ivy reached out and gently ran her hands down Nora's upper arms. "Shall we do the third dialogue?"

"Yes." Nora took a deep breath. "I'm good. I'm ready."

It was a quick, easily-read dialogue, and Nora was smiling when it was complete. "I saw my grandmother's quilt, the one on our bed. The energy felt cozy but important. It was about pieces coming together to make a whole, but what really caught my attention were all the stitches. They represented loving commitment."

"That's Luke's love for you." Ivy watched as Nora's fingers wrapped tightly around her mug. She wasn't massaging it. Didn't gaze into it. It was something to hold while she connected the quilt-energy to her husband's love.

It was several moments before Nora spoke, but she wasn't feeling all warm and fuzzy. "I get the cozy part. And how that energy feels important. It fits. But I have to tell you, my grandmother's quilt never made me feel smothered, and I'm feeling that way with Luke these days.

"If my dad were here, he'd listen to me, talk me through the things coming up, but he wouldn't try to make things easier for me. He'd expect me to take care of myself."

Ivy got it. "He treated you like you were strong and that felt empowering."

"Yes. That's it. When Luke fixed me tomato soup and a toasted cheese sandwich the other night, it just made me want to cry. Crying doesn't do any good."

Nodding, Ivy asked Nora if she could read energy while staying seated.

"Yes. I'm sure I can. Let me shake off this last energy."

When Nora nodded, Ivy focused on what Luke needed from his wife as she explored the impact of the dream.

Eager to unlock the message of the energy, Nora said, "I saw a radio turned on."

"How did that feel?" Ivy asked.

"It was fine. I wasn't irritated by it."

When Ivy told Nora what she was holding, Nora jumped in with a popping insight. "Luke needs me to keep him in the loop, talk to him about what I'm feeling and thinking. Don't you think?" She hurried on before Ivy could answer. "I was quiet, withdrawn the night he made me soup."

"It makes sense to me." Ivy could see the pattern. "His love is about holding the pieces of your life together. If your usual communication isn't there, he tries to 'stitch' the connection by nurturing you."

"Oh my god… it makes total sense." Nora was stunned. Relieved. Amazed it was so simple. "I need to talk to him. It's what we do, especially when we have something going on."

"Why has this time been different for you?"

Nora set her mug aside and looked for an answer in the nameless space we go to contemplate. Heedless of time, momentarily transported, she observed the previous week and saw what was happening. "This time, I'm trying to understand something that isn't solid. It's a dream, not what color we should paint the house.

"It's like watching a movie with nothing but shadows, movement, silence and then trying to tell him what the movie is about. I don't know how to talk about this! What would I say...

"I heard a jump rope on my grade school playground.

"A green presence caught my attention.

"I woke up with the distinct impression that someone had a hold of my wrist!?"

Ivy took mental note of this last statement…a new clue… and answered Nora's question. "You tell him just what you've told me. Share impressions as they come up. Let him know how challenging it is to express what feels so vague and foreign.

"Try to imagine you're walking through a landscape you've never experienced, and he's blindfolded. Report what you are seeing, sensing, noticing. Luke doesn't need a tidy conclusion. He just wants to be with you as you put these new pieces into the quilt of your life."

Tension drained from Nora's body. Like crepe paper streamers at the end of the prom, she sagged into her chair. Ivy scooted a footstool in front of Nora's feet, encouraging her to put them up and feel the relief. "Does it feel possible to have that kind of conversation with Luke?"

"It'll be a challenge but doable, and I think it'll make a big difference. If the shoe were on the other foot, I'd want him talking. Not shutting me out. I'd want to be part of his mind-bending, world-imploding journey."

Nora's laugh was part release, part hope. She slipped off her shoes and put her feet up. "Where do we go now?"

"In case we run out of time, what feels most disruptive in your life? The rug or the silence?"

Nora shook her head. "I couldn't say."

"Then we'll just let the journey guide us. We can always trust the energy field to take us where we need to go."

Nora was fully ready to accept Ivy's advice. Finding the answer to her dilemma with Luke had felt impossible, and yet it had been revealed as smoothly as peeling an orange to expose the fruit. The silence and the rug no longer felt like crushing, monumental monsters.

Ivy rolled her shoulders and adjusted her posture aware that she tended to curl into the conversation when discovery was in motion. "We're going to do something different now. I'm going to tilt your chair back, so you can get more comfortable while I take you into a state of deep relaxation."

"I'm with you."

Getting up, Ivy walked over to the refurbished cabinet where blankets and pillows were stored. "Would you like a purple, green, or yellow blanket?" she asked as she opened the leaded glass door.

Nora looked at the shelves holding pillows and blankets. The green made her uncomfortable. She didn't like purple. "Yellow's good."

Ivy dragged a second footstool next to Nora's chair and handed her the soft, fleece cover. She reached over to the end table and pulled two kleenex out of the box. "One for each hand. It gives you something to hold while you journey into relaxation."

Before sitting on the footstool, Ivy asked Nora to place the pillow behind her head and get comfortable. "Some people like to snuggle under the blanket. Others just hold it on their lap. You tend to feel cooler when you go into relaxation."

Nora tucked it around her feet, pulled it up and across her lap. "Feels like I'm settling in for quite a journey. Will I need a seat belt?"

"I like that image," Ivy smiled. "You are getting ready for a journey, but you'll be traveling in your inner world so no need for the seat belt. Have you ever experienced guided imagery or hypnosis?"

"Nope."

"Then we'll start with what you can expect. The purpose of deep relaxation is similar to clearing for the energy dialogues... going to a quiet state of mind without the inner chatter of your thoughts, feelings, beliefs. It'll feel like drifting off to asleep. You're totally aware of everything around you, but you aren't attached to it."

"Does anyone ever fall asleep?" Nora wondered.

Ivy's eyes lit up. "They sometimes drift pretty close, but you and I will be talking to each other so there isn't much chance of that happening."

"I don't know about that. I'm pretty comfy here, and I haven't been getting much sleep lately."

Ivy liked the way Nora was easing herself into the unknown. Getting information. Challenging that information.

"Imagine you and I walking into an overgrown forest where you have memories hidden in the shadows. During relaxation, I'll be holding the light, but you'll be leading the way. It's your inner world. You are the one who will instinctively know the path we need to follow.

"And this next part is very important... your mind~body~spirit will never let you go anyplace you're not ready to experience. You don't have to worry about anything being too much. Most often, you'll feel more than ready and frustrated because the answers will be just beyond your reach until you're completely ready in every way."

Nora, who had been intently watching Ivy, nodded. "So we'll know if I'm not ready because you won't be able to get me there. I won't have to tell you?"

Ivy confirmed, "You are always in charge. It's your journey. For instance, I might say 'find a comfortable place to sit' and you can tell me you want to lie in a hammock."

"Okay. I'm ready." Feeling like she was getting ready to step out of a plane with a parachute, Nora felt the need to jump without a moment's hesitation. She didn't want to lose her courage. Once she got going, she knew she could handle whatever came up. After all, she had Ivy flying tandem.

Ivy scooted her footstool into a comfortable place next to the chair. "Do you feel comfortable having me touch your arm and your mind's eye... between your eyebrows? That's the site of visual consciousness."

"Yes"

"Good. Close your eyes and take a deep breath."

Eleven ~ Nora

Ivy's first task was taking Nora into quietude. Thoughts of the rug and the silence from the dream made this a challenge. Inviting Nora to imagine a ball of white light entering the top of her head and traveling through her body, their journey began.

Following Ivy's words, Nora learned to feel the vibrating warmth of the white light. It moved slowly from the roots of her hair to the tips of her toes and fingers... a shimmering, iridescent ball. Her breathing became steady and deep.

Ivy touched Nora's mind's eye and counted down from ten to one, encouraging her to feel more and more serene with each number. She was in deep relaxation when Ivy said, "Relaxing, releasing, and letting go.

"Nora, as you feel the white light continuing its calm, peaceful flow through your body, I want you to imagine a perfect retreat. Don't think about this. Let it come from your inner wisdom. A place that's just for you."

Ivy saw Nora's face light up and knew she'd identified her retreat. "Tell me what came to you."

"Ocean beach. Blue, warm water. White sand."

"Beautiful." Ivy could see it in her own mind's eye. "Imagine you are barefoot. Firmly plant your feet in the sand. Wiggle your toes in the warmth.

"This is your very personal retreat. A reflection of your inner world and desires.

"Notice what time of day it is.

"The temperature.

"How the sun feels.

"Notice there is no one else on your beach. No one can come to your retreat unless you invite them. This is a place you get to be fully you... with all of your emotions. A safe place as you seek answers."

Crossing her legs, Ivy asked Nora to find a comfortable place to sit and then nod when she was there. "Where are you sitting?"

"Edge of water. Feet in the water."

"How does that feel?"

"Peaceful."

"As you sit in this soothing, calm moment, I'd like you to travel back to a time in your childhood when you felt the same way. Don't try to remember this. Just let that time come to you. Feel yourself present in that moment."

Nora's eyelids began blinking rapidly. Ivy knew she was time-traveling. "Nod your head when you get there."

She nodded.

"Tell me what you're experiencing."

"I'm at the creek behind my house. Sitting beside it. Want to put my feet in, but I'm not supposed to get in the creek."

"How old are you, Nora? Don't try to figure this out. Just feel your body, look at your feet… you'll know."

"Eight. Nine."

"Good. You're doing well. Trust what comes to you. You said the creek makes you feel peaceful. Do you know why?"

"The sound."

"What sounds are catching your attention?"

"All of them. The birds. Bugs. Mostly the water."

"Is there a lot of water? Is it a large creek?"

"Too big for little girls. I'm not supposed to wade."

"Your little girl likes the sounds of nature. Are there other sounds she likes?"

Nora's head tilted slightly to the left, as though she was looking for the answer. "My little girl likes her radio, but they turn it off when she falls asleep, and that wakes her up." Nora's voice faded with this observation and escalated as an insight struck her. "Bad things happen when it's quiet."

"Bad things? Did your little girl go to the creek because something bad was happening?"

"Yes. We're moving. I don't want to move."

"Who says you're moving?"

"Daddy. I heard him tell mommy we're moving. Then she got quiet. There's no noise in the house."

Ivy prodded. "Does your mommy want to move?"

86

Nora shrugged. Sighed. "I don't know. She just listens."

"Nora, when bad things happen, there's always something about it that makes us feel disempowered. Without thinking about it, just letting your truth speak out, what makes you feel most disempowered when everything gets quiet?"

Ivy watched as the woman sitting in front of her seemed to shrink. Tears began escaping. Ivy had to lean in to hear Nora's barely audible response. "Nothing I can do. Can't make it better."

"But sound makes you feel better. Does it make you feel safe?"

Tears breached Nora's instinctive resistance and ran down her cheeks. "I hum when they turn off my radio, but I have to hum very quietly. Sometimes I hum inside my head so no one can hear me."

"You were a very ingenious little girl… finding a way to feel safe without getting into trouble.

"Nora, I'm going to gently touch your mind's eye. I want you to imagine walking into your little girl's bedroom at night when she's humming. Feel yourself sitting on her bed. See how she responds. Nod when you get there."

As Nora responded to her suggestion, Ivy glanced at the large clock on the wall next to the entry. Time was an inconsistent critter during sessions. Sometimes racing forward and, just as often, standing still.

Nora nodded.

"Are you in the bedroom?"

"Yes. But my little girl doesn't want me to sit on the bed."

"That's okay. Silently, in your mind's eye, tell her you like knowing what she needs. Reassure her. Tell her you won't sit on the bed. Ask if you can stay in the bedroom. Then tell me what happens."

A few moments later Nora reported back. "I can stay."

"Silently, tell your little girl how glad you are to be with her. Tell her you want to hum with her and help her feel safe."

Seconds later, tears streamed freely across Nora's cheeks.

She cried.

And cried some more.

Ivy reached over her and grabbed more kleenex, placing them in her hands. In her own mind's eye, she encouraged Nora to keep crying the healing tears.

When Nora shuddered a sigh, Ivy removed the wads of tissue in her hands. Placing fresh tissues in them, she encouraged her to share her feelings.

Nora's voice was shaky. "My little girl's trying so hard. Feeling so alone. When I asked if I could hum with her, she let me sit beside her. That… it just… it broke my heart... and filled it."

Ivy placed her hand on Nora's shoulder. "You're healing your little girl right now.

"With your feelings.

"With your tears.

"With your attention.

"You're making a big difference. Keep your eyes closed, so we can to do more healing."

Nora's nod was Ivy's go-ahead. "Your little girl feels like there is nothing she can do, so we're going to help her use her voice. I'm going to touch your mind's eye and have her take you to the conversation between her dad and mom. Nod your head when you get there."

Ivy lightly touched Nora's forehead and waited.

"We're there."

"Where did your little girl take you?"

"In the kitchen. Dad and mom are eating lunch. No one's talking."

"You're doing great. Tell your little girl that you're with her. She's safe. Her mom and dad can't respond and both of you are going to hum as loudly as you want. Silently, in your mind's eye, start humming. See if she'll join you.

"Hum as long and loud as she needs to feel empowered.

"Feel the tension flow out of your body as it's released through your hum.

"Nod your head when you're done."

Seconds later, Nora nodded, Ivy encouraged her to take another step. "Let your little girl talk. Encourage her to tell her mom and dad how the silence feels. She doesn't have to be articulate or make sense. She just needs to use her voice. Nod when she's done."

Nora might have looked relaxed, but eye movement behind her lids told Ivy she was busy expressing feelings and thoughts that had been suppressed for years.

While many liked to believe unpleasant childhood emotions and experiences were in the past and naturally released with passing time,

Ivy knew they became embedded in the body. They were stowaways, undetected but threatening to come out at any time.

The courageous woman in front of her was, in this moment, letting go of disempowering energy. Energy that was still affecting her.

A deep sigh. The softening of Nora's face told Ivy she was done. "If you feel comfortable sharing, you'll find the release is even deeper."

Nora didn't hesitate. "My little girl told them their silence hurt more than any words ever could. And when she turned to the comfort of sound, they took that away. Her radio wasn't entertainment. It was a life-line."

"Tell your little girl she's a heroine today. Honor her courage. Ask her if she'd like to go back to your retreat with you."

Nora took only a moment. "She wants to go to the retreat."

"Good. I'm going to touch your mind's eye and count to three. You and your little girl will find yourselves back at the beach.

"One. Two. Three. You're there."

Ivy touched Nora's arm. "Ask your little girl what she'd like to do to celebrate. It can be anything because everything you want will magically show up in your retreat."

Minutes passed. Nora smiled. "The radio's on, and we're swimming. We hummed underwater."

"How does your little girl feel?"

She's happy. I told her she could make all the noise she wants. Anytime."

"Perfect."

Nora added. "She wants to play drums."

Ivy's smile lit up the room. Nora wasn't holding back. She was taking her first journey much further than many. "I love it. Let your little girl choose a perfect spot on the beach. Imagine a drum set sitting there and ask her if she wants to stay on the beach and play or if she wants to come back to your world with you."

In the wonderful world of deep relaxation, it happened in a flash. "She wants to stay."

"Let her know you'll be coming back to see her. Then ask her how she will let you know if she needs you. She needs to be able to signal you."

Moments later, Nora laughed. "I'll hear her drums."

Ivy shared Nora's laughter. "It'll be interesting to see how that works. In the days ahead, if you hear drums, remember it's your inner child reaching out to you. Take a moment and feel yourself back at your retreat. Then ask your little girl what she wants to share."

Nora's heart swelled. She wanted that to happen. It would feel like being handed a warm, cuddly teddy bear. She nodded, her laughter transformed into a softness that was new to her.

"Then we're ready to bring you out of relaxation. I'll touch your mind's eye and count down from three to one. When you open your eyes, you'll feel centered. Grounded. And you'll remember everything that happened.

"Three. Two. One. Open your eyes."

Nora blinked. Stared ahead without focusing on anything in particular.

"It feels like coming through a tunnel, doesn't it?" Ivy knew fragments of Nora's journey would become part of her own memory. When she traveled with clients, it felt as concrete as driving down the freeway to San Francisco.

Unconsciously pulling the kleenex in her hand apart, Nora looked over at Ivy. "That's quite an experience."

"You traveled through time."

"It felt as real as this does right now. How can that be?"

Ivy clenched and stretched her fingers, releasing her immersion in Nora's journey.

"Do you remember me telling you that Einstein showed us that everything that *has been* and *will be* is also right now. Being present with your eight-year-old is as simple as refocusing. That happens more easily when you're deeply relaxed, not concentrating on this moment."

Nora looked around for a place to put her kleenex and laid them on the table. A smile emerged. "I guess tissues work better than seat belts." Just as quickly, she became serious as she looked back to Ivy. "I had no idea I used sound to feel comfortable."

"To feel safe," Ivy clarified.

"To feel safe." Nora tried the feeling on with hesitation. A frown claimed her face. "Safe from what?" It was a question for herself as much as Ivy.

And there was no answer. Not today.

90

But Ivy gave her a way to explore the mystery of why she didn't feel safe. "This next week, keep asking your eight-year-old that question...

"While you're brushing your teeth.

"On your way to work.

"Say things like, 'I'm ready to know.'

"Invite a dream to reveal information."

Ivy reassured Nora. "Today you discovered, that for your child, bad things happened in silence. To balance it out, you also discovered sound made you feel safe.

"With that insight, you'll find silence is no longer such a looming threat. Now you can face it head on and know it's not the attacking ogre. It's the messenger telling you something unpleasant could happen. In that way, silence is your ally."

"An ally?" Nora couldn't line that up with the way it had been spooking her since the dream.

Ivy nodded. "For you, silence is like a fire alarm. It's there to tell you to look out. Be aware."

She shifted her focus. "See if this feels right for you. In your dream, silence wasn't there to scare you. It was there to get your attention. It shouted for you to take action because there was something you needed to know."

Nora looked down at the table with the mugs of cold tea and pile of used kleenex. Ivy's observation slowly sank in. It wrestled with how she'd felt the night of the dream. "I'll have to see how that feels. See if remembering the silence keeps giving me goose bumps." Looking back at Ivy, she added, "But, I'm open. What you said makes sense."

Ivy brought the session to a close. "Your inner wisdom will take you to your personal truth. Trust it in the week ahead.

"If you hear drums… on the radio, in your mind's eye, on television, anywhere… remember it's your little girl reaching out to you. Respond to her.

"She learned that bad things happen in silence. Today you learned that silence might be an ally."

Twelve ~ Lillian

Miriam and her friend, Lillian, greeted Ivy with a double decaf mocha and a fun mystery. The detectives knew life's sparkling mysteries could also be explored with energy. Not all of them were earth-shattering.

Accepting the paper cup with a smile, Ivy sipped while Miriam took both purses to the sideboard. "Chocolate sure feeds my soul. Feels like I'm getting a double dose of wonderful today."

Leading them to the chairs, Ivy asked what they had in mind.

"I feel like I'm going a bit crazy because I know there's something I wish… want… need... to do, but I can't figure out what it is," Lillian shared.

"I have the luxury to go off on any lark, but I keep cleaning house, working in my garden, planning trips instead. It's all very pleasant, but I'm aware of spending time, rather than using it in a way that would more deeply satisfy me."

Ivy smiled. If a picture spoke a thousand words, Lillian's sigh and shrugging shoulders spoke another thousand. "Well, first of all, you're not going crazy. You've simply arrived at your spirit-expression time… and you have lots of company. If our teen years encourage us to seek independence, this is the part of our life journey that inspires us to express our authentic self."

Pulling up a footstool, Ivy settled in. "Why don't we start with your life-line. Share the significant moments… events or feelings that felt like they directed you."

Lillian had Ivy's full attention. Ivy listened for emotions behind the words. She watched Lillian's body tell its story. Paid attention to the pauses and rhythm. From experience, Ivy knew this was where the insights were hiding.

"A pretty ordinary life," Lillian finished.

"Oh, I haven't met an ordinary life yet," giggled Ivy. "I wonder what you mean by ordinary?"

"I haven't done anything significant, nothing that stands out... like Miriam being an energy detective, of all things."

Ivy loved Lillian's itch for more and the need to make a difference. It was a feeling shared by so many at this time in their life journey. With a desire to experience fresh purpose in life, living their pure essence became essential to their happiness. It was oxygen when they felt themselves drowning in complacent days.

As Lillian had highlighted her life-line, Ivy had picked up some clues for what might celebrate her spirit. "While you were sharing your story, I saw two potential paths that might feel significant. How about you, Miriam? Did you pick up on anything?"

"I saw one path I'd like Lillian to check out. Shall we set each other and let her feel the energy? She's been doing dialogues with me, so she knows how to do it."

"That'll make it easy." Ivy set her coffee aside and jumped up, excited by possibilities.

Lillian watched as Ivy and Miriam walked into the open space a few steps away from the chairs. Turning to face her friend, Ivy stood still, closed her eyes, and cleared all inner chatter. Fully open, she waited for Miriam to set an energy that would reveal a potentially self-satisfying path for Lillian.

It was Lillian who would read the energy, but when Miriam placed her hands on Ivy's shoulders, Ivy sensed joy and enthusiasm. That feeling stayed with her even when she noticed Miriam stepping away. Her eyes still closed, Ivy focused on the sensation.

Approaching Ivy, Lillian imagined all her thoughts flowing away on a breeze, then opened up to any insights. An image came almost immediately. Stepping away, she shared, "I saw lines moving toward one point, drawing all my attention to a spot in the distance."

Because Miriam knew Lillian had dabbled with art but never taken it seriously, she watched her friend's reaction and shared what she'd set. "I had Ivy hold the energy of you making art important... seeing yourself as an artist."

The idea challenged Lillian. Not the kind of challenge that would require persistence. It wasn't about facing a learning curve or pushing for a goal. This challenge would mean a kind of soul-searching she'd never allowed herself. The very idea felt like stealing from a cookie jar.

Miriam, excited by the two possible paths Ivy had intuited, urged them to move on to the second energy set. "Step back just a bit, Lillian, and I'll clear my thoughts so Ivy can set me."

Lillian watched Ivy take a deep breath and shake her hands as though drying them off. Then stepping forward, Ivy placed her hands on Miriam's upper arms and closed her eyes.

It was as silent as the inside of a freezer, but Lillian felt energy crackle between them. When Ivy stepped aside and nodded for her to read Miriam's energy, Lillian was sure there would be something there.

It took only a moment before Lillian quickly stepped away and started fanning her face with her hand. "That gave me a hot flash," she chuckled. "I was building a big bonfire, so everyone could roast hot dogs and marshmallows. It felt communal. A coming together."

"I felt the heat too!" Miriam exclaimed. "What energy did you set, Ivy?"

"Lillian creating a Facebook page around breast health." Ivy spoke directly to Lillian. "When you shared your life-line, I sensed that you don't feel complete around your experience with breast cancer. You also lit up when you talked about reaching out to other people to make a difference.

Lillian looked at Miriam. The two life-long friends were caught in a moment, a snapshot of a profound journey they'd shared. This energy possibility held deep meaning for Lillian. If she chose this path, it would be a real stretch, like touching the moon.

Wanting Lillian to have all the available information before she made any decisions, Ivy spoke up. "If you can let go of the energy you're feeling right now, I have one more dialogue."

The suggestion brought Lillian back to the moment. "Absolutely! I want that. These last two sets have been so powerful, I can't wait to see what else might be out there."

After setting Miriam, Ivy stepped away and Lillian read the energy. "This one took me to the time in my childhood when I was learning to dive. It was both intimidating and exhilarating."

"That is what you would feel if you reached out to children and helped them connect to their authentic selves through journaling," Ivy said.

With Lillian grabbing her own face in sheer joy, Ivy explained why she'd set that energy. "During your story, strong emotion emanated when you talked about journaling as a child… and how that empowered you during rough patches."

Miriam added, "Once again, it's about helping others through your own experiences."

"Wouldn't that be fantastic." Lillian started pacing. "Imagine giving kids a tool that would help them with the choices they face."

"You know what I like about this one, besides your enthusiasm?" Miriam said. "It goes to what you were saying about me being part of the energy detectives… doing something that you felt was out of the ordinary. I think that's important to you. Something your spirit craves."

Ivy knew this conversation could easily gobble up the rest of the morning, and she would have enjoyed it, but she had another session coming up. "In the energy field, there's a million possible paths, all of them serving you in a different way. Today you learned three possible paths you can follow, Lillian. Each one is connected to your personal spirit, so you can be sure any of them will take you to the fulfillment you crave.

"You can actively pursue your artistic self.

"You can use Facebook to create a supportive community of women around breast health.

"You can empower children through journaling."

Ivy continued this train of thought. "None of them is better or best. All of them can be changed in ways that resonate with you. You can focus on one or blend any of the three. It's about you choosing the feeling you want to have in your life."

"I love them all," Lillian enthused. "I guess the next step is taking action and not just sitting around loving the ideas."

Ivy hugged her, hugged that very true insight. "Here's one way to start… make changes in your *usual*. Read different books. Drive different routes. Get up at a different time.

"Old habits, old routines, and old thinking will bring you more of what you already know. Anything new will open you up to fresh possibilities."

Thirteen ~ Paul

Paul burned his toast. Watching his Ninja whirl his morning smoothie, he'd forgotten to lift the lever that no longer popped up automatically.

He buttered it anyway. More important things had followed him into the morning from the previous night...

A nightmare with fire licking his heals as he leaped from a roof into oblivion.

A text from his older brother asking him to contact their mother because she was in one of her snits.

Fear that was stalking him once again.

Right now, that fear seeped out of the seams of his wood floor. Climbed the walls. Thickened the air and followed his every step.

Paul knew from past experiences he had to stay with his routines. His inclination was to fall into the chair in front of his window and let the fear consume him. That's what he use to do before he'd started seeing Ivy. While drowning in fear, days would go by when he could barely take care of necessities.

Music was his safeguard.

Turning off the Ninja, Paul closed his eyes and listened to the soothing sound of Fleetwood Mac. His turntable had given this particular album many rides in the past few years. This morning, it had been playing since a little after three o'clock.

Peach slices on the toast didn't hide the charcoal taste, but eating helped Paul hold fear at bay. He sipped his smoothie and watched his next door neighbor weeding. Clyde's long, gray ponytail and battered hat were as much a part of Paul's everyday view as the oak trees surrounding his cabin.

Paul knew Clyde would come by sometime during the day. He'd bring something his wife had baked or cooked, maybe mention the weather, and head back home. Every so often, he took time to tell Paul the oak tree fairies were hovering around Paul's cabin, a sure sign of a gentle soul living within.

Clyde and his wife had no idea how much their quiet presence reassured Paul. He was glad he could help them out when they needed muscle or an extra hand. And glad they didn't know fear sometimes hovered inside his cabin.

Picking up his phone, Paul continued watching Clyde, soothed by the constant movement. It was a far cry from the feeling he had when he looked at his brother's text once again.

He knew Ivy would remind him his true power was the choices he got to make every minute of every day. He agreed... but he'd have to call his mom sometime. His only real choice was whether that was now or later, and things only got worse when he delayed.

Paul stared at his phone wondering if calling his mom would ease or aggravate his fear.

He didn't know the answer.

Fear-days were unpredictable. Like horror movies they kept him on edge with no background music to help him sense what was coming. He didn't know what triggered the stalking anxiety. Why it went away. When it would escalate.

He could only hang on and believe fear would eventually withdraw.

Looking across the table at the lyrics he'd scribbled on the back of his utility bill, Paul read what he'd written for Ivy:

You tell me I can't. Make me feel I won't.
I'm lost in your vision of me.

With words that diminish, spread doubt, nurture dread,
Dreams get lost in the dirt.

He knew Ivy had asked him to write something that celebrated making money using his spirit. God only knew why this shit had come to him instead. Except he couldn't separate making money from his mom. They were as linked as Christmas and candy.

Paul picked up his phone and texted Ivy: Time for another session. Fear is back.

He'd wait and call his mom after a session. Consequences be damned.

Fourteen ~ Paul

Kendra loved the weekly Curious Club she offered kids at the library, but today her own curiosity was ignited. She was focused on the unexpected session Ivy had arranged for the detectives. It was unusual for them to meet two Saturdays in a row.

Pushing the chairs back in place, Kendra glanced around to make sure she'd remembered everything. Neat and tidy was given a little slack as she hurried out so she'd get to the barn on time.

After a quick drive-through at Wendy's, Kendra scarfed chicken nuggets and fries as she drove to the barn. She arrived with her root beer and three minutes to spare.

"What have we got going here?" she asked as she sat in one of the two remaining chairs. "I could barely wait."

The last chair was for Paul. Though he'd given Ivy permission to share "any frick'n thing that might help", she only shared the bare essentials.

By the time Paul arrived, Kendra, Jill, Miriam, and Vanessa knew he needed this time with them because he was being triggered by fear. They knew he had originally come to Ivy with back pain.

Paul wore his shield of confidence as he announced, "I'm here." Taking off his hoodie, he tossed it on the table holding their purses and stepped forward with a smile.

Ivy was out of her chair and next to him in a flash. "We were just talking about you."

He closed his eyes and took in the compassion of her hug before looking back to the other women getting out of their chairs. "Did you tell them I'm no better company than a bear with a thorn in his paw?"

"We're all right with that." Kendra liked him already. She introduced herself and then the others.

It wasn't a handshake kind of moment. Too soon for hugs. Sincere smiles and chatter embraced Paul.

"Actually, I was just saying I have tremendous respect for you," Miriam offered. "Not many young men are brave enough to explore their feelings."

"Or be able to leave the house when fear shows up." It sent a shiver through Jill. "I've been there and know."

Vanessa teased as she wrapped her arm around Kendra's shoulders. "This one was saying the real deal is having the courage to spend 2-3 hours with us. But don't worry. Even though there's a whole lot of female here, we promise to be gentle."

Paul got the impression his fear had met its match. He imagined his *stalker* must surely be intimidated by their openness. By the time they were all seated, he knew he had made the right decision to come.

Ivy got things started. "Paul, I've told everyone that you came to me with back pain and you're currently feeling attacked by fear. Fill us in on any details beyond that."

"First, do you have any carbonated water on hand? Drinking something fizzy takes the edge off."

"Ha!" Vanessa chuckled as she got up and headed for the refrigerator in the kitchen. "Let that be a lesson, ladies."

Paul looked at Ivy for an explanation. "We tease her about always bringing lots of food. When I texted everyone, I said we didn't need to bring anything."

Kendra interrupted. "Don't tell me. She came loaded with bags."

Jill filled her in. "Not loaded, but she insisted we needed some drinks and snacks even if we're together for only a few hours."

Vanessa walked back into the studio with a smug smile, glass of ice, and a tall bottle of flavored, carbonated water."

Thanking her, Paul lifted the bottle and raised his brows... asking permission.

Vanessa got the question. She, with two teenage sons, nodded. "Sure. Drink right out of the bottle. We've got lots."

After one long gulp, Paul held the bottle in his hands and leaned forward. Resting his elbows on his knees, he began.

"It was happening before I came to Ivy. I started feeling like something bad was going to happen. I mean, really bad. Like my gas line was going to explode. Or, if I drove, I'd hit a pedestrian. I could tell myself it wasn't real, but that was like putting a fire out with gasoline."

Staring at his lime water, slowly turning the bottle, Paul seemed to get lost in the fear. He took another sip. A deep breath. "Ivy's helped me find ways to de-escalate the fear so I can function. But... she says it won't go away until I understand the message it's trying to give me. Until I get to the root of why it shows up."

Shaking his head, Paul admitted, "I haven't been ready. Not until this episode. I mean, what in the name of Batman am I doing wimping around my cabin like a kid scared of ghosts?"

Looking around the group, he declared. "So, I'm here and ready, and Ivy said working with you guys would be powerful."

Miriam asked the obvious question. "Since you've been working with Ivy, I'm assuming you know how to work with energy dialogues."

"It's right up there with drumming... I'm good."

Ivy added, "Paul's got it down and he's courageous. He'll fit right in... anywhere we go."

"Paul, tell us what you were doing the day before your fear arrived?" Jill's arms hugged her mid-section, an instinctive response from her days in fear. "Just the main highlights that come up when you think back to that day."

As he sipped his water, Paul started recalling Thursday. "Weeded my garden in the morning. Went to Andy's Market on my way to have coffee with a friend. Read my book when I got home, then had two drum students." His thumb tapping the bottle, it took him a moment to recall the end of his day. "Popcorn. Had some popcorn and looked around YouTube. Went to bed."

"We're going to do a group dialogue for you." Jill explained how he would leave the room and come back and check the energy each of them was holding... moving from one to another.

"Got it." Paul gave Ivy a smile and raised brow. She knew he was all in.

"Do you know where the kitchen is?" Vanessa asked and then encouraged him to dig into the snacks while he waited. "It's the way we roll around here."

"I'm liking this group more all the time."

The sleuths started moving into a huddle as Paul left, but looked up when he spoke from the door. "Almost forgot. Got a text from my brother, Mike, while I was cruising YouTube."

"Okay." Jill spoke up as he slipped into the kitchen. "I want us to hold different aspects of his day that might be connected to his fear." They chose three:

Kendra/*meeting friend*

Ivy/*YouTube*

Miriam/*text*

Vanessa sat back down, and Jill went to get Paul. She found him leaning against the counter eating a handful of peanuts. "We're ready. We have three sets waiting for you… each one focuses on something you did on Thursday. We want to see if any of them triggered your fear."

Paul tossed the remaining peanuts into his mouth, rubbing the salt residue on his jeans as he followed Jill into the studio.

He read Kendra first. "I saw music notes drifting in the breeze, and it jacked me up.

"I was holding you having coffee with your friend."

"So that's all good. We like getting together to jam… or talk music."

Paul moved on and read the energy Ivy was holding. "With you, I walked into a fantasy library. When I opened the books, they talked to me. I wanted to stay, but also felt overwhelmed… like I wanted to open every book and knew I couldn't.'"

"That was YouTube."

Paul laughed. "Get outta here. This stuff makes logic look like nursery rhymes."

In the nods and murmurs of agreement, he turned his focus on Miriam.

Paul took a deep breath as he stepped away. "A fire-breathing dragon… big as a house… in my face. I was trying to back up but couldn't move fast enough."

Before Miriam could share what she'd held, he was hit with an insight that rang absolutely true. He knew it to the core of his being. "You were the text."

Miriam nodded, and Paul looked over at Ivy. "Did I tell them my fears are mostly about fire?"

"I don't think you did."

Paul reached for his bottle of water and finished it. "My worst fear is being burned alive. It feels like there's a fire ready to ignite, and I can't do anything about it."

101

"Then I think Miriam's energy just gave you a big insight," Jill suggested. "There's a difference between believing you *could be burned* and recognizing your fear *feels like* a fire-breathing dragon. It really turned things around for me when I got that kind of distinction."

Crunching the plastic bottle, Paul asked, "What was your fear?"

"My twins, who were five at that time, were going to be kidnapped. I was terrified and absolutely sure it was going to happen."

"Was there a reason?"

Jill shook her head. "No. That's what's so crazy-making about these fear triggers. They aren't based on what's currently happening in our life. They're symbolic."

"So...." Paul was wrapping his mind around this. "When I know the root cause of my fear, I'll be seeing something that makes me feel like a fire-breathing dragon is going to burn me."

"Yes," Jill confirmed.

Kendra jumped in. "Sitting here right now, describe what you think it would feel like to be burned up."

"Sitting here right now, I'm blown away that you guys can talk about this shit like we're sharing recipes or something."

Ivy repeated the question. "How would you describe what you imagine it feels like to be burned up?"

Paul started crunching the water bottle once again. "A lot of pain that I'd be aware of," he began twirling the bottle, "and I can't get away from it."

Vanessa leaned forward. "Go to your inner wisdom and see how this possibility feels to you.... is someone else starting the fire?"

"What do you mean?"

"During your fear attacks, when you think of fire, are you the one starting the fire? Or does the fire come out of nowhere?"

"Oh." Paul got it. "I've never thought about it before, but I'm sure as hell not the one starting the fire." He looked around the circle. "Looks like I need to know who the dragon is."

Ivy nodded. "Want us to create another dialogue for you?"

Paul's face showed his grim determination, but he got up and headed for the kitchen asking if there was any chocolate in the pile of snacks.

"There's some mini brownies," Vanessa called to him.

"You really are the food angel," Miriam said as they pulled their chairs closer.

102

After exploring different sets they might use, Kendra volunteered to get Paul. She brought the carton of brownies out for everyone. Setting them on the nearest footstool, she explained the purpose of the dialogue. "Since the text was from your brother and family related, we wanted to see if there was any strong connection between the dragon and the two members of your family that Ivy thought were significant during your sessions with her."

Anticipation waited patiently as Paul stepped up to Ivy for the first energy reading.

"Job interview came to me."

"How did that feel to you?" Ivy wanted more information.

"I felt like I was dressed to the nines and had a killer resume, but wasn't going to make the grade."

From her chair, Vanessa asked, "Is it safe to say this person in your family makes you feel like you don't meet his or her expectations?"

"That feels right. And following that line of thinking, I lose out even though all my ducks are all lined up."

Miriam added, "You don't get to be yourself and get what you want."

Paul felt the truth of that. "You sure you haven't met my family? You've got them down. Which one were you, Ivy?"

"Your dad's mother." She watched Paul's complexion blanch. "I remembered you telling me your dad had no balls because his mother dictated his every move."

"Is she a big part of your life?" Miriam asked.

"She's the grand matriarch." Paul's disgust wrapped around every word. "I see her as little as possible, but she's got a long arm."

"Is she the dragon?" Jill asked.

He shook his head. "She's more like the ruling queen of the Bascom family. I don't go to her castle anymore or even enter the family realm when she's present. I wrote her off when I went to college. And she wrote me out of her will. We've got an understanding."

Paul wasn't surprised that his statement was accepted, but he was startled to have the circle celebrate his choice. They got that it honored his personal spirit.

He managed the unexpected emotional hug by turning his attention to the energy Vanessa had held. "You were a forest fire."

"The source of your fear?" she asked.

The barn joined everyone in waiting for a possible revelation. Paul walked over and grabbed a couple of brownies before handing the carton to Kendra. She took three and passed it on to Jill as Paul confirmed this energy was the source of his fear. "I felt the same panic… caught in a fire, trying to get away, it coming too fast for me to escape." He looked back to Vanessa. "Who were you?"

"Your mother."

Paul dropped down on a nearby footstool. "Damn. That's a lot like looking for your shadow. It's been there all along. Don't you think so, Ivy?"

"We've walked around her energy many times," she agreed. "It became a significant clue for me because you've avoided following the trail every single time."

"So why didn't you point me in the right direction?" Paul was mostly curious, but there was an edge to his question.

Ivy felt comfortable with it. "Energy work is always about each person finding their own truth. I'm not here to point out answers. My job is to help you explore possibilities that might lead to your own insights."

"I know. I *know* that. It's been very clear. This is on me."

Jill stepped in gently. "It sounds like you're most bothered about taking so long to see the answer rather than seeing your mother as the dragon."

"Can you pass those brownies?" Paul asked as he considered this observation. Vanessa brought the carton to him. He looked at the two remaining treats nestled among the crumbs as he spoke. "Honestly? In our crappy relationship, I've probably called her a dragon. We've been sparing for as long as I can remember."

"I have a dialogue," Miriam announced. "This is an interactive one, so you can sit down and watch, Paul. I'll be setting three people, and they'll physically respond to the energy they experience. You'll get the insight by seeing how the energies relate to each other."

"So they talk?"

"No, it's still silent."

"Okay." Paul finished off the brownies while he watched Miriam set Jill, Kendra, and Vanessa. Pulling a footstool next to Paul, Miriam whispered, "Jill's holding your *mother's* energy. Kendra… your *grandmother's* energy. Vanessa… *your* energy."

The three detectives were already in movement when she looked up.

Kendra/*grandmother* was like a herding dog. She kept trying to bring the other two energies close to her. Jill/*mother* and Vanessa/*Paul* wouldn't comply.

Paul got it... *he could see his grandmother wanted everyone under her thumb.*

What he found even more interesting was the way his mother was confrontational about wanting her own space, while he tried to use their interaction to slip away. But they noticed.

They're on me like bees on honey,.. I can't slip away, and that's what I've been trying to do, Paul thought.

When the dialogue became repetitive, Miriam brought it to an end with, "Okay."

"You nailed the tail on this donkey," Paul announced. "The fire follows my movement no matter how far away I move or try to avoid it."

"That's what I saw in the interacting energies." Miriam was excited that the set provided information for Paul. "Even though your grandmother and mother were in a power struggle, they were very aware of you. There's a forceful energy connection among the three of you."

"Yep." Paul felt the weight of that heavy truth. He'd done everything he could to live his own life, but the bond with his mom and grandmother felt stronger than Gorilla glue.

"Would you like to explore that connection?" Ivy asked. "If you can see what drives it, you'll feel empowered to let it go."

The weight got lighter. "Yes."

"You'll need to head back to the kitchen while we work on it."

Part of the fun of energy work was the way intuitive hits started firing more rapidly as the dialogues unfolded. It took only a few minutes for the group to choose what they would hold for Paul. They wanted him to experience possible energy connections between himself and his mother:

Ivy/*anger*
Vanessa/*money*
Kendra/*guilt*
Jill/*reacting.*

While Miriam leaned back and watched from her chair, Paul started with Ivy. "That felt like a rattlesnake. I was aware it could strike out, but I could also avoid it."

"I was holding anger, Ivy said.

Nodding, seeing the connection, Paul told everyone what he'd learned about his mother and anger during his last session with Ivy.

"We were looking for my energy leak, and it turned out to be my anger toward my mother. I felt angry about the way she reacts to my making money using my creativity. Right, Ivy?"

She nodded and he expanded. "Anyway, that anger is linked to my back pain. You could say she's a pain in the… back." Paul's light laughter got smiles. "I'm surprised my mother-anger isn't the energy connection we're looking for, but it's still a big one."

Miriam adjusted the pillow at her back. "Rattlesnakes won't stop you, but they sure as heck make you more cautious."

Paul's eyes opened wide. "Good point."

Vanessa held the energy of *money* because he'd talked about being disinherited by his grandmother. Paul saw the oak tree fairies his neighbor was occasionally pointing out. Money wasn't the connection.

Kendra's energy was very neutral. "Felt like riding a merry-go-round," Paul said.

Kendra explained, "I was holding *guilt.* Sometimes we feel like we're betraying our family when we're the black sheep. Because we don't fit or meet expectations."

Paul shook his head, "I didn't feel engaged and that pretty much describes me and guilt in my family."

Paul felt his stomach tighten as he checked Jill. "Your energy made me feel like I was being put in a straight jacket. I sensed I resisted, but was overcome."

Paul felt both curious and concerned. Ivy always said information was power, but, in this case, he knew something big was coming at him. Overwhelm was hovering.

"I was holding *reacting,*" Jill revealed.

"Reacting? You'll have to tell me what you mean."

"When I was holding this energy, I was seeing you make choices by reacting to your mom. Defining yourself by going against her expectations."

A kaleidoscope of his life came to Paul's mind's eye. He saw a series of moments when he resisted his mother's influence by rejecting her suggestions and demands.

In grade school, she chose his shoes. He scuffed them up at every opportunity. His friends thought him a hoot.

She signed him up for football in middle school. He was benched more often than not for missing practice.

She insisted he go to college. He packed his car, drove past the campus and kept right on driving. He told himself he was taking a coming-of-age road trip and was labeled irresponsible.

"This is a big one. You know how to peel the skin right off a guy. Shit!"

Everyone moved to the chairs and sat down. "What are you thinking, Paul?" Kendra moved the footstool she was sitting on closer to him.

"I'm thinking that set was powerful. I need time to let it sink in. The straight jacket is how I feel with my mom, so I react. Right?"

Vanessa offered her take on the straight jacket insight. "When your mom pushes you in any particular direction, your personal spirit feels restricted. You feel your authentic self being consumed in the same way a fire would extinguish you. So you react.

Paul nodded, but it was clear he was still trying to sort through the possibilities.

Miriam offered her perspective. "The energy connection between you and your mother is the root cause of your fear-trigger. That connection came up the other day because you got a text and you felt compelled to react. Either call or don't call… it didn't matter… you were in reaction mode. The fire had been started."

"It's amazing how something as simple and small as a text can become an event, isn't it?" Jill knew the pattern well.

"So…" Paul ventured. "The message from my fear is to stop my knee-jerk reaction when it comes to my mom. That's the way I can change our relationship." He was hopeful.

"We'll need to do more work with that," Ivy answered. "You can't use logic and will-power to create the shift. It goes deeper than that. But, we can do another energy set to help you get started."

"Let's go! Let's go… let's go." Paul wanted to leave this Saturday session with a tool.

This time, Paul left the studio to use the bathroom while the detectives brainstormed. They all liked Vanessa's suggestion. "Let's help him identify his super power for responding to his mother."

"Great idea. I choose his *personal spirit*, so he knows what's best for him," Kendra volunteered.

Jill had hers. "Using his *voice*."

Ivy added, "*Writing lyrics*."

Miriam asked, "Does he *meditate*, Ivy?"

"Yes."

"Then that's my choice."

"I want to do something *physical*. Get the serotonin going," Vanessa suggested. "Is there something he especially likes, Ivy?"

"Biking. Walking… yard work."

"I'll hold all of those… whatever feels best in the moment."

Kendra called out in a voice she'd never use at the library, "Paul. We're ready."

One-by-one they explored what might be his super power for overcoming his instinct to react. Lyrics, meditation, and using his voice were positive, but being guided by his personal spirit and being physical were much stronger.

Paul liked both of them. "If I'm weeding or riding my bike, I'm totally in touch with my personal spirit."

"So you've got a two-pronged super power." Vanessa made it sound like gold. Now your challenge is remembering them and using them when you feel that knee-jerk reaction to your mom."

"I'm not sure I'll even know it's happening."

Jill had an idea from her own experience. "Make a deal with yourself. You won't acknowledge your mom's demands in the moment it happens. Have a go-to response like, "I'll get back to you on that." Give yourself all the time you need to be physical. To connect with your personal spirit. And only then, give her an answer or take action that serves you."

"I like it, but it'll be hard."

"Of course it will!" Kendra laughed. "But not as hard as suffering through another fear-storm."

"You got me there."

"You can do it," Ivy assured him. "If you can heal your back pain, you can do this."

"Damn right I can."

Miriam raised her arms with a loud, "Yes!"

Paul watched as each detective joined her, and then he joined the chorus of the powerful chant. Their 'yes' affirmation felt as powerful as drumming. Everyone picked up on the beat and their bodies responded. They moved as instinctively as a cat smelling catnip.

As he grabbed his hoodie, hugged each one of them goodbye, and walked out to his car, Paul knew the journey wasn't over. They had been very clear this was just a giant step in the right direction, but he felt lighthearted. Even joyful. It had been the weirdest, most amazing Saturday afternoon of his life.

Fifteen ~ Nora

Nora much preferred taking her car to an independent mechanic. She knew that, like her dad, they had to build their clientele with excellent service and reputation. She'd been told Rick Parks had both.

He was also on her way to work and offered a loaner-car. Nora drove up to his garage thinking her previous mechanic's retirement might be a blessing in disguise.

Before she turned off the ignition, a friendly face emerged from the shaded workspace behind two open garage doors. "You must be Nora Ruben. I'm Rick. Why don't you just drive on in, right here," he pointed. "Into the left stall."

Leaving the sunlight behind, Nora eased her car forward until he shouted, "Good. That'll work just fine."

Her car door was opened with flair and a smile, but Nora didn't notice. Gripping the steering wheel, staring at her hands, she fought off the light-headedness that had followed her into the cool shadows.

Hesitantly reaching for his offered hand, Nora stepped out of her car seeking the solid ground with legs that felt hollow. She used her voice to overcome a silence that hovered around her like the Grim Reaper. "You have a nice place here. It reminds me of my uncle's garage."

"Mechanic or car buff?" Rick was oblivious to Nora's internal drama. She responded to his casual question and felt more settled.

"Both, actually. He worked for my dad but refurbished cars in his spare time at his home garage. You might have known them. Kevin and Neil Torrence?"

"Dang me, if I don't! You couldn't ask for more go-for-it guys if you wanted to get into a bit of trouble." Rick was lit up with a memory.

Nora felt like her clothes were the only thing holding her up. "Trouble?"

"As a kid, I'd stop by their garage for a candy bar when I was supposed to be running an errand. They'd let me hang around, hand them tools. That kind of thing. Who knows. Maybe I've got my own place now because of those afternoons."

Nora looked around. The smell was the same, but Uncle Neil's garage had been as organized as a library. "Do I need to sign a work order before I leave? I'm on my way to work."

"Nah. I'll just give your car a complete servicing and call if anything unexpected shows up. You good with that?"

Her wooziness easing up, Nora agreed.

Rick headed for his office in the back corner of the garage. "Follow me, and I'll get the key to your loaner."

Nora walked by the shelves lining the left wall, saw the light coming out of his office. It sprayed the floor at the end of the shelves, and her feet became heavy. Her heart beat crawled into her throat. Shivers up her spine warned her to turn around, but her feet kept moving forward. They turned left at the end of the shelf. Crossed the threshold to his office.

"Here you go, ma'am." Nora looked at Rick holding the key in a bright blue key ring. "It goes to the gray Corolla right outside. Cleaned it just this morning."

She didn't know where she found her voice. How she walked out of the garage. Or how she drove herself to work. But Sally, being a perceptive receptionist, kept her moving through the day.

By the time Nora was getting ready to pick up her car, she recognized what had happened. Somehow, entering the garage had triggered something dark from her past. It had consumed her when she was at Rick's. It had lingered throughout the day. And she was damn well going to find out what had spooked her. She might have walked unaware into an unpleasant memory, but some of her greatest breaks in divorce court came with the unexpected.

Sixteen ~ Nora

With Ivy at her side and the barn feeling like a friend, Nora was immersed in deep relaxation. She'd gratefully followed Ivy's guided visualization. Leaving her tension behind. Nora listened to the whispers of her inner wisdom.

The meditation had taken her to her safe, ocean retreat when she heard Ivy's reminder. "Even though your adult self came ready to dig in and find answers today, don't be surprised if your inner child, who experienced this memory, resists. She dissociated for a very good reason, and, for her, that reason still exists. She'll have to learn to trust you."

"She *can* trust me."

"I know." Ivy's smile was gentle. Nora's passion for children was going to be an unflinching force in her healing journey. "Do you feel yourself sitting on the beach? Your feet in the surf?"

"Yes."

"Go to the feeling you had when you were in the garage. Don't let it take over. Let it move through your body as a messenger knowing you are safe with the sound of the surf. Nod your head when you feel connected."

Ivy watched to see if Nora could go back to that feeling. "You're doing great," she encouraged. "Let the sensation be with you. Know you recognize this exact feeling from another time. You have an inner child who's been living with this feeling and is ready to share with you.

"Silently, in your mind's eye, tell her you're ready. You will believe anything she has to share. She can trust you."

Ivy gave Nora a few moments and continued, "Look down the beach to your right. You'll see your inner child coming toward you. Nod when you see her."

The nod came quickly.

"Silently, ask her to come sit with you and see how she responds. Accept any choice she makes and tell me what happens."

Nora's voice was nearly a whisper. "She was coming toward me, but stopped."

"That's okay. Thank her for showing up. Ask her what she needs to feel comfortable."

"Her blue bike. So she can leave if she wants."

"Look behind you, Nora. Her blue bike is leaning against a palm tree. Move slowly and take it to her. Stop if she gets concerned or agitated."

Ivy watched Nora's expression move from serious to serene. "She has her bike. We're sitting together."

"Wonderful. Tell her how much you appreciate her being with you. That you recognize the courage it took for her to come to you. Let her know she can ride away on her bike any time she doesn't feel safe."

"She likes that."

"How old is she? Don't try to figure it out. Just let the age pop up. You know the answer."

"Six. She's wearing her favorite Sunday school dress. I'd forgotten about that pink thing."

"Let her know how fun it is to see it again. Reassure her that she is totally safe on the beach. No one can come unless they're invited.

"Tell her you came today because you got scared and thought she could help. Ask her if she'll help you."

"Yes. She's nodding yes."

"Silently, tell her what you experienced Monday morning at the garage. Ask her if she remembers feeling that way."

Nora recalled her physical reaction to the garage. Even though nothing happened, she'd felt on high alert and anxious the entire time. She knew the feeling from watching movies, when the music told you all hell was about to break loose.

Ivy watched Nora's eyelids become active. Saw tears building in the corner of her eyes. "What's happening?"

"My little girl doesn't like garages. She doesn't like it when her daddy takes her to Uncle Neil's."

"Why?'

Nora appeared to recede into the chair. She held her kleenex against her eyes. "The green swirl is back. It's intimidating me."

"Is it in your uncle's garage?"

"Yes."

"How big is it, Nora?"

"It's everywhere. I don't like it."

"Is your little girl with you?"

"Yes. She can see it. She's doesn't like it either."

Ivy sought more information. "Ask her why she doesn't like it."

The kleenex stayed firmly pressed against Nora's eyes when she answered. "It knows."

"What does it know?"

Nora's deep frown froze. Her long-held belief was still in charge. "If I tell you, you'll call me a liar. No one believes little girls. They tell stories that can't be true."

"I'll believe you. Let your little girl know that you and I will believe anything she tells us. Let her know that her story will be a great help to you."

Nora shook her head. "It's too icky. We won't believe her."

"What's icky, Nora?"

With the tissue hiding her eyes, Nora didn't move. Time and space opened up for answers. Ivy watched Nora's breathing and knew she was not avoiding the question, and then she looked like she'd eaten a lemon. Her mouth and tongue were trying to get rid of the taste.

Nora shivered as her little girl spoke. Each word stretched out in monotone aversion. "Something   icky   in my   mouth."

Ivy placed her hand on Nora's arm. "Tell your little girl we believe her. Hug her. Tell her she was very brave, and we know she doesn't tell lies. Nod when you know she believes you."

Tears came in an avalanche… sobs released by a secret revealed and accepted. They fractured Nora's reserve, cascading through her and into the safe space of Ivy's barn.

Ivy held her hand still. She knew any soothing movement would stop the free-flowing release of feelings. Coming from an ocean of pain, these tears from the past would seem endless. Nora might wonder if she'd drown, but Ivy knew they wouldn't last long and every tear brought profound healing. Each droplet was pulling long-held trauma out of every cell in her client's body. Ivy knew something wonderful was happening.

She took the wet kleenex from Nora and handed her more tissues until sobs turned into deep, shaky breathing. Rubbing Nora's arm, Ivy spoke. "Hug your little girl. Tell her you believe her. That she was very brave."

Ivy waited. Whatever was happening in Nora's inner world, it seemed like an angel was now present. Serenity and joy were radiating as Nora's face relaxed.

"How does your little girl feel?"

"She trusts me."

"Because you believed her?" Ivy asked.

Nora nodded.

"Ask her what made her feel powerless when the green swirl showed up."

"She was all alone."

Ivy moved forward. "Are you still in your uncle's garage?"

"Yes."

"I want you to feel the green again."

"It's here."

In deep relaxation healing, Ivy worked with both her client and her client's inner child. Though it would have been confusing if anyone had been listening in, it felt completely natural for Ivy to be with Nora and her inner child at the same time.

This unique and powerful communication was possible because, in the energy field, there was no dimension of time. Nora, Nora's inner child, and Ivy could transcend the concept of time to come together… work together… talk among themselves… and heal.

"Nora, let your little girl use her voice. Have her tell the green swirl that she's no longer alone. She has you, and you will always believe her… whatever she tells you. She doesn't have to make sense. She can scream. Throw a tantrum. Mumble. And all the time you'll be standing beside her, hearing and supporting her. Nod when you're done."

In these kinds of moments, Ivy often felt she could see her clients stepping into sunshine, escaping the low-lying fog of their emotional wounds. From one moment to the next, they looked younger.

"She's done." Nora felt replete. Worn out and calm, she was an explorer sitting on the top of the mountain after a steep climb.

"Now I want your adult-self to talk to the green swirl," Ivy said. "Let your little girl experience your current power to stand up for children.

"Say everything she needs to hear to feel understood and believed. As you do this, notice how the green dissolves. Keep talking until it's gone."

Ivy glanced at the clock not knowing if minutes or hours had passed in the Place-Of-No-Time. She needed to start pulling the pieces together rather than guide Nora to new insights.

"The green is gone."

"Hooray! Celebrate with your little girl. Dance. Cheer. Whatever feels right for her. Working together, you made that swirling, shaming energy go away. Nod when you're done."

When Nora nodded, Ivy asked how they celebrated.

"We rode away on our bikes. I have one now. The same color."

"Wonderful. Ride to your ocean retreat. Let me know when you arrive."

"We're here."

Ivy touched Nora's shoulder. "Tell your little girl she gets to stay here and can talk to you anytime. Whenever you think 'blue bike', you'll know she's calling to you, and you'll come to the retreat to be with her."

Waiting just a moment, Ivy continued. "Nora, I want you to find a quiet place on the beach. You don't need to bring your little girl. She's safe and can play. Nod when you're seated."

The nod was immediate.

"I want you to know that you saved your little girl today. She's been caught in that moment since it happened, and you have taken her out. She's now released from her trauma and free to explore the world feeling safe. Being believed. And you'll feel that in your own life.

"In the upcoming days, you might notice how little things change. It will happen automatically, without you trying, because of what you did today."

Gently rubbing Nora's shoulder, Ivy continued. "I'm going to bring you out of relaxation, but first I want to ask you a question. Let the answer pop up. If it doesn't come to you, that's okay. It just means it's not time. What happened to your little girl's mouth?"

Nora's skin flushed red. "Penis in her mouth."

"Whose penis?"

Nora shook her head. "Who would do that to a six-year-old child?"

116

"In the days ahead, your little girl might be ready to share that. Trust what comes up, even if it doesn't make sense. You're holding that information in your body. Let it talk to you."

Seventeen ~ Nora

Continuing the conversation that had begun in the car, Nora and Luke were lost in the tangled jungle of what had been uncovered that afternoon. The box holding their favorite sausage pizza from Antonia's sat between them on the kitchen table waiting for them to dig in. The wine bottle remained uncorked.

"What do you mean when you say 'the green' seems to know something?" Luke needed more information.

"During my first session, I experienced a momentary menacing sensation… a thick mist of green suddenly showed up and disappeared just as quickly… off to my left. It was a presence that felt like it knew." Nora thought back to that moment. "It made me feel ashamed."

Luke had already learned how important it was to listen without delving for details. That could come later, as the thread of Nora's story became clear. He nodded and waited.

"The green showed up again when I was in deep relaxation… at Uncle Neil's garage. It knew what happened to me there."

Nora looked down. Rolled her paper napkin. Unrolled it. "Oral sex," squeezed passed a whisper. Her lips compressed as those two words hit the air.

She had felt the physical sensation with Ivy. They had talked about what that meant to her little girl. But this was the first time Nora had said the damning words out loud. She felt slimed. And freed. She wondered if Luke would believe such a thing could have happened to her.

He responded in a heart beat. "Do you know who did it?"

"Ivy asked too. The answer didn't come, but I think it's pretty obvious that it was my uncle. It was his garage." She twisted the napkin, trying to stay with the feeling. "Luke… I just remembered the office in his garage was painted green. Pea-green, ugly, dark green."

"The green that knew." Luke saw the connection. "It must have happened in his office."

"That's why I felt so weird when I walked into Rick's office on Monday."

"Was it green?" Luke asked.

"No, but it felt the same. The door was at the end of the shelves. It was off in the corner. No windows. The way the overhead light shined on the floor outside the office door."

"The walls knew." Luke didn't try to hide the grim wave that washed over him. "Do you think it happened just this once?"

That caught Nora. It dragged her into a rabbit hole where a labyrinth of possibilities waited for her. "I don't know."

"Maybe it doesn't matter."

Nora's temper flared. "Oh, it matters all right. It matters a lot. I'm wondering if my uncle liked messing around with little girls?" She stared at the pizza, recognized it was getting cold. "Maybe my dad caught him, and that's why he suddenly dropped out of my life."

As they played with this conceivable scenario, Luke picked up a piece of pizza and nibbled.

Nora followed suit and couldn't taste a thing. Her mind wandered. Unfamiliar feelings pulled her in unexpected directions. "I don't know how it fits, but a client I saw last week is coming to mind. She's like a fly landing on our conversation. I keep swatting her away, and she's back."

"Don't swat at her. There must be a reason she's getting your attention. What is it about her that you recall?"

Taking another bite, Nora let the appointment play like a video. Feelings from that meeting passed through her. "It was the warm scarf she was wearing. Seemed odd that she was wearing it in this weather, but I assumed she wore it like a light sweater."

"So we're talking about fashion?"

As Luke made that observation, Nora was hit with an insight. "It made me intensely uncomfortable, and I'm realizing I never wear scarves or mufflers. Nothing around my neck."

He hadn't thought about it before. "And no turtlenecks." Both of them knew turtleneck gifts were taboo.

A puzzle they didn't know existed took them into their own reflections. Pieces from the past began forming a pattern. Luke got up and grabbed a dish towel. He gently draped it around Nora's neck.

"What the hell! Why did you do that!?" Tears glistened in angry eyes. Trembling hands yanked at the cloth.

"Maybe we're figuring out why you don't like things around your neck." Luke sat down and took the towel. "What are you feeling right now?"

"Scared. Overwhelmed." She was fighting the sobs welling up, a tidal wave of emotion held in check by blinking eyelids.

"It's okay to cry."

Shaking her head, Nora looked at him through a tunnel from the past. "Crying doesn't do any good."

Eighteen ~ Nora

This time, Julie wasn't with Nora in the dream.

The bed moved, carrying her into the corner, once again. The bare walls and eerie calm held Nora in place as surely as a coffin nailed shut. The shadows from the single overhead light bulb terrorized. She grabbed for safety and found her hand wrapped around a flannel shirt. Heart pounding, Nora felt her scream caught in her throat as she opened her eyes.

"You okay?" Luke hovered over her.

"Yes. It was the dream again." Remembering that movement helped the last time, Nora started shifting her feet, her hands. She sat up. The dream gradually left her body, leaving visual impressions and stunned senses.

She could hear the deathly silence.

Taste the fear.

See the light fighting the shadows.

Smell anguish.

Feel the flannel in her hand.

Luke reached over and turned on the bedside lamp, thinking light might help Nora move out of the dream. At the very least, he would be able to see her face on this moonless, cloudy night. "You made the same strangled sound."

"I was aware of trying to scream."

"It was more like talking underwater."

"Or gagged." Nora was as surprised as Luke as the description tumbled out of her mouth. The words hovered between them.

"Were you gagged in the dream?"

"No. I don't have a sense of being gagged. Is that how I sounded?"

Luke thought about it. "Not really."

Nora snuggled back under their quilt. For comfort.

Luke laid down beside her. "Was this the same dream as before?"

"There was the bed thing again."

Nora shivered. "The light bulb was there... casting shadows like something was lurking.

"And the bare walls."

Nora turned on her side facing Luke and adjusted her pillow. "The silence was just as eerie and bone-chilling. I wish you could be there with me and experience the otherworldly sensation of the soundless movement. It's like everything's alive."

Luke reached out for Nora's hand. "Similar to your session with Ivy and the green walls knowing?"

"Sort of... but, in my dream, it's not as obvious. The silence doesn't just sit there. It hovers. The walls aren't just walls, they're.... they." Nora looked for the right words to describe her surreal experience. "They're very real, and I get the feeling they're painted with dark secrets."

As he had many times since the first dream, Luke grappled with something beyond him. Nora's healing journey was taking him to foreign landscapes wearing a blindfold. And while she did her best to paint a picture with words, he very often had to trust it would all make sense as they moved forward. Together, they were exploring a world neither of them had known existed until a month ago.

"Are you scared? Are you still trapped in the dream?"

"No. Moving helps. Talking about it makes all the difference. Just wish I felt more in control during the dream."

"Maybe you could start telling yourself you'll scream out loud if the dream comes back."

"So, I'd try to yell when everything starts moving... before the fear becomes too strong." Nora's subdued giggle was a final step out of her dream world. "You might want to consider a hair-raising howl might be more disturbing for you than my struggle to scream."

"I'll manage."

Luke and Nora weren't snugglers, but this night Nora moved toward him, and he wrapped his arm around her waist. As she grabbed the quilt to warm her shoulders, she froze. "Luke, I forgot something from the dream. There was a flannel shirt on the bed that wasn't there last time."

"You don't like flannel."

"I know, but I grabbed it when I was scared. I think I was just grabbing for anything, and it was there. That's what woke me up. It jolted me right out of the dream."

Luke waited to see if there was more.

There was. "I felt like I'd grabbed a boa constrictor."

Nineteen ~ Nora

Nora felt out of her body. There was a feeling of floating above the car as Luke drove them to her mother's condo.

She was also determined.

She'd woken up Thursday morning knowing she needed to look at old family photos. Something told her there was an answer to be found.

"Thanks for using your Saturday to visit my mom. I need you there to deflect her, so I can look at the pictures without her hanging over my shoulder. Do you mind?"

"Not a bit. I'm thinking I'll ask her to come help me pick out your birthday gift. Maybe take her to lunch."

"That's a fantastic idea. It'll give me lots of time. You really are my hero, you know."

Luke smiled. Nora declared someone her hero almost daily. He always liked joining the ranks.

When they arrived, her mother was ready with coffee and breakfast muffins. A fresh bouquet sat on the coffee table. Everything was immaculate. Tasteful… just as Nora would expect of her mom.

Nora tamped down her impatience and sipped her coffee, trying to think of something to say when every thought was taking her back to Neil's garage. Her hero stepped forward with a question about the condo association. That was sure to start a conversation.

Nora nodded. Smiled. Even found a relevant question about a troublesome neighbor before asking if the photos were available.

"Oh yes, Dear. I laid out all the boxes and albums on the dining room table. Are you looking for anything in particular?"

"Not really. I had my car serviced last week and it made me think of Uncle Neil's garage. Thought it might be fun to see if you have anything from that time."

"I'm sure I do. Probably in the dark blue album. Or in the boxes. Would you like me to help? We can have a morning of reminiscing."

Luke spoke up. "Actually, Caroline, I was hoping you'd do me a favor. I'm trying to find Nora something special for this birthday and was hoping you'd help me."

Nora felt a pang of unfamiliar sadness when she saw how much Luke's request meant to her mom. She thought about the way her mom loved... quietly doing tasks for others from a distance. Unknowingly, Luke had found the perfect way for Caroline to be part of her daughter's birthday.

"I'd be glad to help, if Nora feels okay with both of us abandoning her."

"I think it sounds like a wonderful plan. I know Luke would like your help."

"You're sure?" Caroline needed assurance.

"Honestly. I would like the quiet time to look over the photos. Go with Luke. It'll make all of us happy."

It took ten more snippets of conversation to convince her mom to leave, and Nora's usual impatience with Caroline was surfacing by the time the two walked out the door.

Pouring another cup of coffee, she headed for the dining room table.

Pulling the faded blue album toward her, Nora sat down as her heart started fluttering. *This is ridiculous. I'm just looking at photos.*

Her skin responded, tingling until it made the hair on her arms stand up. Nora opened the blue album knowing it could be Pandora's Box holding more questions or a crystal ball with answers.

She guessed she was about four years old in the first photo. It was summer, a favorite picture she remembered well. She was leaning against her dad's knee in their back yard. That's what she'd always noticed before, but, today, Nora saw something more. Her mother off to the side, standing at the barbecue. There it was. Her childhood family dynamics in a nutshell. She and her dad the focus, while her mother kept busy at the edge of their relationship.

Picking up her coffee, Nora stared across the room feeling a deep shift in attitude. Her dad took one step down off his pedestal. Her mom raised a notch in her regard as Nora thought of different kinds of love.

Flipping the page, she saw it was Christmas. She was standing in front of the decorated tree between Uncle Neil and her dad. Nora looked past the nostalgia, noting the body language. Her dad had pulled her close with his arm hugging her shoulder. Neil's arm was above her, his hand on her dad's shoulder. *Was dad feeling protective?*

Nora stared at her uncle. She expected repulsion. Anger. She felt detached.

Turning the pages, glancing at the passing images, Nora watched herself grow through her fifth year. At her sixth birthday party, someone had caught her glee as she opened a Barbie doll, her gift from Uncle Neil. He sat beside her smiling.

She remembered his gift vividly. Today, she wondered about the possible significance of that curvaceous figure. Gazing at the photo, she went to her inner wisdom to find her truth. She felt the joy of Barbie and the hours of play it had given her.

As the following pictures appeared, nothing grabbed Nora's attention until she turned a page and saw Neil's garage. There was no need to check with her inner wisdom. She felt the same light-headedness she'd experienced at Rick's garage.

Nora looked at her uncle standing in front of the building on a sunny day and suddenly realized she hated him. She pulled the photo out of the plastic pocket and set it aside. *I need to keep looking at him and his garage until it no longer affects me.*

There were more pictures of the garage. Her dad leaning over an engine. Neil and her dad sitting on the well-remembered, discarded dining room chairs with beer in their hands. Neil pumping up the tires of her blue bike. Her wearing overalls and drawing in the dirt in front of the open doors.

The last one caught Nora's attention. *No joy there. That's not a picture of me playing. I look like my dog ran away.*

This photo was set aside with the other one as she started flipping quickly through the pages. When she reached the back, she reversed and kept going until she returned to the first page of the album.

Nora was struck to the core of her being. The predominant expression she saw on her little girl's face throughout the album was not happiness. *How did I not know? All the times I've looked at the family photos, and I didn't notice how seldom I smiled.*

To confirm her impressions, she quickly looked through the album one more time. This time, she saw how young she was when she was orally raped. Tears fell on the picture of her sixth birthday party... tears for the little girl who played with dolls and liked to ride her blue bike.

When Luke and her mother came through the door, Nora was sitting on the sofa with three photos in her purse. She had no idea how she was going to chit-chat when every fiber of her being wanted to be in the car with Luke heading home. Nora knew her mother had no idea anything was out of the ordinary when she kissed her goodbye and thanked her for getting the photos out.

Before Nora had closed the car door, she said, "First chance you get, pull over." She nodded her head when Luke looked over to make sure he understood her request.

In a shopping mall parking lot, in front of Target, she pulled out the three photos and handed them to Luke.

He saw her standing with her dad and uncle in front of a Christmas tree. Playing in the dirt in front of a garage. Sitting on her dad's lap in a reclining chair. All about the same age.

"What am I looking at?" Luke knew he was missing something significant.

"The flannel shirt my dad's wearing, Luke. It's the one from my dream."

Twenty ~ Nora

Nora had considered calling Ivy to move her Wednesday appointment up to Monday, but her own schedule couldn't be re-arranged to make it possible. She'd stuck with her regular appointment and suffered for it.

Parking her car outside the barn, she shook her head against the dizziness that had been erratically showing up since seeing the photos on Saturday. The vertigo was a fickle invader, arriving and leaving with no apparent pattern but never totally disabling her. She'd been able to walk, talk, and pretend for all the world that everything was normal.

This time, dizziness attacked with vengeance. Moving cautiously from her car and into the barn, Nora sensed it was because she was going to be with Ivy and no longer had to hold it all together. Ivy would know how to disarm this light-headed menace.

Without a greeting, Nora headed straight for her usual chair and plopped down. She watched Ivy take her purse and set it aside. "Dizzy," Nora announced.

Pulling a footstool over and sitting down, Ivy took Nora's hand and started tapping her upturned palm. "Silently, in your mind's eye, tell the dizziness you know it's come with a message. Let it know you're ready to have the information revealed. That you will believe whatever unfolds to move your healing forward.

"Tap with me, Nora. Good. Keep tapping your palm with me. Tell your dizziness that you can't listen to the message while you feel light-headed. Ask it to leave your body and sit in my chair. Thank it for arriving with such a strong message. Confirm you're ready. Ask it to leave and be an honorable witness to what you're about to discover. Keep tapping until your vertigo is gone."

Together they tapped as color returned to Nora's face. Until she was able to look up, look into Ivy's eyes and nod.

With an encouraging smile, Ivy asked, "All gone?"

"Pretty much all gone. Good enough."

128

"You brought a friend with you today." Ivy glanced over at her chair where she'd sent the dizziness.

"Friend? I don't think so."

"Then a messenger with powerful information that will serve you. Do you know what it's about?"

Nora shared the new piece of her dream... the flannel shirt. "You need to know I've always hated the feel of flannel. Makes me feel like I'm touching cold vomit."

Ivy nodded. She got it.

"Luke and I've been talking about the way the pieces of this mystery are coming together. My dad could have been wearing that shirt when he left me at my uncle's garage... the day I was orally raped in Uncle Neil's office. So now I associate flannel shirts with that trauma. It's also possible the photo of me in front of the garage and drawing in the dirt was from that day. The timing fits."

Ivy listened for the clues. "So we have the flannel shirt, green office, and a troubled child. When I take you into deep relaxation, I'd like you to focus on those red flags rather than the story you and Luke surmised."

Ivy continued, "Our stories come from our thoughts, feelings, and beliefs. They help us understand our experience, but they reflect our conscious awareness. They confirm what we believe.

"To find your personal truth, it's important to leave your story and go to your inner wisdom. You'll find information beyond your awareness there."

That rang true for Nora as she thought of the story she'd harbored about her mother for as long as she could remember. When the story shifted because of her insight about the way her mother loved, their relationship had started changing. "So you're saying don't convict until I have all the information. My subconscious has a file I haven't investigated yet."

"Exactly. Remember that your dizzy-messenger is wanting you to see something you haven't recognized yet. If your story revealed all the answers to this mystery, your vertigo wouldn't be hovering and insisting you keep looking for answers."

Ivy got up to get Nora a pillow and blanket. "When you're thinking about the clues you've found, you can only use your current memory of the past. When we work with energy, there is no dimension of time, so you get to time-travel. You get to be in the moment of dissociation and experience it from that frame of reference."

Handing Nora the pillow and blanket, reaching for the kleenex for her to hold, Ivy's expression spoke of possibilities. "While others stood on the shores and discussed the flat world, Columbus sailed out to see what there might be beyond beliefs. That's where we want to go. Beyond your beliefs and into your truth."

Nora leaned back and made herself comfortable. 'Going beyond beliefs' had caught her attention, but she let that thought go as Ivy began taking her into deep relaxation.

Ivy's voice lulled and invited. "You've come to your retreat today because dizzy-energy has arrived with a message, and you're ready to know what's beyond your awareness. Sit at the edge of the water and let your feet feel the warm, gentle surf lapping the edge of the sand. Watch the waves and let the soothing sound move through your body. There is no silence here. The ocean is a safe place, giving you a gentle, constant melody.

"As you sit in your sanctuary, I want you to see the energy of your dizziness. It's hovering there, above the water, right in front of you. Notice its color. Its shape. Nod when you see it."

Eyes closed, Nora moved her head to the right. "It's an orange tornado with a red center."

"Silently, in your mind's eye, tell it you're ready to hear its message. Trust whatever comes to you, Nora."

After waiting several minutes, Ivy nudged. "Don't think about it. It's already there. What came to you?"

"I saw my little girl drawing in the dirt."

"Go to your inner wisdom when I ask you this question. Is she feeling dizzy?"

"Yes." The image of her little girl became vivid for Nora. "She doesn't look up. She's sitting there because she's dizzy. Not drawing. Just moving the stick. Doesn't know what to do."

"I'm going to touch your mind's eye. On the count of three, go to your little girl. Be there for her.

"One. Two. Three."

"She's not looking up. I don't think she knows I'm here."

Ivy guided. "Talk to her. Ask her if you can sit beside her."

"I'm in front of her. Sitting."

"Tell her she's not alone. That you can help her feel better. Ask if she wants to sit on your lap."

"No, but she likes me to be with her."

"Ask her if you can make a physical connection by touching her knee."

"Yes."

"Gently massage it. Make soothing circles with your fingertips and see the orange tornado flow out of her knee. Hum for her so she's not caught in silence. Nod your head when your little girl's dizziness is gone."

Ivy watched as Nora gently massaged her own forearm. She knew the movement in this time and space was transferring to her little girl. "When you sense she's aware of you, talk to her. Tell her you've been feeling light-headed too. Is her dizziness gone?"

"Yes."

"How old is she?"

"Six."

"Tell her you want to know what happened to her. What made her feel dizzy. That you'll believe anything she tells you. This time she won't be alone. You'll be there, holding her hand."

"She said she'll show me, but I'll think she's lying. I told her I promised I would always believe her."

"That's good. You're doing great, Nora. I'm going to count to three. Go with her. Trust what comes to you… any pieces of insight that you see, feel, taste, or hear."

When Ivy touched Nora's mind's eye, Nora simultaneously watched her little girl *and* physically experienced what her little girl was seeing… the shelves in her uncle's garage… light splashed on the floor… green walls. "In my uncle's office."

"Is your little girl alone?"

"No."

"Does she like being in the office?"

"No. Doesn't want to be here. Scared."

"Who's with your little girl?"

Nora shook her head from side-to-side. "Grabbed my arm."

Watching Nora's active eyelids, Ivy encouraged. "Trust what you see. Believe your little girl."

Nora reached for her throat. Pulling down on it, she began whimpering.

"What's happening, Nora?"

"Something wrapped around my throat. Soft. Getting tighter."

Ivy watched closely for any sign of deep distress, but Nora's voice was flat, defeated when she spoke up. "He wrapped a rag around my throat. He's pulling it tight while his penis is in my mouth."

Ivy's response was firm. "Nora, I want your adult self to be fully present in the office. Your strong, protective self. Go to your little girl. Make her safe. Nod when she feels safe."

Without hesitation, Nora nodded.

"Take the rag off her neck."

"It's off."

"Hug her. Tell her you love her spirit. Say what she needs to hear, so she can feel loved and safe. Nod your head when you're done."

Her mouth closed, Nora's lips moved as her soaring emotions and passion for children exploded into personal power. Ivy could feel the energy vibrating throughout the barn. *More healing energy flowing through this space*, she thought as Nora nodded.

"Can you put your arm around your little girl? Maybe hold her?"

"I'm holding her. Her legs are wrapped around my waist."

"Beautiful. Holding her, I want you to go to your inner wisdom. What made her feel most disempowered in this moment?"

Nora knew. There was no doubt for her little girl. "Green walls watching. Making me feel shame."

"Have her talk to the green walls. She gets to say anything she wants. Do anything she wants. She can paint the walls a different color. Go at them with a sledgehammer. Let her react to them until she feels the shame leaving her body. Encourage her with cheers and hugs."

When uncovering layers of truth in a dissociated memory, survivors often start with what they are ready to see.

Nora had been ready to recognize a presence that was intimidating and made her feel shame. Until now, the green wall held these feelings. She hadn't yet recognized the wall represented a person.

"Who is the green wall?" Ivy took a chance that Nora was ready for a deeper understanding with that question.

The answer was instantaneous. Clear. Decisive. Nora felt a cold wave wash over her. "Uncle Neil."

"As your adult self, confront him. Tell him how your little girl's abuse has affected your life. How his knowing shamed you then, and you are still carrying that emotional wound. Call him out on his lewd participation in the same way you would a perpetrator in court."

From grim, to strong, to calm, Nora's expressions revealed her silent confrontation with her uncle.

The silence was abruptly shattered with a whispered revelation. A deep knowing extinguished the last ember of Nora's instinctive denial. "It was my dad."

Four words. Words spoken as quietly as striking a match, but igniting changes that would enrich Nora in ways she couldn't imagine.

Without tears, with the same numb detachment of her little girl drawing in the dirt, Nora described what she experienced. "I was talking to my uncle about the shame. As that silent, horrible movement from my dream swept over me, I turned. My little girl was standing in front of my dad… in the office. He held the rag. Told her come to him, and it didn't do any good to cry."

Now the tears quietly flowed. Nora didn't blot them away. Ivy wasn't sure she was aware of them, though they ran across her cheeks and into her ears as she lie reclined. "He was wearing the flannel shirt."

"What made you feel powerless in that moment, Nora?"

Stillness answered. In a home where silence kept secrets, using her voice to tell her truth was like growing wings to fly away.

With a sigh, Nora swiped at her tears, found the words. "No one to tell. No one to help me."

"I'm going to count to three now, Nora. When I touch your mind's eye, I want you to take your little girl to your law office. Take her there so she can tell you her story. So you can work with her and she knows there is someone to help her."

While Ivy waited, Nora felt like she was watching a movie.

Her little girl arrived. Sally treated her as she would any client and ushered her into Nora's office, where she took notes while Nora's little girl told her story.

Both Nora and Sally praised her for being so strong, for all the choices she made to hold her life together. They hugged her. Celebrated her. And then they asked her if there was anything else she needed.

She just wanted to tell her truth and be believed.

In this Place Of No Time, Nora felt like she was gone for hours. It was only a few minutes for Ivy when Nora nodded to indicate she was done.

"How does your little girl feel?"

"We both feel… complete. Yes. That's it. Complete. The piece that was taken from us that day is now ours… not theirs."

"Both of you did a courageous thing today. Your little girl trusted you with her story, and you saved her by believing. I'm going to touch your mind's eye and take both of you back to your retreat, so you can celebrate.

"One. Two. Three.

"What does your little girl want to do? She's been re-experiencing that moment every day since it happened. It's been in your body. And now it's gone. It's over."

"She wants to ride her bike."

"Oh yes! Get your bike out and take off with her. You get to ride anywhere… into the land of fairy tales or movies or on the moon. Ride your bikes. Feel the freedom. Nod when you're done."

Freedom's a timeless energy. It has no ups or downs. There's no forward or backward. It takes you into a bubble of now, of being present in the moment. When Nora nodded, she was radiant.

"Ask your little girl if she'd like to stay at your retreat where she can play and always be safe or if she'd like to come out of relaxation and be with you."

"She wants to stay."

"And, once again, if you think of your blue bike, remember that it means she's asking you to pause for a moment and listen. It doesn't have to be a big event. It can be just five minutes, being open to any impressions or images."

Nora smiled. "I'll do that."

"Feel the huge leap you took today in claiming your personal truth. What you did will guide your choices and responses in new ways, and you'll find a new shine in your life.

"Look around your retreat. It's a reflection of your inner world, and I want you to see if there is more to explore."

Nora's complacency dimmed. "I hear the jump rope at my grade school playground again. The slap. Slap. Feels ominous."

"Tell that energy you'll come back next week to see what it's wanting to share. Does that feel right to you?"

"Okay."

"Assure it that it doesn't need to haunt you or disrupt your life. You won't forget that it's talking to you."

"I said 'same time, next week.' And I don't break appointments." Nora was firm. Determined.

"I'm going to count down from three and bring you out of relaxation. You'll feel grounded, centered, and remember everything that's happened.

"Three. Two. One. Open your eyes."

"Did you know?" Nora's eyes flew open, and she watched Ivy carefully. "I think you knew."

Ivy shook her head. "I never go to conclusions. They don't even appear on the horizon. To the core of my being, I know you and I are traveling in your energy field of infinite possibilities, and only your inner wisdom can find your truth."

"Did you suspect?"

"Did you?" Ivy responded.

"Never." Nora shook her head. "Never in a million years."

"How does this truth feel?"

Nora was surprised that she wasn't blown away. "Maybe if he was alive I'd feel different, but I'm more focused on what happened to my little girl. That's more real to me and only a card-carrying bastard would do such a thing. If I met a man like that today, I'd want to hang him up by his balls. Does that shock you?"

"Of course not. I think your professional work has helped you overcome a hurdle many survivors experience at this point in their healing. Not only do they feel the jolt of a parent-child cord unraveling, they have a hard time overcoming our culture's pressure to hold parents in high regard."

"You're right. I've seen enough dysfunction to know all is not what it seems or others wish could be. It turns out my dad was a jerk. I can deal with that."

Ivy knew Nora's feelings about her dad would very likely travel a convoluted journey in the weeks ahead, but this was certainly an empowering place to start. And it was so very Nora to be protecting the child above all else.

Nora had a burning question. "Do we know if my uncle also abused me? Why did I feel such hate when I saw his photo? That was right from my inner wisdom."

"We don't know if he abused you, but even if he was only aware, your feelings about him aren't surprising. Survivors often feel safer venting their emotions on the people associated with the abuser."

"That makes sense, but I'm keeping my mind open about whether my uncle also abused me."

Twenty-One ~ Hannah

None of the detectives had met Hannah before today. With a faint smile, she came into the barn fighting the frown that had become attached to her problem. "My friend, Maddy, came to you guys a couple of years ago. She thought sharing with you would help me get a different perspective."

All of them did their best to make Hannah feel comfortable as they explained how they worked. She listened and nodded while keeping her hands busy turning her wedding ring, rubbing the diamond. She was both wide-eyed and subdued, as though meeting a movie star who had struck up a conversation.

Ivy was the one who was able to quickly summarize energy concepts. Vanessa wrapped up the explanation. "If you have any questions about what we're doing as we seek insights for you, feel free to ask."

"Okay. I will."

"Tell us why you're here today." Hannah felt Miriam's warm regard. When she asked thought-provoking questions, Miriam had a way of looking at you that made you want to crawl into her lap.

"Lucas is fifteen, and it feels like he's in his terrible-twos. Before that, he was the easiest kid in the world."

Kendra recognized his attitude from her work with children at the library. "How's that showing up?"

"He's contrary. His grades took a dive spring semester. Thank goodness, he doesn't throw tantrums, but he's getting pretty good at whining." Hannah had a hard time meeting the eyes of the women sitting with her.

Shame's come to roost, thought Ivy as Hannah continued. "I guess I want to know what's changed for him, so I can figure out what to do. His moods are pretty much running the family."

Miriam leaned forward in her chair, "So it's you, Lucas, and who else in the home?"

137

"Brad, my husband, and our younger son, Alex."

All eyes were on Miriam. "Perfect. You've done a great job of giving us enough information to get started. Now it's time for us to find insights about Lucas that will empower you."

"Does it always work that way?" Hannah asked. Curiosity drove the question. Hope was a passenger.

"Every time!" Miriam spoke her truth with a fairy's smile. "Ladies, it's time to talk to energy. I have a set."

Hannah watched as everyone stood up and moved into the clear space in front of the chairs. Fascinated by the silent choreography, she felt pulled into the curious process. Anticipation about what would happen sat on one shoulder. Concern about what she was going to learn sat on the other one.

Standing in a loose line, Ivy, Jill, Vanessa, and Kendra closed their eyes and let their thoughts, feelings, and beliefs take a back seat. In the silence, they waited for Miriam to approach them one-by-one.

Miriam also cleared her mind. As she went from one detective to another, she focused on four different energies she thought Hannah would find helpful then sat next to her. "Here's your first insight.

"Ivy, what did you experience?"

"I was in a box, looking for a way out."

Laying her hand on Hannah's arm, Miriam spoke loud enough for everyone to hear. "I set Ivy as your husband's energy in your current family dynamics."

"That sounds right. He's spending a lot of time in the garage and taking care of the yard."

Miriam nodded and asked for feedback from Jill who had left the line and rushed around pulling things from the air. "I felt like I was tearing through the grocery store grabbing things off the shelf. But it wasn't random. I was trying to gather specific things for a recipe but felt too hurried to stay focused."

"I set Jill with your energy, Hannah." Miriam gave her arm a reassuring squeeze. "Do you get any insight from this?"

"I can relate to what Jill described. Lucas' moods make me feel frantic." Hannah took a long, deep breath. "I'm so glad I'm here today. I feel better already… seeing what I'm feeling is powerful. It gives me a little distance." She found her first full smile of the day. "Now I'm a tornado-hunter instead of the tornado."

"Frantic is a good word for what I experienced," Jill confirmed. "It was like the store was closing in five minutes, and there was no way I'd be able to find everything I needed."

The little bit of extra weight Hannah carried sagged against her chair. Her kind, brown eyes darkened. "That's it. I feel like I'm always working against the clock. I need to calm Lucas before Brad gets home. Get through a confrontation before I drop him off at school on my way to work. Get him out of the bathroom, so everyone gets their turn. I'm exhausted by the end of the day."

"I can see why." Miriam's compassion felt like a jolt of caffeine for Hannah's beleaguered spirit. It helped her focus as Miriam asked Kendra to share what energy she'd experienced.

"I was just floating… a fluffy white cloud drifting away from the storm on the horizon."

Miriam looked at Hannah. "That's what your younger son is feeling."

"He doesn't seem very affected, does he?"

Kendra agreed. "He feels detached, although he's aware of the storm in your family."

"Do you think that's bad?" Hannah asked Kendra.

Kendra thought about how she felt in the energy Miriam had set. "Remember, I could have had a thousand different emotions, but I was floating. I was just staying in my own corner of the sky… not feeling trapped, not trying to get away, not feeling pushed away. It seems like you can feel okay about Alex."

"So I can let *that* worry go… that's a huge relief," Hannah said more to herself than anyone else. Looking at Miriam, she surmised, "The last one must be Lucas' energy, right?"

"Yes," Miriam confirmed. "What did you experience, Vanessa?"

"I felt like I was in a playpen, and I didn't like it."

"A playpen? What does that mean?" Hannah didn't know how to translate the image into information about Lucas.

Miriam had the answer. "It means we have a clue."

"I've got a set for exploring the clue," Kendra volunteered.

As the detectives worked through the dialogue Kendra set, it became clear Lucas felt he was being treated like a baby, not the young man he envisioned.

A second dialogue revealed the key issue for him was his parents' troubled marriage. Jill had set Ivy as *dad*, Vanessa as *mom*, and Kendra as *Lucas*.

Ivy/*dad* moved away, turned his back on the other two.

Vanessa/*mom* stood still, watching *dad's* retreat, twisting her wedding ring.

Kendra/*Lucas* ran between the two trying to bring them together.

Hannah was stunned. "How did you know? How does he know?" She was convinced no one had picked up on her husband's increasing distance. Like a magician distracting the audience to perform a trick, she believed she was covering what was really going on.

The detectives sat down with her.

Jill answered the question of how she knew. "When we're setting different energies, we know our sixth sense is the surest pilot. In this case, my intuition was nudged by what you're doing right now."

Jill looked at Hannah's hands. She was, once again, twisting her wedding ring from side-to-side. She offered a supportive smile as Hannah's eyes glistened.

"Brad and I are having a bit of a rough time, but it's not about Lucas."

"It may not be about him, but the energy dialogue showed us it is the root cause of the change in Lucas," Jill confirmed.

"I didn't even know he was aware."

Vanessa stood up. "Ivy, I have a set for you."

Hannah watched, momentarily pulled away from wondering how Lucas knew. The dialogue took only a moment.

Ivy didn't move as a scene played out in her mind's eye. Still standing near Ivy, Vanessa asked her what she'd experienced.

"Talk." Ivy's giggle caught Hannah's worry off guard, slipped under her supermom cape and tickled her. "I was surrounded by Goofy, Mickey Mouse, and Donald Duck… all of them talking… all at once. What did you set?"

Vanessa smiled at Ivy's reaction. "You were what Lucas needs from his mom. What he needs, so he can release the feeling of being trapped in the playpen."

The image popped up again for Ivy and another giggle bubbled up as she turned her focus on Hannah. "I think Lucas wants you to talk to him about what's happening with you and your husband. The

140

dialogues show he no longer wants to be treated as a child, left out of the loop. Alex is okay with it, but Lucas is reacting."

"He's moody, reactive… because I'm not being honest with him." Hannah could see that. "It's going to be hard. I'm not really sure what's happening myself."

"If you feel comfortable sharing some possibilities about what might be going on between you and your husband, we could check them out… see what the energy is around them," Jill suggested.

Hannah didn't hesitate. She had a new feeling. Hope had been released making her feel lighter. She wanted more of that.

Jill got up. "If you guys could step away, Hannah and I can come up with some dialogues."

The other four detectives moved over to the window, letting the view of the meadow fill the time. Jill sat down next to Hannah and explained how she could be part of the energy reading. Hannah would focus on four different likely causes of discord as she went from person-to-person.

Hannah was game. When she'd decided on four potential hurdles in her marriage, Jill called everyone back to the floor.

Hannah walked out to the four silent women standing in a relaxed line. One-by-one, she completely concentrated on each of the four options she'd chosen, then turned to Jill to see if she was done.

Jill waved her back to her chair and they watched…

Ivy seemed to be a butterfly in flight.

Vanessa sat on the floor. She seemed to be a child putting a puzzle together.

Kendra moved from side-to-side and seemed to be bouncing a ball.

Miriam stood still. Stiff.

When the movement stopped, Jill nodded to Hannah. "To share the energy they each experienced, you can call on them in any order that feels right."

Hannah was intrigued and called on Ivy first.

Ivy reported a soft, languid movement through space.

Hannah blushed. "You were sex."

Vanessa described her energy as happily playing with Legos.

Hannah liked that insight. She had set Vanessa with the upcoming remodeling project for their home.

How about you, Kendra? "Hannah asked.

"I was totally weaving through the basketball players on the court, dribbling like LeBron James."

"I guess that means Brad is finding a way around his sister's constant demands. That's a good sign, don't you think?"

Jill agreed. "If he's feeling like LeBron James on the basketball court, he's doing fine."

Jill and Hannah waited to see if the energy Miriam held would be the answer they were seeking. "I felt like a square peg being hammered into a round hole."

Hannah was silent. Not the quietude of musing, but the noiseless place of remorse. In the same arena as guilt. "Brad's been wanting to quit his job and become a consultant, and I've completely resisted. To me, it feels too risky to switch gears in the middle of raising a family."

Ivy commiserated. "Financial security is deeply rooted in our culture. It's such a loud expectation, it can shut out other possibilities. It pressures us to focus on making money when there might be other valid considerations. Your response was very natural."

Vanessa spoke up. "But today, Hannah, you've discovered there's another truth. It's your husband's need to grow, maybe express his personal spirit or feel the wonder of being challenged in a new way."

Jill added, "Maybe he's not pulling away as much as he's going inside himself. That's pretty common when we're trying to meet expectations that no longer feed our spirit."

"Everything you're saying feels right. I think I knew it, but chose to ignore the signs, so I didn't have to be brave." Hannah's confession was as much news to her as it was to the detectives.

"Which brings us to something truly wonderful about working with energy, Hannah." Miriam pulled the pillow from behind her back and laid it across her lap. "Instead of focusing on what you might lose... and attracting that kind of unwanted experience... you can think about all the ways Brad's change can enrich your life... and attract a different reality."

Jill jumped in. "The energy field delivers what we're focused on. Every time. What you're feeling, thinking, and believing is the ultimate power for you to achieve financial security.

Miriam added, "The extra perk is this... it's fun to think about wonderful possibilities. It's like inviting sunshine to the picnic instead of ants. Whatever you think about is sure to show up."

Hannah realized this kind of thinking is what her friend, Maddy, had been talking about since her session with the detectives. She smiled. Now it was sinking in.

She looked around the circle of women and thought her first conversation with Lucas would start by expressing appreciation. He had brought her to this afternoon with the energy detectives, and it looked like her world was about to change. In her journey with them, Hannah had realized energy insights very naturally opened doors to communication as they revealed a new perspective.

Twenty-Two ~ Susie

Text messages were flying among the five energy detectives. It all started with a request from Susie on Friday afternoon: Could I have an emergency session with the detectives on Saturday?

Ivy: I can ask. What's the emergency?

Susie: Parents leaving house Sunday. Want to find photos.

Ivy's group message quickly moved into a buzzing hive of exchanges.

Vanessa: Why does she need session for that?

Jill: Scared

Miriam: Agree. Available anytime.

Kendra: Work till 1:00

Miriam: Could locate photo with energy work. Afternoon is good.

Vanessa: Good idea. 3:00? What's happening Ivy?

Ivy: Susie's taking charge. 3:00 is good.

Kendra: Looks like it's working.

Kendra: She sneaking in?

Jill: Not ready to confront dad. 3:00's good if home by 5:00

Vanessa: Me too

Ivy: 3:00-5:00 then

Jill: She going alone?

Kendra: Hope not. Husband?

Kendra arrived in full detective mode. Her curiosity barometer was spiking wildly.

Jill came with a list of energy dialogues that might help them locate the photos in Mr. and Mrs. Cassidy's house.

Vanessa breezed in with a container of ginger cookies. She went directly to the kitchen to set out cups and the selection of teas.

Miriam walked to the window and gazed at the sky with Ivy and Susie. "This is interesting. It was stormy the last time we got together."

Ivy gave her a quick hug. "Pretty decisive energy out there. What do you think… cozy or ominous?"

Miriam had no doubt. "Cozy. I can feel it building a cocoon for us."

Muffled chatter called them away from the window. The dusky afternoon settled by the fire like a sleepy dog. The six women were ready to explore.

"Tea's ready to go. Cookies too," Vanessa announced as she took a seat with her plate and cup.

Kendra headed into the kitchen wondering if there might be a Pepsi in the refrigerator. She liked washing her sugar down with more sugar. "I want to know how Vanessa stays so frick'n slender with all the baking she does."

"You sure you want to know?" Jill teased.

"Some of us just weren't cut out to start the day running," laughed Kendra. "Vanessa's like a gazelle. I'm a pasture animal."

"We need all Mother Nature's critters." Ivy followed them into the kitchen and piled five cookies on her plate.

Kendra glanced at Ivy's plate. Her look would stop a student half-way through unwrapping a candy bar at the library.

"Homemade spicy ginger." It's all Ivy said as she chose her tea.

It wasn't long before everyone was seated and waiting for Susie to share.

"I want to find the photos Dad took." There was none of her usual vague confusion. Finding her truth had cleared the fog of dissociation. "They're mine."

Vanessa agreed. Loved her decisive determination. "So what's your plan, and why are we here?"

"You said you'd help. Last time, when we unearthed the photos. You told me to let the impact settle, and you'd be there if I needed help."

"How can we help?" Vanessa wanted to get to the nitty-gritty.

"Tomorrow afternoon my parents are heading to IKEA. It'll take them over an hour each way plus all the time they'll take looking at stuff for their kitchen remodel. I figure we would have at least four hours to look for the photos my dad used as a weapon."

Jill almost laughed at the look on Vanessa's face. It made her think of someone being pushed into a swimming pool during a formal party. While Vanessa was incredulous, Jill understood the deep need for tangible action. "I'm open to the idea, but first I'd want to know why you want to find the pictures."

Ivy interjected. "Jill's question is important, Susie. None of us want to do anything that might leave you feeling weakened or vulnerable."

"No. It wouldn't do that." Susie's clarity was reassuring to everyone. "Last time, Kendra said something about my warrior being one of the pieces I lost to the camera. No matter what happens, even if you guys say you won't come, I feel like I'm taking that warrior piece back."

"You know your dad will probably realize you've been at the house. Especially if you find the photos." Vanessa was always the voice of calm reason.

Susie lit up. "Yeah. I know that. What's he going to do? Ask me to return the secret pictures he took when he was supposed to be tutoring? He can't do anything. And he'll know I know."

"Is that your purpose then?" Jill asked.

"No. It would just be an added benefit. By finding and taking the photos, I'm declaring I'm no longer his victim. This happened to me, and I'm not going to pretend it didn't happen."

"I want Susie to experience some energy." Miriam jumped out of her chair and waved everyone out onto the empty floor.

After setting four energies, she guided Susie. "Feel the energy of each one and see which one feels best for you."

Miriam stood off to the side, too absorbed in what was about to unfold to sit down.

As Susie moved among the four women, reading the energies held by each one, Miriam was confident a plan regarding the photos would be revealed. Susie's feedback was swift and sure:

"Jill was a statue, something strong, important to others.

"Ivy was the ordinary feeling of eating bacon and eggs for breakfast.

"Kendra was Jell-O… wiggly and yellow.

"Vanessa felt like a clothes dryer, and I was clean clothes being tumbled."

Excited, Miriam shared what she'd set...

"Jill, the statue, was going to Susie's parents' house tomorrow and looking for the photos.

"Ivy, ordinary bacon and eggs, was waiting to take action.

"Kendra, Jell-O, was going directly to dad and asking for the photos.

"Vanessa was doing nothing about the photos. Dropping the whole idea."

Everyone looked at Miriam. She turned to Susie. "Which one felt like it would most honor your spirit?"

"To serve my spirit, it would have to be Jill's energy. The statue. Being something strong for others feels like a new path that would be good for me."

Miriam looked across the informal circle. "Did you get any hits after I set you, Jill?"

"I knew I was a statue. I knew I was feminine energy. Like a pioneer woman or Susan B. Anthony… a trailblazer."

Nothing in previous sessions with Susie indicated she could be that kind of strong, independent woman. All the detectives thought it was a big leap from her inclination to cower. It was like asking the shy child hiding at the edge of a boisterous classroom to give an impromptu speech.

Susie surprised herself as much as them. "It's okay. I want to show up. My dad and his camera taught me to hide. Not anymore."

An experience that shapes a survivor's sense of self fades away as they embrace what was hidden in the shadows of their childhood. Finding the root cause of past trauma unlocks personal power. Susie's brave work with Ivy and the detectives had given her that opportunity.

"Oh boy," exclaimed Kendra. "Looks like some, or all of us, are going to have an adventure tomorrow."

"Breaking and entering?" Vanessa might be an energy detective, but she was an Honor Society president at heart.

"No way," Kendra answered with a sassy excuse. "Susie's just asked a few friends to come over to her parents' house on a Sunday afternoon."

"For tea?" Vanessa's brow got lost in her bangs.

Laughter and tension were often inexplicable companions of energy sessions. Tears. Giggles. Amazement. Relief. Joy. Surprise. Acceptance. There were so many precious moments when truth was the guiding light. Faced with doing something that was so right for Susie's healing, but challenged their natural inclination, the women responded to Kendra's sass with their own silliness.

"No." Jill knew the *perfect excuse* and maybe a good idea. "We're going over there to go through Susie's stuff. There are things she wants now that she's angry with her dad."

Vanessa nodded. Smiled. "You're good. The quiet rebel."

Jill laughed. She was feeling exhilarated for Susie. For herself. She knew it was part of her own continuing journey to heal. "If the neighbors come over to see what's happening, we'll just explain that the energy field brought us."

Kendra started giggling. "We're detectives gathering evidence of suspicious activity."

Susie cracked up. "Oh my god. I'd love Nosy Rosie from next door to hear that. Let's be sure to tell her that we've been talking to my dearly departed sister."

Standing in a bonding circle of laughter, all of them could see the hilarious absurdity of telling the truth to explain their serious mission. Ivy wiped away laughing-tears and tried to suggest they do some dialogues to locate the photos, but she broke into more giggles when Kendra suggested Vanessa bring a bag of her goodies. "We'll use them like they do in movies when they bring a slab of meat for the guard dogs."

"I have a dialogue to get this going." The image had come to Miriam before they got off track. She turned to Ivy. "You ready?"

Silence and stillness washed exuberance aside. One-by-one, five energies were set, and Miriam sat down to watch. *This is wonderful*, she thought. *Like watching children look for Easter eggs.* Each woman was comically busy and completely focused on their respective tasks without regard for the other energies.

"That was interesting." Ivy broke out of the dialogue first.

"It really was." Vanessa sat down beside Miriam. The others gathered around her like moths to a light.

"You're going to like this. What did you experience, Vanessa?"

"I had the distinct impression of opening drawers or cubbyholes. Maybe one of those antique pharmacy cabinets with lots of little drawers."

"Did anything happen when you were doing that?" Miriam asked.

"No. I was just looking. It felt good though."

"How about you, Susie?" Miriam could tell she wanted to be next.

"I had a similar experience except it wasn't a lot of drawers. It was one big drawer, and I needed to look very carefully."

"Anything happen for you?"

"Not really. Just the feeling of looking and the importance of doing that."

"I had a similar sensation," Kendra added. "Except it wasn't a drawer. I was looking down into something that was dark inside."

Miriam was a bit puzzled. "What would you guess you were looking into?"

Rubbing her eyebrows, Kendra once again felt herself looking down into… "A big vase with a small opening."

"I saw you reaching into it," Miriam laughed.

"I couldn't see inside, so I had to stick my hand way down, but it was empty."

"We've got a theme going here," Jill piped up. "I had a hard time getting into something with a door, a small door. When I finally opened it, there was nothing inside."

"There *was* something where I looked." Ivy hadn't realized the significance until hearing everyone else was searching and not finding. "Whatever you set for me had something in it."

"It looked like you were putting that 'something' in a bag," Miriam said.

"I thought I was pulling items out of an ice chest."

Miriam clapped her hands together. "This is truly fantastic. I didn't think it would be so clear! I set each of you looking for the photos. Ivy was looking into a box."

"What kind of box?" Jill pulled the footstool she was sitting on closer as though that would elicit more information.

"I just set 'looking for the pictures in a box'. I didn't have anything particular in mind."

Suggestions came pouring forth: cardboard box, file box, shoe box, cigar box, jewelry box, wood box, toy box.

"Do you remember any boxes in your dad's study, Susie?" Ivy asked.

The young woman looked at her lap, recalling the dreaded room as it was when she was a child.

Jill added, "Metal box?"

Susie shook her head.

The hush was rife with contained excitement.

"The brood of hens are quietly waiting to be fed the answer, thought Ivy.

In her mind's eye, Susie looked around the study and then doubled-checked, scanning the bookshelves, remembering the coat closet. "I remember two cardboard file boxes sitting on a shelf. They had labels on them, but I don't know what they said."

"He'd hardly label them," Vanessa observed.

"But it's the kind of place you'd store something like that." Jill could imagine them filed neatly by year. "Do you remember him ever getting into them?"

Susie shook her head. Finding the photos that would prove her dad guilty was waging a war in her stomach. Glancing at the women helping her solve her mystery, Susie was beyond glad she wasn't doing this alone. She knew she couldn't. *When a word like 'box' feels like a terrorist, you need allies like these at your side,* she thought. Her voice was shaky when she spoke up. "There was a closet in my dad's study. The door was always closed."

"Was it locked?" Kendra knew that was the first place she was going to look.

Twenty-Three ~ Susie

They met at Ivy's at 11:30. The detectives' respective Sunday plans had been changed or canceled because no one wanted to miss the search of Mr. Cassidy's office. Each woman tingled with nervous, excited energy. The thrill of venturing away from the barn to pursue a mystery tipped their usually smooth, organized flow on its side.

Vanessa brought her van. Susie slipped into the passenger seat. "So I can give you directions."

"Anyone need to use the bathroom before we take off?" Ivy stood at the barn door, ready to close it.

Jill headed that direction. "Good idea."

"Probably should." Kendra followed behind.

Susie jumped out of the van apologizing. "Been having a little diarrhea this morning… stress induced… do you think?"

Miriam settled on one side of a bench seat at the back. "It's not like we have an appointment. Since we're just guessing mom and dad will leave by 1:00."

Vanessa agreed, but felt most comfortable when sticking to a plan. Plans were the guards she'd instinctively put in place during her own abuse with an impetuous father. She fought the unease creeping into her thoughts by asking a question. "Do you think we'll find anything?"

"I really do. And *in a box*." Miriam never doubted what they learned in their energy dialogues.

"You know the box Ivy saw could be a locked safe." Vanessa had woken up with this thought.

Kendra stepped into the van with nothing but her cell phone in its red, leather case with a $20 bill slipped into a pocket. "You guys jazzed?"

Ivy was right behind. "I'm more jittery."

"You're nervous? Why? This isn't Mission Impossible." Kendra laughed. "Though it *is* totally outside our usual mode, I'll give you that."

Ivy settled her small purse between her legs and looked back at Kendra. "I'm a whole lot woo-woo, but I tend to use the crosswalk instead of jaywalking. I like avoiding circumstances where I could get caught."

"My thoughts exactly." Vanessa spoke into the rear view mirror.

"No diarrhea," Susie announced as she settled back into the passenger seat next to Vanessa. "Jill wants to know if you want her to lock the door."

Ivy leaned across the empty seat and shouted. "It's okay. No need to lock it."

Jill jogged to the van and jumped in. "Let's go!"

Vanessa pulled out, noting they were now ten minutes behind schedule. After their chaotic departure, she headed down the road thinking to herself, *I don't need to be in charge of anyone but myself. It's okay. I'll keep us on track. Sunday traffic will be light, especially this time of day.*

She was the only person who was quiet as they made their way to the freeway and then joined the stream of cars with their own Sunday plans. If the number of words tossed from one end of the van to the other was any indication of this day's success, raiding Mr. Cassidy's study was going to be a stellar triumph.

Vanessa was calculating the miles and time, convinced they would arrive at the Cassidy's within minutes of one, when Susie leaned over. "You need to find a gas station. There's an exit coming up right over this hill."

"Find a 7-11," Ivy suggested. She wanted some Peanut M&M's.

"Or a drive-in," Kendra spoke up from the back. "I could use a soda."

"Ladies… we've only been on the road about an hour." Vanessa couldn't believe it.

"Pleeeeease." Kendra could whine with the best. It tickled her to sound like some of the students she heard at the library.

"There's the exit. I'm pretty sure there's a 7-11 off to the right. That would work for me." Susie was close to her home turf now.

Purses were grabbed and seat belts undone before Vanessa shifted into park. Everyone piled out with the same frenzy that afflicts disembarking airplane passengers.

Miriam, Ivy, and Kendra zeroed in on their favorite comfort foods.

Jill looked for something healthy. It was like seeking water in the desert.

Vanessa chose ice water. Then chose not to argue when she was charged.

Susie grabbed a bag of peanuts as she joined the cluster of mercurial anticipation at the counter. "We're just two exits away," she announced as they scurried across the parking lot like quail crossing the road.

Swallowing her first bite of a Mars bar, Kendra asked, "So how are we doing this? How will we know if they're gone?"

Susie opened her peanuts. "We can drive by. I'll know."

"Sounds like a solid plan." Vanessa's doubt was obvious, but they went with it. As they turned down Oak Tree Avenue, everyone looked out the right side of the van.

Susie guided. "It's the sage green house. White trim. See it coming up?"

"Slow down, Vanessa." This from Miriam who was leaning across Kendra to get a good look.

"I'm going 15 mph. We don't want to look like we're casing the joint."

"Pretend you're looking for an address," Jill suggested.

"That's not going to make sense when Susie steps out of the van." Vanessa felt like she was a chaperon on a grade school field trip.

"There it is. Everyone look!" Jill directed. "Are they home? I didn't see any movement. What do you think, Susie?"

"I'm not sure. Turn around and go by again, Vanessa."

Vanessa barely kept herself from rolling her eyes. To the core of her being, she needed logic, not the disjointed reactions of her cohorts. Susie was still unsure. "Drive to the end of the block and go down the alley. I'll jump out and sneak into the backyard. I can check to see if their car's gone."

Tamping down her impatience, Vanessa pulled up close to the fence. Susie slipped through the back gate while five hearts pounded in the silence of suspended time.

When the gate swung open, all eyes were on Susie. "Car's gone." A collective sigh soared through the van.

"Back into the driveway, and I'll open the garage door so you can back in." Susie had found her *Superman cape.* "We're here to clear out my personal effects… remember?"

With ease and joy, the van took the vacated space in the garage. The garage door was lowered, and five detectives followed Susie into the house through the kitchen.

"Dad's office is over here." Susie led them across the living room to a door off the front entry. She looked at them, placed her hand on the knob, and everyone crossed their fingers.

It was unlocked.

They swarmed into the space they all knew well from their energy work. Susie went to the shelves behind his desk. Miriam and Jill began looking through his desk. Vanessa immediately investigated a metal file cabinet.

As intended, Kendra headed straight for the closet door. It had been converted into a storeroom for office supplies. On a shelf just above her head, she eyed two well-used cardboard file boxes. One was labeled 'Lesson Plans'. The other 'Tutoring'. She took both off the shelf, setting them in front of the closet.

Susie noticed. Responding to a strong pull, she joined Kendra at the boxes. Together they knelt down and opened the lids. While Susie looked through the hanging files of 'Lesson Plans', Kendra started thumbing through the files in the 'Tutoring' box.

Nothing out of the ordinary popped up until Kendra got to the three files at the back. Those files were marked 'Students'. Each one contained a manila envelope. "Susie. Look."

Both of them eyed the unmarked envelopes. Stared at each other.

"You look," Susie said.

Kendra lifted the flap, glanced inside. Gave a 'yes' nod.

"We found them?" Susie whispered.

Kendra nodded again.

Louder this time, Susie called to the others. "We found them."

Kendra opened the other two envelopes. A glance inside each confirmed they also held incriminating photos.

Every person was convinced they knew what the next step should be. None of them were in agreement. Jill put her hand on Susie's arm. "What's best for you?"

"Let's take them to the barn… where I feel safe. I just want to get out of here now."

"Great idea." Kendra handed the envelopes to Susie and put the file boxes back on the shelf. "Do you feel done here?"

Glancing at the bookshelves behind her dad's desk, Susie shook her head. She walked over and grabbed his camera. Handed it to Vanessa. "Anything else?" she asked the group.

"Well, if it was me, I'd want to check out that laptop sitting on his desk." Kendra knew it would reveal his computer search habits.

Susie walked toward it. "What would you look for?"

"I'd start with his 'Favorites'. Check his online history."

"Do you know how to do that, Kendra?" Ivy was once again walking the tightrope of appropriate.

"No problem if he isn't using a password."

"Do it." Susie opened the computer.

Kendra's gotcha-smile lit up her face as she looked at the screen. "We are meant to do this... no password."

"No locks. No hidden drawers. No password. Don't you think that's kind of crazy?" Vanessa ventured as Kendra sat down at the desk.

"Arrogance." Ivy had seen this over and over. "Lack of empathy and arrogance are two hallmarks of abusers. They get to hide in plain site because no one wants to believe that someone *they know* could do such a thing."

Everyone wanted to get out of the house as quickly as possible, so Kendra scanned quickly and made a list of websites Susie might want to check out later.

The chatter that had marked their journey earlier was gone. It had been silenced in the oppressive energy of the study. Miriam did ask Susie if she might actually like to look around the house and see if there was anything else she wanted to claim.

There was nothing.

Kendra closed the laptop.

Vanessa looked around to make sure everything was back in place, and they left with three manila envelopes, the camera, and a list of websites.

Twenty-Four ~ Susie

The kitchen table at the barn. That was the destination. Having a plan kept Vanessa confident as she drove back to the freeway. Like the other passengers, her adrenaline and exhilaration were soaring.

Jill was the most verbal. "I don't know how you can even drive, Vanessa. I feel like I'm popping out of my clothes. My skin. Susie, I couldn't believe it when you grabbed the camera. And I was so, so proud of you!"

In that single act, Jill's own defiance had exploded. She now knew she could challenge her deeply embedded need to avoid those with power. The skill she'd honed to survive would no longer hold her in check.

Ivy looked at the smiles and joy shaping Susie's profile in the front seat. "Are you still glad you took it?"

Glancing at the camera sitting by her feet, Susie twisted in her seat to see Ivy. She spoke to everyone. "I'm glad.

"Super glad.

"More than glad.

"It was like I didn't have any other choice. It needed to be done, and I needed to be the one to do it."

"What do you think your dad will do? Does that scare you?" Jill would have been terrified to be so overt.

"No, I'm not scared. It's become pretty obvious to me that my dad's a coward. Controlling kids with a camera is false power. Don't you think?"

Miriam offered her thoughts. "I think the house fell on Mr. Cassidy today, and his power turned to dust, like the Wicked Witch in Oz."

"I love that." Susie added to the image. "We were the Kansas tornado. The wickedness of Oak Tree Avenue has been vanquished."

"Are you thinking this will stop him?" Jill wondered.

Susie was clear. "I haven't really thought about that. It's more about him losing power over me. After today, he's dust in my life."

156

Remembering the dialogues celebrating Susie, Ivy added. "You get to be pretty. And smart."

"This is going to change your relationship with your mom, you know." Vanessa watched the road and spoke loudly so everyone could hear.

Susie wasn't so sure. "Maybe. It pretty much depends on what I choose to do. If I decide to pretend nothing happened, they'll go right along with me. My coward dad and clueless mom."

Kendra couldn't let this pass. "You don't believe your mom knew what went on behind those office doors?"

Susie felt dark, moist energy fill the van. "You think she knew? Why?"

"I was remembering my reaction when I was set with her energy," Kendra said. "She seemed disengaged more than clueless."

Susie knew the revealing energy about her mom was there, but she didn't want to listen. She labeled it mom-would-be-very-upset-if-she-knew and turned to denial. "I don't think she knew. She would have stopped it."

Susie looked down at the envelopes sitting on her lap and thought, *No. Mom didn't know. And I can't tell her.*

Vanessa caught the shift in Susie and took the pressure off by asking the detectives a question. "So… are we adding 'breaking and entering' to our resume?"

The animated, sometimes funny, and often self-reflective discussion continued until they were all gathered at the kitchen table in the barn.

Mr. Cassidy's three packets of incriminating photos were an unsettling centerpiece.

Kendra wanted to dive in.

Jill was suddenly nervous.

Ivy watched Susie and was reassured by her steady, curious state.

Miriam was sure Mr. Cassidy's energy force had followed them… as witness to his daughter's empowerment.

Vanessa asked if anyone wanted tea. There were no takers.

Susie opened the top envelope and took out the first photo. Her face turned white as she slapped it onto the table and covered it with her hands.

Kendra gently pulled it away. Her worst fear was confirmed. Two naked little girls, strangers to her, stood stiff and straight, their faces as blank as an erased whiteboard.

One-by-one the image was passed around the table in a silence that damned the injustice of violated innocence.

Miriam's fingers shook as she laid the photo down and placed her hand over Susie's. "Do you know these two?"

Susie shook her head... it felt as heavy and disconnected as a bowling ball. She barely heard Vanessa's voice that seemed to come through a wind tunnel. "Did you ever consider this possibility?"

"When I opened dad's computer, I had a flash of being young and naked. It was a physical sensation, like a twitch, that was gone as fast as it came." Susie turned her hands over and squeezed Miriam's. "Maybe it didn't happen to me. I don't remember taking my clothes off."

Miriam's suggestion was tenderly offered. "Do you want to continue? Maybe another envelope has different kinds of images."

Susie felt like she'd been plopped down on a bucking bronco with no choice but to hold on and ride it out.

Susie knew she had to have answers. She knew the time was now. But reaching for the second envelope took more courage than anything she'd done so far. In slow motion, she dumped the entire contents in the middle of the table.

It was all there:

Each photo showed a naked child.

Boys and girls standing in provocative poses.

No smiles.

No light in their eyes.

Each detective, who had been set as a tutoring student of Mr. Cassidy's, remembered how it felt to be trapped in his menacing arrogance. The images horrified each and every one of them. Helpless shame emanated off the prints. For these caring women, there was no feeling of triumph for finding the perpetrator of the children's abuse. They knew each child had been deeply wounded.

Shuffling through more than two dozen photos in the second envelope, Susie didn't see herself or her sister.

Going back to the first envelope, Susie dumped it on top. A quick search made it clear these photos were taken first. When Mr. Cassidy was simply taking photos without posing the children. Neither Susie nor Crissy were included.

Susie grabbed the third envelope with purpose. Anger had overtaken shock. She lifted the flap at the top and shook out the last set of photos.

And there she was. From a 5×7 inch rectangle, her little girl looked back at Susie. Thin. Naked. Defeated. Eyes that didn't look into the camera but sought refuge on the floor.

Rage stepped up and saved Susie from collapsing. One after another, she picked up several photos of herself and started ripping them in pieces so small they looked like blackened snowflakes.

No one made a move. They barely breathed. None of the detectives wanted to stop the raging energy that was declaring war on Susie's abuse. They silently waited for the tears that were sure to come.

They weren't surprised when she screamed, "How did this happen, and I didn't know! How is that possible!!?"

Everyone turned to Ivy. "We talked about this during your private session, but I can totally see how these photos are taking the abuse to a new level for you.

"Though it feels crazy and impossible, it's more common than you might imagine for people to have traumatic experiences they can't recall. It actually comes from the wonderful way our mind protects us.

"When we experience a traumatic event that makes us feel powerless and at risk, our mind instinctively processes what is happening in a different way than an ordinary memory. You could say it grabs the moment and tucks it into the primitive part of our brain. It keeps it locked up until we feel safe enough and strong enough to consciously connect to it."

Still trembling from fury that had taken charge, Susie took a deep breath. "I sort of remember you talking about this... dissociated memories. But this! This seems too big to get lost in my brain. I don't get it."

Miriam leaned over and put her arm around Susie's shoulder. "Dissociation happens because it was *so big*. So awful. So revolting and degrading. It was more than your little girl could handle and still continue living in the same house with your dad. So she was protected by this biological response."

Tears shined in Susie's eyes and began washing her grief-stricken face. "Did Crissy dissociate?"

"We can't know for sure, but it's very likely," Ivy answered.

"But if she did and didn't know this happened, why did she take her life?" Susie was trying to understand while shock and rage ebbed and anguish rose to the surface. It squeezed the heart of everyone around the table. Each, in their own way, wished they could take on some of her pain.

Jill knew the answer to Susie's question. "The thing is… when we dissociate, we aren't aware of what happened, but the trauma continues to affect how we feel about ourselves and our place in the world. It still drives our choices."

Vanessa picked up the kleenex box that always sat on the table and set it in front of Susie. She was right there for her when Susie realized, "My sister felt all kinds of feelings that brought her down, she just didn't know why."

"Yes." Miriam nodded and added. "Abused children often think it's who they are, rather than a reflection of what they've experienced."

Susie was deflating, like the air slowly seeping out of a balloon. The adventure and empowerment of finding the photos were giving way to the aftermath of today's discovery. "I'm ready to go home," she announced.

"Do you need a ride?" Vanessa knew everyone present felt the pull of wishing Susie would stay so they could offer their support. She also knew that responding to Susie's request was the support that would mean the most.

All the detectives believed one of the most valuable things they offered was truly hearing what a client wanted and responding without question. For many clients, having their needs heard and having their requests honored was new. It was muscle as they lifted themselves out of the past.

"Would you mind?" Susie was relieved.

"Not a bit. Ivy, do you want to drive Susie's car? I'll bring you back."

"Maybe one of the others could do that, and I'll ride along with you two." Ivy wanted to use the drive to Susie's home to give her some ideas for navigating the days ahead. She knew three suggestions she wanted to cover.

Writing down the thoughts and images that grabbed Susie's attention. Taking note of them would help her feel empowered rather than bruised by them. It would invite further exploration that could honor her personal spirit.

Naming the different emotions that were sure to arise would encourage Susie to allow her feelings rather than push them away.

Consciously choosing to have *conversations* with Crissy would help Susie begin integrating the dissociated memory into what she presently knew about herself and her sister.

Jill pushed her chair away from the table. "I'd be glad to follow with Susie's car."

Vanessa, Ivy, and Susie stood up to leave. Susie didn't say anything about the photos. When your world has crumbled, details cease to exist.

Twenty-Five ~ Nora

It had been a bittersweet weekend. Though Nora would have gladly skipped her birthday celebration, there was nothing better than having her daughters home. A junior in college, Anastasia was dedicated in her quest to be a vet. Madeline was enthusiastic about her budding career in high school administration. Nora anticipated the conversations they were sure to bring home.

The visit didn't mean just clearing the calendar and changing sheets on the beds. It raised issues Nora had never imagined becoming part of her life. Neither she nor Luke intended to keep what was happening a secret, but the idea of sharing overwhelmed Nora.

She was already feeling a bit raw. The jump rope slapping on the asphalt lingered like a boogeyman ready to pounce. She knew the trigger might suddenly demand her attention in the same way dizziness had unexpectedly shown up at the garage.

As they'd discussed how to manage the weekend, it seemed best to postpone any revelation. There wasn't a way to open that door just a little. Their daughters were far too curious and intelligent to accept just a peek.

They were also perceptive.

Nora went into the weekend feeling like she was on guard. Would Anastasia and Madeline notice the changes in her? She wasn't the same woman they'd known all their lives. Neither was her relationship with Luke.

Nora was now easily accepting Luke's affection and attention. Luke had taken on household tasks that had traditionally been Nora's exclusive domain. They'd added a new language to their conversations with words like inner child, energy insights, green walls observing, silence haunting.

Nora had wondered if they could go back to how it use to be... just for the weekend. Then realized they couldn't. The changes were too deep, coming from a new personal truth that couldn't be denied. She went into the weekend knowing their daughters were sure to feel the difference. She just didn't know if they would ask about it.

By Sunday afternoon, it seemed the weekend would come to a close with nothing significant coming through the cracks of what was usual. Nora was thinking she'd navigated the visit without waves as the family headed to Sundaes & Such for the weekend finale.

Waiting in line at the ice cream parlor was part of the tradition, and today's line was out the door. Madeline loved this part of the experience. Noticing Luke holding Nora's hand, she whispered loudly to Anastasia, "Aren't they cute?"

"I have noticed a bit of lovey-dovey going on this weekend. I think it's a good thing we've moved out and left them alone."

Nora rolled her eyes.

Luke laughed.

Continuing the fake whispered exchange with her sister, Madeline added, "He's hanging out in the kitchen too." Madeline turned to her dad, "What's with that? Cooking spaghetti? Loading the dishwasher? You've always been never-seen-except-to-eat."

Luke defended himself with a chuckle. "I know my way around the kitchen."

Madeline hugged both parents. "Well, I think you two are on a second honeymoon, and I'm happy for you. Maybe it's time to get that puppy you've always wanted, Dad."

Nora felt the same rush of distress she always experienced when they talked about getting a dog. She changed the subject as the line moved inside the door. "No one does ice cream like this place."

Luke agreed, and it wasn't just because it tasted so homemade. "They've never been stingy with their scoops."

"What's their special today, Mom?" Unlike Nora who always had Coffee Bean Blast, Anastasia liked trying different flavors. She couldn't see the sign, but Nora could if she stepped off to the left between the two tables.

Getting herself in position to see the menu board, Nora looked between the couple ahead of her. It was then a deep voice from a chair nearby broke through the surrounding chatter.

"Step over here. Crying's not going to help."

Nora froze.

Like a whip across a slave's bare back, the callous demand rendered her helpless.

163

The words reached a defenseless corner of her being.

Nora could only stare at the little girl who had wandered into the line and was being pulled back to the nearby table. For her, everything around the little girl instantly faded leaving the child in a mental spotlight. The man's statement reverberated, off-key and clawing... "Crying's not going to help."

"Nora?" Luke's arm circled his wife's waist. Recognizing the sudden trance, he gently pulled her against him. He knew talking and movement would help. "Did you see the flavor? Let's check it out."

She kept gazing at the child, but moved as Luke guided her forward. Just a few steps. But away from the table. "Can you see the sign?"

His hand moved up and down her side. He kissed her cheek and whispered, "You were looking at today's flavor for Anastasia. Look up at the sign. You've got this."

The tunnel that had consumed Nora slowly released. Silent terror was gradually pushed aside by the room's chatter. Luke's voice wrapped around her, soft armor to face the challenge.

"Coconut Dream, Luke." She turned and looked into the calming brown eyes. Nodded. "It's Coconut Dream."

"Want to leave the girls here and walk a little?"

Her adamant, "No," was softened by the plea in her eyes. "Let's be with them and see if we can make this normal." That, more than anything, was what Nora needed in this moment.

"They're debating the best route to San Jose in the Sunday afternoon traffic. Find your smile, and we're back in business."

Nora dug deep. Found a smile to mask disconcerted. She focused on her feet and walked the few steps back to their place in line. Then interrupted her daughters' conversation. "Coconut Dream sound good, Anastasia?"

"Oh, yeah. That's what I want. With their fudge topping and slivered almonds." Her enthusiasm was a balm for Nora's receding discomfort. It set off a lively discussion of what everyone wanted to order. By the time they got to the counter, Nora was convinced her daughters couldn't tell she'd been triggered.

Twenty-Six ~ Nora

Wednesday's appointments had become a life raft for Nora. She now trusted the process. Knew they would find the pieces to make sense of the puzzling experiences she had between sessions. These answers and insights felt like glue holding her life together.

Nora didn't know it, but being confident about her healing path was clearing the way to her dream-memory. But first, her healing journey was taking her in another direction.

Nora might believe the jump rope and man's voice were a direct link to the dream, but Ivy didn't assume. She knew memories were stepping stones, letting survivors go at a pace that served their well-being.

At the moment, Nora was in deep relaxation after telling Ivy what had happened at Sundae's & Such.

"Feel yourself at your beach retreat. This is your Place-Of-No-Time, Nora. A safe place where you get to find answers. Look around. Your 6-year-old is there. Check in with her. See if there's anything she wants to share. Give her a hug. Nod when you're done."

A moment later, Nora smiled and spoke up. "She wanted animal crackers. I gave her three boxes."

"Perfect. I love that. She's feeling good?"

"Yes."

"Tell her you've come to get more answers. That you need some time to yourself because another inner child needs your help. Let her know you'll be just down the beach, and she can keep playing. Then find a comfortable place to sit."

"I'm under a palm tree. On a soft chair."

Ivy's voice held a smile. "Snuggle into the softness. Focus on the timeless rhythm of the surf. Let the sound soothe you. You are safe. Can you feel that?"

"Yes."

"Good. Let that safe energy float around you. Fill your body. It's an energy that's a friend of your personal spirit. It invites insights.

"As you sit in your chair, I want you to remember the sound of the jump rope on your grade school playground. It's been spooking you, but today, right now, be aware it's been coming to you as a messenger. It's been trying to get your attention because it has information to take you forward in your healing journey. Without thinking about it, using your inner wisdom, let yourself know the message."

Nora didn't hear the message. It felt more like driving around a sweeping corner and being confronted by what was ahead. "I need to follow the maze inside the black-and-white block of my dad's love."

"Good work… trusting what came to you. Silently thank the jump rope for the message. Then focus on the soothing surf again.

"You have a little girl who knows the sound of the jump rope slapping the asphalt. She knows the moment when her dad's love turned into a maze. Ask her to come to you. Let her know you want to hear her story. Nod when she arrives."

Ivy could see Nora was *trying* to make it happen. She intervened. Trying to make it happen was a lot like trying to dribble a rock. "Relax. Release. Connect to your inner wisdom, Nora. Feel that place inside that just knows. Then, in your mind's eye, look over to the left. Look down the beach."

Nora nodded. "She's there. Walking toward me… slowly."

"Thank her for coming. Make her feel welcome, appreciated. See if she'll share your chair with you. Tell her you want to know what happened that day on the playground."

"She wants to sit on the sand. I'm facing her."

"How old is she?"

"Eight." Nora's face lit up. "She's wearing the new dress I wore on the first day of school in third grade. I felt so grown up."

Ivy responded. "Does she feel grown up today?"

"No. She looks like the shattered, defeated kids who come to my office when their parents are getting divorced."

"Tell her you can see she's upset. That you care. Ask if you can hug her."

Watching Nora's face, Ivy knew the moment her little girl had accepted the hug. She saw the same kind of relief a parent feels when their lost child is found. Being able to nurture, embrace, and support an inner child was always a tender moment. It brought to mind teddy bears, sleeping babies, and doting grandmothers.

Ivy moved Nora toward the answers she was seeking. "Ask your little girl if she'll show you the time she was jumping rope at grade school and something happened she'd never expected. Something upsetting."

"She says okay."

"Hug her and tell her she's very brave. That you'll be with her, close by."

"She likes that."

Ivy set things in motion. "I'm going to count one-two-three and touch your mind's eye. Trust whatever you see or experience. Notice your emotions or how your body feels. Don't try to make sense of it… just let your truth unfold. Remember, dissociated memories come like pieces of a picture rather than a movie.

"One… two… three. Go with your little girl."

Ivy watched the changing expressions around Nora's eyes. As long as there was activity, she didn't want to interrupt. When Nora's face became still, Ivy asked, "What's happening?"

Short breaths registered in Nora's rapidly rising and falling chest. Ivy waited. Then nudged again. "Where are you?"

"My dad. He came to get me after school."

"Was that unusual?"

Nora frowned. "He… it… she doesn't want to get an ice cream cone with him." Nora shook her head. Her forehead worried. "She's licking the cone but doesn't want it. Something's not right."

"What's not right, Nora?"

"We're at the ice cream parlor. He's just sitting at the table. Not talking. Agitated."

Ivy looked for more insight. "Ask your little girl to show you what agitated him."

"Oh. Oh." Nora was startled. "We're at Uncle Neil's garage."

"Does that upset your little girl?"

"Dad and Uncle Neil don't laugh. Or talk. Not good."

"Ask your…"

Nora spoke up, "Dad grabbed her wrist. Told her to 'step over here.' He's taking her to the office."

"Follow your little girl, Nora. She needs you to be her honorable witness."

167

Ivy watched Nora's fingers tighten around the kleenex she held. Watched her face register serious before turmoil took hold. Then settle into resigned. "What's happening?"

Nora's lips moved. Ivy waited while she found her voice to bridge an eight-year-old experience with the present moment. Sadness oozed out of the words. "She's determined not to cry. Knows it doesn't do any good."

"Why does your little girl want to cry?"

Though Nora's body had been storing all the emotions from this traumatic moment, it didn't release them now. It continued protecting her from being overwhelmed so she could see her truth. Her description was colorless. "Oral rape. Rag choking her."

Ivy's voice was strong. "What is making your little girl feel most disempowered right now?"

"She was having fun on the playground. Everything changed."

"Nora, I want you to see your adult self walking into the office and stopping the rape. Let your little girl know she's not alone. Hug her. Nod when she feels safe."

Several moments later, Nora nodded. "I pulled her away from him. Took the rag off her neck. She's in front of me, my hands on her shoulders."

"Now I want you to confront your dad. Say everything your little girl needs to hear. That this wasn't her fault. Not her shame. She's not to blame. That he's broken her trust. Use your voice to comfort your inner child and place all responsibility on your dad."

When Nora was done, Ivy asked her to imagine her little girl standing up to her dad with Nora at her side. Saying and doing anything she needed to feel empowered.

Ivy waited patiently. The calm silence around her gave no indication of the confrontation in Nora's mind's eye.

Her eight-year-old yelling, "I hate you!"

Her eight-year-old pushing him backward. Then pushing again, with both hands.

Adult-Nora pushing with her little girl until his chair fell over, leaving him sprawled on the floor.

As lines of determination around Nora's mouth were erased, Ivy knew the inner child had released pain and disempowerment. That meant it was leaving Nora's body where it had been stored since the day of this trauma.

When Ivy counted to three and took Nora and her little girl back to the ocean retreat, she talked about the gift this memory would bring. "At eight-years-old, you learned it wasn't safe to be in the moment... having fun. The sound of the jump rope was a messenger from your personal spirit taking you to this insight. Now you and your inner child can be spontaneous... experience joyful play. How does that feel?"

"It makes me realize how serious I've been. How I'd rather bring my work home on the weekend than plan something I'd enjoy."

Ivy offered an observation. "How you felt *safer?*"

Nora nodded. "Yes, safer."

"When you leave today, I'd like you to imagine your eight-year-old leaving with you. Imagine her sitting in the passenger seat, buckled up. Going into your house with you.

"She remembers how to play. Let her start guiding some of your choices about how you spend your weekend or evenings. Share that adventure with her."

It was another weird-feeling idea for Nora to embrace, but she took a deep breath and nodded.

Ivy brought her out of deep relaxation.

"So, my eight-year-old is here?" Nora asked.

"Feel her presence, just like you have learned to feel any energy," Ivy responded.

Nora answered, with a wonder-filled voice. "She's standing beside me."

"Any time you think about her, notice where she is and what's she's doing. Have fun with that. Tell her she's free to wander around the barn while we finish your session. Or she can sit in the other chair and watch."

Laughing, Nora said, "She's already exploring."

Her momentary lightness swiftly turned solemn. "His abuse was a pattern, wasn't it?"

"Go to your inner wisdom. What's your truth?"

Nora had no doubt.

Ivy agreed. "The red flag was the upset your little girl felt from the moment your dad showed up on the playground while you were jumping rope. Everything appeared normal, but she sensed all was not what it seemed. It went beyond reading his body language and his quiet demeanor."

"Exactly." Nora could see that now. "It was like the air got thick."

169

"Her inner knowing at odds with outward appearance," Ivy said. "That's what wrecks havoc with a child's perception, until they no longer trust what they know."

Nora looked down at the wad of kleenex she held in each hand. Sighing, she set them on the end table. "I don't think this memory was about my dream because there's no bed, light bulb… rug."

"You're right. Those clues are still a mystery," Ivy agreed.

"So how do I get there? I'm ready to know." Nora's exasperation was a good sign.

"You can't make these dissociated memories surface, but you could start consciously inviting the memory. Ask the child connected to the dream to come forward. Affirm you're ready. That you will believe whatever is revealed."

Nora accepted the suggestion. She *was* ready.

Ivy added another recommendation. "Invite serendipity."

She responded to Nora's wide-eyed surprise with an energy insight. "Serendipity is much more than a random coincidence. It's the energy field bringing together empowering elements of an intention we're holding.

"Think about the serendipity that helped you solve the mystery around the jump rope… how you were getting ice cream at the exact moment a man would say, "Step over here." Words that were a trigger for you… in the presence of a little girl."

"I hadn't thought about that." Nora was a bit surprised she hadn't put the two together.

"Serendipity is an ally creating a noteworthy event to catch our attention."

"You make it sound like a friend," Nora teased.

"It can be. The important thing is this… to get to your memory, trust serendipity enough to let it guide you."

Looking at Ivy, Nora's gaze held a whole lot of tired with a touch of overwhelm. "Every time I think I'm feeling solid in this energy work, you throw me another curve ball."

"And you keep catching them," Ivy laughed.

Twenty-Seven ~ Nora

Nora's news at the following session was the most mysterious of all. Nothing had happened during the week.

"I've been so used to being herded by emotional events and erupting triggers, it felt strange," reported Nora.

"Do you know what it feels like to be relaxed?" Ivy asked.

Nora sat up straighter. The insight pushed as surely as a hand on her chest. "I've never thought about it."

"Relaxed is different than distracted." Ivy's smile promised more. "*Distracted* is television, reading, coffee with a friend, iPhone games. *Relaxed* is an energy that guides you smoothly through time.

"If you look back on the past few days, did it feel like your client appointments unfolded with ease? Or, maybe, shopping at the grocery store was a breeze?"

Nora started nodding as she reviewed her past week.

Ivy took off her cardigan. Settled back in her chair. "Your eight-year-old learned it was dangerous to relax and trust the organic flow of the energy field. She adopted a need to control everything around her to protect herself in an unpredictable childhood.

Today we can celebrate that she no longer has to be in charge because you confronted and dealt with that memory. Now she's feeling safe. She gets to relax and that means you do too."

"I thought the jump rope memory was about me learning I can have fun. I had no idea control and relaxation were an offshoot." Nora wanted more. "You're telling me *relaxed* is an energy. So is *control* an energy too?" Have I shifted from one kind of energy to another?"

"Everything's energy, and you just nailed it."

"I have to say… it seems like being relaxed would've felt good, but I found it a bit disconcerting."

Ivy laughed. "And yet I'm sure you'll quickly learn to live in a reality that is not so unpredictable."

Nora's shrug said she'd wait and see if that prediction came true.

"Another thing came up this week. Luke and I were thinking I probably became a divorce attorney because of my abuse. It made me want to protect children... and believe them. Do you think that connection is possible?"

"I totally agree." Ivy felt the energy of her personal spirit move. It ceased hovering around her shoulders and started soaring around her and Nora.

"I believe every person's deep passion is born in a trauma or life-changing challenge from their past. With survivors, that gift is more obvious."

Nora hesitated, but still asked. "Is your work from a trauma you experienced?"

Ivy's dynamic eyes softened with vulnerability. They glistened with unshed emotion. "Definitely."

Nora felt a deepening connection as Ivy shared her story. "Though personal spirit is always present, my healing journey made me realize I'd become disconnected. Feeling detached from personal spirit, I looked to others for answers.

"Reconnecting was the single most amazing and soul-feeding part of my journey. Probably the most courageous.

"It felt like being turned inside-out. Like my vulnerable, soft-self was in charge of my choices and responses.

"But, when I learned to lean into that gentle source of power, my life became a treasure of wellness and possibilities. I came out the other side passionately wanting to help others connect to their own personal spirit."

Nora had learned that a non-response to her clients often brought forth more information. Heart in hand, she waited and hoped Ivy would keep talking.

"I truly believe open awareness and communication with our spirit paves the road for honoring our authentic self," Ivy said.

"That's when neither guilt nor feelings of responsible dread cloud the energy of our good intentions.

"It helps us recognize that every single person has something valuable and precious to give others.

"It gives us the freedom to find ways to share what we have to offer.

"I want that for others who are seeking it."

In the quiet understanding pulling the two women together, Nora saw how their passions aligned. She spoke up. "You want to heal people after the trauma. I keep trying to prevent or diminish trauma by empowering kids through the emotional upheaval of divorce."

Nora jumped up and motioned Ivy out onto the floor. "I want you to do me a favor. I've checked how Luke's and my mom's love feel. Now I want to read the energy of *how I love*."

"Of course. And I'll add another set I'd like you to experience. That way, you won't know which energy you're reading. Sometimes, when you know the energy being held, you wonder if you are affecting the outcome."

Ivy shook off the conversation. Became clear so they could start the first dialogue. "I'm ready when you are."

The energy around Ivy was strong and easy for Nora to read. "Messy. I saw a house with great curb appeal, but the inside needed some serious organization. Everything's waiting to feel settled in… like when you move into a new house. Hope that wasn't how I love."

Ivy didn't soothe Nora's chagrin with an answer. "Here's the second set."

That reading was also clear for Nora. "This is funny. I was in my backyard, but it was filled with birds, and I was taking care of them. Talking to them!"

Ivy asked, "Did you feel like you were nurturing them?"

"Yes… encouraging them to fly. They weren't in cages."

"That is how you love, Nora. Your love is nurturing. Your love gives others their wings."

Joy and relief filled Nora. "I didn't dream it would be that gentle."

Ivy hugged her. "I'm not surprised."

Nora placed her hands on Ivy's shoulders. Her gaze held Ivy in place as much as her touch. "Thank you. Thank you for all the ways you're opening me up to the soft side of myself."

"Ivy met her gaze. "Thank you for sharing your courageous journey with me.

"And that brings us back to the first set… where everything appeared good on the outside but messy on the inside. I was holding the energy of how you're feeling at this time in your healing."

Nora broke away, laughing. "A perfect description. Let's get to work and clean up some of that mess."

During the remaining time, Ivy took Nora into deep relaxation and used the clues from her dream to see if she could get more information.

It wasn't time.

Nora wasn't ready.

Her emotions trapped her in a fog of fear as surely as a witch's wand casting a spell.

The silently moving bed in the corner frightened. It felt as terrifying as a chasm opening up under her feet in an earthquake.

The bare walls haunted. Now alive like the green walls of her uncle's office, bringing a message she was unable to hear.

The single light bulb launched shadows where she needed light.

The silence still felt like it was wrapping around her ankles and pulling her under.

The rug dared her to trespass where its meaning could be found. And promised retribution should she stray into the moment she'd dissociated.

Assuring Nora all these clues would be revealed when she was ready, Ivy took her back to the ocean retreat where the deep relaxation had started. She asked her to imagine swimming in the gentle, warm surf. She suggested the smooth, silky water would pull all Nora's fears out of her body and leave her free to move about in the week ahead.

"If you want to get closer to your truth, you could spend some time writing down any feelings you have about your dad... past and present. You've done a stellar job of seeing what happened to your little girls, but that's different than expressing your feelings. Getting in touch with them could loosen up your fears about the dream."

Nora nodded.

Counting down three to one, Ivy brought her out of her deep relaxation.

"Don't feel discouraged," Ivy said as she took the blanket from Nora. "Today was a powerful session. It moved you forward."

Nora pushed on the lever, moving her reclining chair into an upright position. "While I was swimming in the ocean, I smelled laundry soap. It turned my blood to ice."

Twenty-Eight ~ Paul

Like a warm Chinook wind, Paul blew into the barn. Ivy turned to greet him and thought his smile might be curling his toes.

"Rode my bike over, and that's a good five miles," he announced as he headed into the bathroom.

Ivy had no idea why he'd requested a session or where it would take them, but it was clear Paul's fear wasn't hovering.

She settled into a chair, and opened up to any insights that might be trying to get her attention. When he walked out of the bathroom, drying his hair with the hand towel, she wondered if he noticed her surprise.

"Ended up sweating like I was going on a prom date." Tossing the towel over the back of the chair facing Ivy, Paul sat down. "Didn't expect that to happen so early in the day."

"Your back's feeling pretty good then?"

"Today it is, but I'm not completely out of the woods." He leaned back in his chair and crossed his legs. "That's why I wanted to see you. Thought we might have a few loose ends to unravel."

Ivy pulled a footstool in front of her chair. "What would you like to get from this session? Has fear shown up in these past three weeks?"

"Nope. You ladies kicked its ass. Nothing even close."

"You're the one who kicked ass… by your openness to new perspectives. When we step outside the circle of familiar people in our lives, it's easier to learn new things about ourselves. That's when emotions like anger and fear break away from their mooring."

It was important to Ivy that her clients take credit for their shifts and growth. She never wanted them to believe their power to change relied on others. Because it didn't.

"Your life's been showing you that reacting doesn't change things. In fact, it strengthens the energy connection because you had to be constantly thinking about what your mother wanted.

"Simply trying to focus on new thoughts doesn't work either."
Ivy's smile was filled with compassion.

"Logic won't work because we are mind~body~spirit beings. We
have to listen to our body and have a conversation with our personal
spirit to get to the root of what's causing us to react. We have to update
the information at that level. That's when the energy pattern changes,
and we start experiencing a new reality."

Ivy leaned forward. "Does that make sense to you?"

"Yeah... I get it. You've talked about it before. But a person has to
be ready to challenge their old belief to make that happen.

"Excellent point." Ivy returned his smile, then asked, "Tell me how
things are going with your mom, and then I'll take you into deep
relaxation. Now that fear is no longer stalking you, we have a very
good chance of getting to the root of your back pain."

"Actually, I thought standing up to her would be harder than it is.
Every time she suggests anything, my response is, "I'll get back to you
on that, Mom." And I'm getting really good at walking away or cutting
her off, ignoring her texts if she doesn't drop it." Paul's face looked
young, triumphant, like he'd just outrun his older brother for the first
time.

"Are you using physical activity to find the answers?" Ivy was
remembering the super power he found when working with the
detectives.

"Now that part's more challenging. The exercise, or whatever, was
supposed to help me connect to my personal spirit, but I'm not always
sure if that's happening. Sometimes, it feels like it could be old
thinking."

Paul ran his hands through his still-damp hair. It had nothing to do
with combing out the wisps that were sticking out at odd angles and
everything to do with taking him back to feeling doubtful. "Like the
other day when mom wanted to drop by my house. I did the whole 'I'll
get back to you' thing, then did some push ups. But I was so dead set
against her coming, I didn't know if I was 'hearing' my spirit or not.

Ivy got that. She also knew old reactions would get less persuasive
over time. "It's not so important that you got it right. You didn't
react... and that's what is healing."

Paul leaned forward, clasping his hands at his knees. "Get this.
Mom asked me over for dinner to meet her new personal assistant.
Who was she trying to kid?! I knew she was trying to fix me up.

"My first thought was… why in the hell would I want to meet a P.A in hospital administration? But," Paul tilted his head and paused, purposely encouraging Ivy's curiosity, "I chose to go running and listen to my spirit. By the time I got home, going to dinner seemed like the right thing. *Going felt like sunshine. Not going was a foggy day*."

"Very good," Ivy exclaimed.

"Turns out, much to my mom's surprise, this girl's passion is singing. Working as a P.A. is her day job. She's coming over this weekend, and we're going to work on some music."

Ivy felt goose pimples from head-to-toe. "Magic happens when you let your personal spirit guide you.

"And the more you trust that guidance, the more you'll want to fly," Ivy mused. "Now, let's recline your chair and see what your back's trying to tell you."

Twenty-Nine ~ Paul

Deep relaxation made Paul feel like a spelunker. What Ivy called clues or messages, he saw as openings to caves where he'd stashed difficult, childhood experiences. She'd shown him that simply storing them out of mind didn't banish their effects on his life. Going into those caves and bringing the hurtful memories out into the light set him free.

Today, when she touched his mind's eye and counted one-to-three, he was transported to his retreat in a flash. The cool, pine-scented forest he'd chosen as his safe place in previous relaxations felt as real as the reclining chair.

He especially liked the sessions when Ivy used deep relaxation. It was much more vivid and tangible than energy dialogues, like being in a movie rather than sitting in the audience.

This was the state of mind that had connected Paul to inner children from memories beyond his awareness. Each time, as the session came to an end, Ivy had him imagine the children were safely remaining in his retreat. Today, she asked about them. "What's happening with your three boys?"

"They're doing good. Building a fort." Paul's physical energy unwound and reshaped until Ivy had the impression of him at ten years old. Curious. Ready for adventure.

"You made that possible, you know. Doing the energy work to take them out of their stressful circumstances allowed their playful natures to soar. Notice what each of your boys brings to the project. Do you see any particular talents or attitudes?"

Amusement washed across Paul's face. "My 7-year-old's a complete goof-ball but good with the hammer. The 10-year-old was born to build. That fort's going to be a solid masterpiece."

When Paul became still, Ivy waited to hear about his 3-year-old. "My little guy's something else. None of them know it, but he's the one who's really in charge. I think it's because mom hasn't crushed his spirit yet."

"Go to your inner wisdom, Paul. Tell me how old you were when your spirit first felt crushed."

"Six."

"Look past the fort being built, deeper into the forest. See if that six-year-old will show up today. "

"He's by the path leading to my memory-caves. Looking bummed-out."

"Ask him if he wants to show you what made him feel so down."

"That's why he showed up."

"Good for him. Tell him you're going to follow the path with him. That it will lead to the cave that holds the memory he wants to share. Nod when you find the cave."

Ivy watched Paul's face for signs of what might be happening. She was surprised when he announced they were already inside the cave. "What's happening?"

"He's showing me the stick town he made for the beetle he found. Describing it in a lot of detail."

"What upset him?"

Subdued, Paul responded. "Mike bombed it with rocks." His voice revealed it was so much bigger than his older brother butting in.

Ivy commiserated. "How does your six-year-old feel?"

Paul's inner child responded, "When I started screaming at Mike, he laughed. Said it was just a stupid pile of sticks.

"Mom was even worse. When she came out to see what was happening, she went off about me being too old to cry over some sticks. And what was I doing in the dirt? She'd sent me out to practice my pitching."

Indignant, feeling like a pacing, caged-lion, he growled. "She wanted baseball. I didn't."

"What felt most disempowering to your little boy?" Ivy asked.

Paul sighed. A long, deep, sad sigh. "I felt good when I was building the stick town. Like I was doing something only I could do. It mattered to me. But not to them."

Ivy wanted to be sure she understood. "Did if feel like two powerful people in your life weren't recognizing an expression of your personal spirit?"

Nodding, Paul added his twist. "They made me feel like a piece of shit."

Ivy saw an energy pattern coming together. "They challenged your self-worth and that's huge, Paul. Our self-worth helps us express our personal spirit. It's an essential element for setting boundaries, and our boundaries tell others how they can treat us."

Ivy gave Paul a few moments to consider this insight before continuing. "Look around the cave and see if there's another energy hovering."

"Yes. I see it. It's so big, I thought it was fog or something."

"I want you and your little boy to walk into the middle of that energy. It's an encompassing ally. Trust your inner wisdom and recognize the force surrounding you."

Paul knew immediately. "It's anger."

"Does that make sense to you? Anger is an energy that helps you set boundaries. In the face of feeling diminished, it can be an ally."

Her question brought Paul more clarity. "At nine years old, the summer before fourth grade, I started rebelling."

Ivy wanted to take Paul and his inner child back to the retreat to explore this insight about rebelling, but first they needed to empower his six-year-old. "Let your adult-self show up where your little boy was building the stick-town. Interrupt what Mike and your mom are saying. Ignore them and talk directly to your six-year-old.

"Tell him what you think about his project. That he's ingenious. That you respect the way he stayed with it to create a unique town. That you love the idea of building a town using nature's materials. Give him honest praise until you can see he's able to believe you."

Rubbing her hands together, Ivy waited several minutes. A softness enveloped Paul, then shifted. She sensed tension. Anger. "What's happening, Paul?"

"My little guy's feeling pretty damned good. So I told him to tell Mike and Mom they could get off the bus if they didn't like where he was going. He reamed them up one side and down the other. Told them he didn't care what they thought."

"Does he feel empowered?"

"Yep."

"Then I'm going to take the two of you back to your retreat. Do you feel complete here?" Ivy asked.

"We're done. Let's go."

181

Ivy touched Paul's mind's eye as she counted. "One. Two. Three. You're back at your retreat. What does your inner child want to do to celebrate all the great things he heard from you about his project?"

"He's over at the fort."

Ivy laughed. "Of course."

Paul chuckled. "I think he'll fit right in."

"While they're building, I'd like you to imagine meeting your mom at a picnic table. Somewhere you feel comfortable. She's sitting on one side and you're on the other side. Nod when you're there."

Paul nodded.

"As you sit there, I want you to feel yourself moving through time until you're in the summer before fourth grade. Feel your size. Feel your mother's presence... how you depended on her in a hundred ways. How she was in charge of your home and you."

In deep relaxation, Paul felt himself becoming short and thin... all arms and legs. His upper front teeth were still coming in. As he looked across the table, his mother seemed tall. In the deepest part of his awareness, he knew she was in charge. "I'm at the picnic table with Mom."

Ivy waded in. "We can't understand our childhood wounds if we look at them through a telescope made of our life experiences. Our child views events differently than adult-selves. We need to experience the wounding moment from the perspective of the child.

"Paul, I'm going to make a statement, and I want you to take it to your inner wisdom to see if it feels true. During the stick-town incident, your little boy recognized his personal spirit was being dismissed, and he felt powerless. Anger showed up."

"Nailed it."

Ivy continued. "To overcome those feelings, he found ways to thwart his mother's power. Let your body talk to you now. It holds your story. Don't guide it, just listen. Observe. Feel."

"My back's aching."

"Listen to what it's telling you."

Paul adjusted the pillow behind his back. Became animated. "It's so obvious, but I just didn't see it before. My backache got me out of doing things I didn't want to do... mainly sports but other things too. I got out of Thanksgiving over at my grandmother's... a couple of times. Then there's the time mom made me stay home from a hike with my friends... she wanted the garage cleaned.

"I'd get a backache when she was pushing me to do something I didn't want to do."

Ivy responded, "I'd interpret that as your body helping you honor your spirit needs. Your back pain was an excuse your mother could understand when her demands made you feel powerless and angry. Does that sound right to you?"

"Totally. What I felt, emotionally, didn't mean crap to her. But she couldn't argue with physical pain. The doctors could verify that."

"Congrats! You've found the gift from your backache. It gave you a valid reason to refuse her expectations.

"You have to know how your behavior or symptoms have been serving you if you want to achieve permanent change. Otherwise, you would see them as something randomly happening to you. You wouldn't recognize you had a relationship that you could change."

Ivy rubbed her hands together. "Let's reconnect with your nine-year-old who's still sitting at the picnic table with your mom. I want your adult-self to sit down beside your little boy. Look at your mom and tell her why you've been having backaches over the years. Tell her you'll no longer need them as an excuse. Instead of your back helping you to honor your spirit needs, you're going to be using your voice. Nod when you're done."

When Paul nodded, Ivy initiated another energy experience. "Your mother's power over you began long before you were aware her expectations didn't fit your personal spirit. It's an energy connection that was firmly in place by the time you were nine.

"I want you to look across the table and see the energy that comes from her and attaches to you. It's an energy that doesn't serve you, and you get to disconnect from it. Tell me the color and how that energy looks."

"It's red darts coming at me. I feel like a target."

Ivy could imagine his mother's controlling energy becoming embedded each time he tried to stand up to her. "You're going to release those darts using your voice. Silently, in your mind's eye, say, 'My voice is my power.'

"Do it over and over. Shout it out. Feel the darts dropping away from your body. Let the painful punctures heal as your voice soars to the far reaches of our valley."

Moments later, Paul declared the darts gone.

"Now I want you to recognize that every time your back ached, you were sending your mom anger energy. You were creating your own strong, energy connection. It's time to untangle your energy from hers.

"You can do this by focusing on everything that makes your spirit soar. Do that now and witness the tangled energy fade away. Think about your drumming, bicycling, cookies, reading, gardening. Let your heart song flow through. Nod when you're no longer energetically connected through anger."

Ivy knew this session would likely be the last… at least for a while. Today, Paul was an energy astronaut breaking free of the gravity that had held him in orbit around his own mother earth.

"Man, that feels good." Paul opened his eyes without the usual countdown from Ivy. "I feel freed up."

Ivy nodded. "You are freed up. We tend to have repeating thoughts that validate what we know, and those thoughts create the backbone of our beliefs. Now you are free to have new thoughts about your back."

Paul reiterated what Ivy had said so often in their time together, and laughing, she joined him half way through… "And our thoughts, beliefs, and feelings create our reality."

Their session ended with all the fanfare of a wave returning to the sea, but both of them felt the timeless, compelling expanse of what they'd shared.

Thirty ~ Nora

Joslin's starchy reception room was softened by fresh-cut flowers Nora had never noticed before. Today was different. She wondered if they'd always been there, and she was just now noticing her surroundings... one of those gifts of healing Ivy had talked about.

As she followed the receptionist to the treatment room, Nora leaned into the yellow roses tucked into an antique pitcher and took a deep breath. It was no surprise to her when she smelled nothing. Smell hadn't been her thing for as long as she could remember.

As she undressed, Nora scanned the Pooh quotes framed next to Joslin's credentials. Her office might be professional and efficient, but the massage therapist was as cozy as hot cocoa on a winter day.

After lying down on the warm Biomat and covering herself with the soft, flannel sheet, Nora read the quotes attached to the ceiling.

The quiet knock on the door came quickly. She answered, "I'm ready."

Joslin's smile said she had all the time in the world. Reaching for Nora's right hand, the massage therapist began pulling gently on her fingers. Her deep voice purred. "What can I do for you today?"

"Nothing specific. I'm just giving myself a treat."

"Look at you! Showing up without your usual sore neck and stiff shoulders. As Pooh says, "As soon as I saw you, I knew an adventure was going to happen.'"

Sighing into the soothing finger sensations, Nora suggested, "Let's go for more of that relaxing touch... all over."

"Sounds good. Are you warm enough?"

Nora was slipping into indulgent tranquility as Joslin placed a pillow under her knees and adjusted a heated wrap around her neck. She was soft-butter by the time Joslin's talented fingers had kneaded her feet and moved up her legs.

Suspended in pleasure, she barely noticed Joslin move from her lower body and lift her left arm.

She wasn't aware when tears moved across her temples and into her hair.

Then subterranean panic robbed her breath and seized the moment. Her face was suddenly on fire, and her eyes flew open.

Joslin moved the massage away from the trigger spot below Nora's left elbow. Picking up her hand, Joslin made gentle circles in the palm and talked. "Stay lying down if you can. Take a deep breath." Joslin counted for Nora and inhaled with her. "Now exhale as I count down from seven." Together they breathed until Nora asked for a kleenex.

Wiping away the tears, she asked, "What happened?"

"As I moved up your forearm from your hand, I noticed you started crying. I think we reached a spot that's connected to some significant body memory. It happens during massage... more than you might think."

Brushing her dampened hair back with her fingers, Nora thought about sharing her childhood abuse. For a second.

"Are you aware of the bump you have here on the inside of your forearm?" Joslin asked.

Picking up her arm, Nora looked at the spot. "Yes. That bump came up a few months ago. Maybe late winter. I had one like it before, and it's nothing serious."

"I was massaging that area when your body reacted. The bump or the faint scar running across it might be connected to an accident. Do you remember anything?"

Nora looked closer. Her scalp tightened. A vaporous sense of loneliness settled in her chest. "I've never noticed that scar. I don't remember getting hurt there."

"Well... it might have happened a long time ago. Seems like it would have been pretty significant to still be evident. Maybe it happened when you were a toddler or baby. By your reaction, I'd guess your body is still holding the event."

Again, Nora started to say something about her work with Ivy, but her instinct for privacy was too strong. The words were firmly locked behind her self-image. Instead, she asked, "Do you think our bodies talk to us?"

"I've never thought about it that way, but I do know our cells are constantly exchanging information with the energy field. In fact, our cells are a hundred times more sensitive to energy signals than physical sensations."

Joslin gently massaged Nora's hand. "They also store our experiences. You could say cells hold our autobiography, and, sometimes, forgotten parts of our story come up during massage."

Joslin reached out and gently touched the bump and scar. "You started crying when I worked in this area. Were you feeling sad?"

"No. And I'm good now. Do we have more time?"

A quick glance at the clock showed them Nora had another twenty minutes. "Let me work on your neck and shoulders," Joslin suggested.

Nora tried to relax. She tried to enjoy the magic of Joslin's pushing, prodding, and rubbing, but she kept thinking about serendipity. Was this one of those moments when the energy field was using a bump and a scar to signal an empowering revelation?

Thirty-One ~ Nora

For four days, Nora had thought about the faint, two-inch scar just below her elbow on the soft skin of her inner arm. Mostly, she couldn't believe she'd never noticed it before.

She'd massaged it now and then, wondering if it would bring more information. Nothing came. Nothing compelling or mystifying. Just a low-grade loneliness she could blink away with work, music, or her current novel by Amanda Quick.

Once again, she was in the reclining chair at Ivy's barn, depending on her to make sense of the inexplicable. With the count of one... two... three... and the cool touch of Ivy's finger between her eyebrows, Nora was transported to her deep relaxation retreat.

The sound of the waves immediately soothed. Her two little girls from previous memories were playing Monopoly. And, because the retreat reflected Nora's inner world, a puppy had appeared.

She reported her observations to Ivy.

"Does that feel good? Did you have a dog when you were young?"

"No, but I always wanted one... just like this golden retriever puppy that showed." Softness suffused Nora's face. "My little girls named her Paws."

"Spend time with them and nod your head when you're ready to find answers about your scar."

When Nora nodded, Ivy asked her to walk down the beach and find the perfect spot to sit at the edge of the water. "Put your feet in the gentle lap of the surf. Embrace the softness surrounding you... the whispering breeze, the smooth sand, the fluffy clouds.

"You've been wanting to understand your dream, and serendipity might be guiding you with the scar. Acknowledge any fears you might have, knowing you are always safe in your healing journey. Let the anticipation of answers bubble up inside you. Remember I'm right here beside you, and you will only uncover what you're ready to know."

Watching Nora's hands relax around each kleenex she was holding, Ivy began their journey. "Look down the beach and see if you have an inner child who's been waiting for you… one who knows about your dream."

Nora's surprise was evident. "Yes, but she's way down the beach. I think she wants me to come to her."

"Walk slowly toward her. Talk to her. Tell her how glad you are to see her. Ask her if there's anything she needs to feel comfortable."

"She wants her new, red, birthday bike."

Ivy was glad Nora's inner child was so forthcoming. It was a good sign. "Look over at the palm trees on your left. Her bike is there, waiting for her."

Nora nodded. "She's walking toward it. So am I. She wants to ride it in our old neighborhood."

"I'm going to touch your mind's eye, and both of you will be transported there. You'll both have red bikes. Nod when you're there, riding."

Nora nodded.

Ivy asked, "How old is she?"

"She just turned ten."

"Ask your little girl if she knows about the scar on your arm."

If they hadn't been inside, Ivy would have thought a dark cloud passed over Nora. The air around them thickened. "What's happening, Nora?"

"She got off her bike. We're sitting on the curb near my childhood home."

"Using your inner wisdom, read her energy. What's she feeling?"

Nora felt it crawl inside her… the crushing, silent solitude from her dream writhed liked maggots in rotting food. "She feels all alone… like everyone she knows is gone."

"Ask her if she'll show you what makes her feel this way. Tell her you want to know. You care. You'll believe anything she shares with you."

Nora shook her head. "She's just staring ahead."

"Tell her you had a dream and felt so alone it scared you. That everything shifted until you didn't know what was real."

Nora's breathing hitched. "She's looking at me."

"Tell her your dream."

189

Nora didn't know if she could. Not in this realm where she had no control. Not here, where bikes and puppies could appear. She stared at her little girl and couldn't find the courage.

Her ten-year-old was fading when she felt the light pressure of Ivy's hand on her shoulder. "Wiggle your toes, Nora. Feel the pillow at your back. Your inner wisdom will never allow you to get swallowed up by the memory.

"You can open your eyes at any time and be present with me, but, right now, your little girl needs you. She lived what you know from your dream. She's here today asking you to witness her story, so she can release it. Is this the right day for you to do that for her?"

Nora crushed her kleenex, rubbed them against her eyes. The answer crackled, as though coming through a failing walkie talkie, "I want to do this."

"Tell your little girl you're ready now. That you forgot the two of you don't have to do this alone. Right now, you have a spirit guide who is showing up to help you. Feel the guide's presence. Feel its energy, and tell me what it looks like."

Nora's lopsided smile told Ivy the guide had shown up. "It's a big dog. Floppy ears. My little girl's hugging him."

"I want you to hug him too," Ivy responded. "He's come because he's a spirit guide that guards. Feel his protective presence."

"I can feel it. I'm ready."

"Ask your little girl if she will take you to the moment when she felt so deeply alone."

"She will if the dog comes too."

Ivy knew her agreement was huge. "Yes. All three of you will travel together. I'm going to count one-to-three and touch your mind's eye. Hold your little girl's hand and go where ever she takes you. Trust whatever you sense, see, or feel.

"One. Two. Three. Go with your little girl."

Nora's eyebrows became active. Her head tipped from one side to another. Ivy waited a few moments, then asked. "What do you see?"

"It's completely black. I can't see anything."

"Is your little girl with you?"

"I'm holding her hand."

"Look to your left, Nora."

"Still black."

"Do you smell anything? Or sense anything?" Ivy asked.

"It feels silent like my dream, but I'm not scared."

Ivy tried breaking through Nora's resistance that was being represented by the black.

She had her reach into her pocket and find a flashlight. Nothing was revealed.

She had her walk forward.

Look upward.

Feel what she was walking on.

None of these opened up an insight.

"Nora, this black space is a portal that will take you to answers about your scar and maybe your dream. I'm going to count to three. Feel yourself leaving the portal. Let it open up to light and insight. One. Two. Three."

Nora's scalp tightened. PANIC!… panic that felt like coils of deeper darkness snaking toward her. "I want to go back to my retreat."

"One. Two. Three. You're back at the beach.

"Listen to the surf.

"Your little girl and your floppy-eared spirit guide are with you."

Ivy gently touched Nora's shoulder. "Feel your feet firmly grounded in the sand. Take a deep breath. Nod if you're ready to come out of relaxation."

Nora nodded.

"Let your ten-year-old know she gets to stay at the retreat. She can be with your eight-year-old, six-year-old, and her guide until you come back."

"She likes that."

Ivy smiled. She could see the inviting, safe, child-friendly retreat as clearly as the inside of her barn. "Tell her you'll be coming back. That you still want to know about why she felt so lonely. How she got the scar.

"Tell her she did a fantastic job today. That you love her courage and will always believe what she shares with you.

"Then ask her how she could get your attention in the days ahead, just in case she has something more to share before our next appointment."

Nora sighed. Ran her fingers through her short, black hair that was just beginning to soften with gray. "My scar will tingle."

"Good. If that happens, remember to pay attention to any feelings or thoughts you've just experienced... or that come up as the scar tingles."

Ivy brought her out of deep relaxation.

Profound disappointment etched Nora's face. "My little girl showed up, and I was too scared to go with her."

Ivy didn't see it that way at all. "She came, and you dared to travel toward the dream as far as you felt comfortable today. Next time, you'll go deeper into the landscape of the memory."

"That's not good enough. That's like telling me it's okay if a thug is stalking me because I'm headed to the police station. I need to run there or fight back.

"I need to fight for her. Don't you see that?" Nora couldn't look up. Didn't want to see Ivy's eyes when she was feeling so much like a two-year-old in a tantrum.

She resented Ivy's calm response but listened to her continued insight. "I totally get your need to take control of this mystery, but the answers have been stored in your body through your five senses. You can only *sense* your way to them. Your strongest feeling today asked you to wade, not dive, into the unknown."

Ivy reached out and lightly touched the area of Nora's scar. "I know you don't intend this, but when you are shaming yourself for not fighting for the answers, your ten-year-old is also feeling the shame. What would you want her to take away from this day?"

Nora looked up, met Ivy's compassion with her own empathy for her inner child. "I'd want her to feel like a hero for coming forward. A super hero for standing in the black void with me." Sighing, Nora realized, "That really was something, wasn't it? To be in the dark silence and not be scared."

"It really was," Ivy agreed. "It would have been very natural for you to pop out of deep relaxation at that point. So, in a way, you could say you *did fight* for your little girl. You challenged yourself to stay, to see what might be revealed."

Nora's relief was as strong as catching a falling baby. More than anything, she didn't want to leave her ten-year-old caught in the web of a traumatic moment. Now that she had learned going into dissociated memories released the emotional hold on her inner children, she couldn't fail this child who loved her bike and had the courage to ask for help.

"I stayed until panic started creeping in."

Ivy squeezed Nora's arm. "That's another way you fought for your child. You choose to step out of panic. Instead of pushing through, you showed your little girl that she got to leave and come back another day. You empowered her."

"You see this so differently." It was as close to whining as Nora had ever expressed. "I feel like I'm falling out of the sky, and you tell me I'm flying. And then I see it. I really do. But I want to see it without you pointing it out."

"Oh… that will happen. I can only point it out because I've traveled the landscape so often. It's all new to you."

"Okay." Nora acknowledged Ivy's insight. "So, if I tell you I feel like I'm flailing around in this landscape…

"scared out of my mind that I won't get to the memory to save my ten-year-old…

"at the same time, I'm scared out of my mind that I'll find the memory…

"what's your advice as I leave you for another week?"

"I'm thinking drum lessons."

"Are you kidding me?"

Ivy smiled. The idea had popped up so spontaneously, she knew it had to be perfect. "It's about you making sound… loud, demanding, thrumming sound. I know it will both soothe and empower you at the same time. It will open that black portal."

Nora threw up her hands and mumbled something about the way Ivy was always asking her to venture into uncharted territory. "Okay. I'll do it. How do I get started?"

"I'll connect you to a young man named Paul. He'll totally understand that it's not necessarily music. It's about personal empowerment."

Thirty-Two ~ Nora

Driving to Ella's house, Nora wondered if they might share a cup of coffee today. In the past two years, their relationship had been easy conversations before and after meetings about the Growing Lives Foundation. They were connected by a shared passion for the organization Nora had established for children. Their parting refrain was always, "We should have coffee sometime."

Pulling into the driveway, Nora anticipated looking at some of Ella's stored furniture that might be used in the house the foundation had just purchased. She thought they might have that cup of coffee... wondered if she would tell Ella about her memory work. If there was anyone who would understand, it was the director of the foundation.

Ella's home was a perfect reflection of the lovely lady. There was no particular style, but the down-to-earth combination was a statement in itself. Cozy and inviting, it was organized with just enough loose ends to make you feel relaxed.

Ella greeted Nora with a hug. "The furniture's in the basement. They are some older pieces we accumulated when Richard's parents died, so we don't have to worry about the kids damaging things. I think they'll feel more comfortable than with something new."

"I agree. It'll feel more like home. Your offer is just what the kids' house needs."

Ella's laughter was rich, a heart song released. "You'll be doing us a favor if you take the entire collection. Richard has plans for that corner of the basement.

"Set your purse on the table there, and I'll take you down."

Listening to Ella's comments, Nora followed her through the sunny kitchen and down the well-lit stairwell. "The sofa's pretty much your traditional grandmother-style. You know, cabbage rose fabric in pinks and greens. It'll blend well with sticky snacks and shoe tracks."

Laughing, they reached the bottom of the stairs and turned to the left. An extra refrigerator and the washer and dryer caught Nora's attention as they moved past them to the doorway leading to the furniture.

Her scalp tightened.

Ella's animated chatter became a hollow echo engulfing Nora in suspended time… time that split her apart. A wisp of her slipped away, hovering above and looking down at what was happening. The rest stayed with her body giving every appearance of being fully present as she nodded, looked, and agreed.

Ella began dislodging the stacked furniture. She pointed. She pulled pieces out. Her words bounced as though they were nothing but balloons bumping against the furniture.

Their eyes met. Green, gentle eyes with a question snapped time back into place. "What do you think? Will this be a good start?"

Nora was present again, mostly whole, though she felt like she'd been reassembled by the Star Trek's transporter, and it had lost track of some molecules. "I think you've got a real treasure here."

"Oh good. I was hoping you'd find it usable. We'll make arrangements to get it moved when the house is ready."

Nora turned around. The doorway waited for her. Paralyzing dread fought with anxious desire to get out of the basement. Like a haunted house, she knew her fear wasn't real, but she was ready to jump. To scream.

Consciously paying attention to Ella's description of her husband's plans for the room, Nora made her way back to the kitchen. Each word was a distraction creating stepping stones for Nora.

"Do you have time for a cup of coffee today?" Ella asked.

"Oh gosh. Not today, but thank you. I need to get going."

Reminding Nora to grab her purse, Ella walked her to the front door. There were hugs. Goodbyes.

Nora reminded herself to breath as she walked to the car. Felt release when she sat behind the steering wheel and shut the door.

Looking down at her purse, the basement doorway flashed in her mind's eye. Seeking her keys, shaky fingers dug into her bag.

She ached to get home. It beckoned like a warm fire in the middle of a snow storm.

Nora looked over her shoulder to back out of the driveway. Sitting on the back seat was the portable drum set Paul had loaned her earlier in the morning. Relief snapped into place.

That's what she needed.

That's what she craved.

Knowing she got to go home and spend the afternoon drumming felt like being tossed a life jacket as the ship went down.

Thirty-Three ~ Nora

Nora had come to the session angry about having another dissociated moment in her friend's basement. Sitting with Ivy, she had tersely outlined what she now knew.

… the deep loneliness, the scar, and the panic brought on during her massage.

… her scalp feeling like it was shrinking when she turned left at the bottom of the stairs at Ella's

… a nebulous aversion to the appliances in Ella's basement

… prickling foreboding around an everyday, garden-variety doorway.

Nora hadn't liked Ivy starting her deep relaxation with reminders… that her memory would come as she was ready for it… that it was important to honor the guidance of her inner world. She didn't want band-aids and kisses on what felt like a gaping wound.

Ivy's gentle voice had taken Nora to her retreat, but her raging determination was in charge. Her ten-year-old was ready. So was she.

"Is your ten-year-old waiting for you?" Ivy asked.

"She's got her own drum set, and she's whaling on it. Feels like a wild, desperate chant calling me."

"Go to her and find a drum you can beat. Let the sound roar. Bellow. Howl. Let your inner wisdom and your little girl know you are ready today. Nod when you feel your body is ready to give up the secret it's been holding."

As the seconds passed and Ivy waited for her to nod, Nora's expression changed. Tense became subdued. Resolute lines around her mouth vaporized with the drum beat Ivy couldn't hear. She surmised the drumming must be creating a strong bond for Nora and her ten-year-old.

Nora nodded.

Ivy began. "Ask your inner child if she's ready to show you what caused the scar."

"She's ready. She grabbed my hand and we're walking down the beach."

"Ask her to stop along the way and look at the surf with you."

Nora answered a moment later. "The surf's high today. Huge, crashing waves."

"Is that how your little girl is feeling. Something big coming at her?"

"She says we could be washed away."

"Notice your little girl's dog-spirit is joining you. Remind her she's not alone this time. Ask her if she needs her bike too."

"She wants to know if we can come back to the beach if we need our bikes."

"Absolutely," Ivy answered. "Tell her to say, 'bike,' and the two of you will be standing on the beach in that very second."

"She's ready."

Ivy felt herself slip into the calm Place-Of-No-Time that guided her. "Trust whatever comes to you, Nora. Don't try to figure it out.

"One. Two. Three. Go with your little girl."

"It's black, again."

"That's okay," Ivy assured. "It's just a portal, and today you have information that will help you move through it to get answers. Something at the bottom of your friend's basement stairway triggered you. Go with that feeling."

Nora felt every cell in her body congealing in resistance until she felt her little girl's hand in hers. Squeezing it, she felt movement surrounding her. The skin on her head tingled. Tightened.

The darkness turned to gray. In the lifeless shadows, the basement stairs of her childhood home appeared.

Silence took over. It was a noiseless, shifting force, moving the bottom of the stairway directly in front of Nora.

"Stairs." It was all she could utter before the cement floor seized her attention and light slithered across it. Survival screamed at Nora. She knew not to enter the creeping light.

Gripping her hand, Nora's ten-year-old stepped forward… into the ominous glow.

Nora felt the pull. Not in her arm, but in her chest where her lungs collapsed into shallow panting that accepted the challenge.

She followed.

Slowly, a doorway became illuminated. Nora turned toward it. She dug deep and found the courage to follow her little girl through the opening.

The smell of laundry soap poured over her. Like syrup, it stuck to her skin and filled her nose with a thick, sickening-sweet floral scent. The smell was a quicksand of anguish sucking her in, trying to drag her under.

"Bike."

Nora felt snatched from suffocating despair. It was as if she had been in a plane, and the pilot had pulled her out of a nosedive. Ivy's finger firmly pressed her mind's eye and she heard, "One. Two. Three. You're at your retreat, Nora.

"Listen to the surf. Go to the drums with your inner child and find a rhythm that matches the sound of the waves. Nod when you feel fully present on the beach."

Ivy watched, looking for physical clues about Nora's state of mind. Her face held intention, not distress. Her hands were holding the kleenex firmly, not in clenched fists. "Take a long, deep breath and feel your feet firmly grounded in the sand."

Nora took several deep breaths. "I'm ready to come out of relaxation."

"Is your ten-year-old feeling centered and grounded?" Ivy asked.

"The waves aren't crashing any more. She's chewing bubble gum and playing the drums."

"Tell her you'll be coming back. That she did some fantastic work today. Celebrate the way she keeps showing up for you."

When Nora nodded her head, Ivy brought her out. She waited until Nora looked at her. "What are you feeling?"

Nora reached inside the neckline of her t-shirt and rubbed her neck. "I made it through the black portal. And, god, I wish I'd stayed, but "Bike" popped out of my mouth. It wasn't a conscious choice. I didn't see it coming."

Pushing down on the lever to raise the back of her chair, Nora continued. "It's amazing how I could be that scared, and now I'm sitting here talking to you. Both feel equally real."

"They are," Ivy confirmed. "Whether we're in deep relaxation or in conscious attention, we always experience what holds our focus. In one moment you were focused on your ten-year-old's experience. The next moment you were focused on a retreat you've created for yourself. In this moment, your focus is with me. You're shifting your awareness."

Nora got it. "I think that's the power of memory work... it's not you telling me what happened. It's me experiencing it again with adult awareness."

Ivy took the yellow blanket Nora handed her. "What did you experience today?"

"We went to the bottom of the basement stairs of my childhood home. The floors were cement. The space was shifting, like in my dream.

"When I felt that movement, I totally wanted to leave, but I knew I'd be upset with myself... and I was aware of my little girl holding my hand. Man! She has a whole lot more courage than me."

Nora shook her head in disbelief, "I don't get that, but there it is. She's the one who stepped into the light on the floor. I don't think I could have done it on my own.

"That's when the doorway appeared." Saying it out loud, jolted Nora with an insight. "The way the basement stairs and doorway were arranged at Ella's was just like my childhood home. At the bottom of the stairs, you turned left to go through the door. But today, I was already at the bottom, facing the stairs, so the doorway to the laundry room was on my right."

Like an embedded reporter, Nora was both observer and participant. "I didn't want to go in."

She sat forward, rolling the tissue in her hands. Her active eyes told Ivy she was probably seeing more than she had during relaxation.

That happened often. It was one of the reasons it was so valuable to talk about the memory experience after coming out of relaxation. Information could get overlooked in the high emotions.

"I can't imagine why the laundry room would feel like the devil's own haunt, but the smell of the laundry soap hit hard. It felt like my heart exploded. That's when I needed out."

"Do you remember what your feelings were in that moment?" Ivy asked.

"Like I was going under. Sucked into swampy violence." Nora's eyes widened. "I don't like that. Horrible happens in chaotic places not a laundry room."

Shifting her feet off the footstool, Nora placed them on the floor as though instinctively seeking to ground herself. Her eyes locked with

Ivy's. "How are we going to get answers when, apparently, I don't want to know the answer?"

"There is another way. I think you could get there more easily and quickly if we brought your mystery to a group I call the energy detectives."

"Energy detectives? There's such a thing?" Nora's doubt made Ivy smile.

"It's a group of five women, including me, that has lots of experience using energy to solve personal mysteries. They could seek answers without the fears that are holding you back. And… you could witness, rather than experience, a lot of the unfolding information. It would feel less intense."

Nora felt like she was being offered a hand while clinging by her fingernails to the slippery wall of an endlessly deep chasm. She wanted someone to save her. "Did you say it would help me move forward faster?"

Nodding, Ivy said, "You'd have five energy guides working with you and for you to get answers."

"Do I know these women? Won't they know everything about me if we call them in?" Nora looked into the chasm holding her answers and still couldn't imagine allowing that. It would be giving them permission to crawl into the weak spots she guarded.

"I don't know if you know the other four, but I can tell you this… they are as honorable and caring as you. Nothing learned during the session would ever leave the barn."

"You totally trust them, then."

Ivy was firm. "Totally."

"I'm going to have to think about it."

"Of course, and while you think about it, consider this… they will learn some things about you, but you'll also be learning about them. As you know, energy work comes from our inner world. They can only seek answers by revealing themselves, so you'll become part of a circle of empowered women who dare to venture beyond the pale."

Thirty-Four ~ Susie

"I know I should've been able to let Susie's situation go, but I can't tell you how glad I am that we're meeting with her again." Haphazardly Miriam filled a bowl with fruit she'd brought. Grapes skittered across the kitchen table at the barn. Two peaches were sure to sport bruises.

"Of course, you want to know what's been happening since she left." Vanessa set her carrot cake in the middle of the table like an artist seeing exactly what her painting needed. "We might not have expectations for the people we work with, but it's natural to wonder how things are going. Especially when there are so many questions left unanswered."

Kendra blew through the kitchen door with verve and a bag of corn chips. "I can't wait to hear what Susie has to say. I've imagined a hundred scenarios."

Fifteen minutes later everyone was sitting around the table digging into the taco salad.

Placing her napkin on her lap, Susie sighed. "It feels great to be back with you guys. Do you ever have someone look for more life challenges just so they can meet up with you again?"

Jill laughed. "That's probably why this group formed. We kept wanting more."

Humor swept around the table. "Then we ran out of personal mysteries, so we had to invite others to bring theirs," Miriam teased.

"That's actually pretty much our story." Kendra piled corn chips on her plate and doused her salad with hot sauce. "What's your story, these days, Susie? I'm dying to know."

Susie looked around the table. "I'm dying to share. These past three weeks, I've imagined sitting right here and sharing everything."

"Go for it." Kendra let her curiosity off the leash. "Did you hear from your dad or mom?"

"No contact from Dad, which isn't out of the ordinary. Mom calls like usual and acts like everything is normal."

"Maybe it is for her," Jill volunteered. "She might have no idea we invaded the office and took the photos."

Susie agreed. "I don't think she does, but dad certainly knows. "I sent him an email and told him he had to stop all tutoring, or I would tell mom what was happening in his office."

Jill was stunned. Couldn't imagine confronting him so boldly.

Kendra whooped.

Ivy smiled. Loved that Susie took such a big step without needing it validated by them.

Vanessa understood how maintaining the appearance of a closely knit family could depend on stifled communication.

Miriam wondered how Susie's husband fit in all this. "What does Noah think about your brave action?"

"Oh. I haven't talked to him about it yet." Susie saw no contradiction in continuing the pattern of keeping secrets within family dynamics. "I'll do it sometime but not right now. I don't want his observations. I need to feel stronger."

"So you haven't shared this big change with anyone," Miriam summarized.

"That's why I was so excited about spending time with you guys. So much has been going on."

Miriam grabbed one of the rogue grapes and put it in the fruit bowl. "We'd love to hear everything."

"First of all, things are getting better with my husband. All this healing work has helped me see that the conflict in our sex life was leaking into other areas. He thought he was being romantic and encouraging me to believe I was pretty by fawning over my body."

Vanessa saw it immediately. "That made you retreat. The more he praised your looks, the more it hooked into your pornography experience."

"Exactly. So that's sort of smoothing out cause I'm not pushing him away as much. I can see now that I wanted to be married, but didn't really want any kind of intimacy."

"Your clothes have even changed," Jill observed.

Susie liked Jill's smiling celebration. It tickled the same place wildflowers touched. "You noticed."

"Today you showed up wearing a t-shirt that isn't two sizes too big. And that lavender really makes your eyes pop."

Susie's soft laughter was gilded with golden pride. "I thought so." She topped her salad with two slices of avocados. "I bought it the same day I registered for some online classes."

This is better than Christmas gifts, thought Ivy. "My goodness! What are your plans?"

"I'm going to finish school and get a degree in law."

Every fork hung in mid-air. Not one of the detectives could connect the dots.

Susie's enthusiasm tumbled into the void. "I want the power to do something about pornography. Law seems like a good path. Don't you think? I want to be an activist, maybe get into internet law."

Murmuring agreement flowed. Enthusiasm bubbled. Susie took the floor.

"I've joined an online group for survivors of childhood pornography, and it's clear nearly everyone continues to feel powerless. They haven't found the pieces the cameras stole."

The five women listened to the budding advocate as Susie shared her ideas for making a difference. Their hearts beating as one, they were once again witnessing the way healing spread. As natural as a river flowing to the sea, its power couldn't be contained to one life.

"So," Kendra ventured into unfinished business, "are you convinced some of your personal photos are on those websites we found on your dad's computer?"

"I don't know. I left the website list here with the photos, but it doesn't really matter whether it's me or another child. I can't let it go." Susie pushed her hair behind her ears. "I need to get a new haircut."

Deflection might work with others in her life, but these women could spot it a mile away. Vanessa was the one to ask. "What's the next step around the photos and list?"

"That's why I asked for this meeting. I want energy insights to guide me because I keep going in circles when I think about it."

Kendra ventured into the tender spot Susie might be avoiding. "Is it safe to say you've decided to focus on others who've been affected by pornography and leave what happened in your family floating under the radar?"

There was nothing in Kendra's voice or inflection that felt accusatory, but Susie could see how it might look like she was letting her own house decay while wanting to rebuild others'. "Do you think I'm sort of skipping a step?"

"No, not at all." Kendra was quick to respond. "There are no best steps… no map to follow when we're moving out of childhood trauma. I just wanted to know, so I could be sure I'm with you on the path you're choosing."

Susie looked around and saw it was true. As always, there was complete acceptance in the air.

Vanessa confirmed this. "Each one of us would make a different choice, and all of them would be perfect. The path we choose reflects our individual experience, our personalities, and the lasting effects of our emotional wounds."

Susie made her path clear. "As long as dad has stopped taking pictures, I just want to forgive him and move on. I don't see the point in ruining mom's life by bringing the dirt out now. It won't bring Crissy back. It won't make me feel better."

Ivy felt the need to speak. "The interesting thing about forgiveness is how it feels like we're putting an emotional wound behind us. Yet, it can be another way of managing denial."

Miriam was riveted as Ivy continued. "To give ourselves body-cleansing, deep healing, forgiveness has to come from the perspective of the person who had the experience. When we're working with memories, that person is who we were at the time of the trauma, not who we are today."

Miriam thought about the forgiveness she'd offered in the past, now seeing why it had felt hollow. "You're saying that it's the childhood-Susie, the one who experienced the photography sessions, who has to forgive her dad. Not the Susie sitting with us."

"Yes, but I'd add this… It's totally okay for this lovely lady to say she is forgiving her dad so she can move on. She just needs to realize it's not part of her healing. It's a way of saying, *I'm done for now. I know a lot has changed, but I need to keep this moment feeling the same.*"

Thinking about herself, as well as Susie, Miriam asked, "So, at a later date, Susie could work with her inner child to experience deep healing forgiveness?"

"Absolutely." Ivy spoke directly to Susie. "If that comes up for you in the future, you would want it to be about the way it's affected you.

Your focus would not be on your dad. He's the one who must journey to find forgiveness for himself."

"I understand that part, but what do you mean by body-cleansing forgiveness? Does that mean what I'm doing now is all in my head?"

"Exactly. You're using logic. When your child forgives, it will come from deep emotions, and that's what will change your energy pattern.

"Remember, our thoughts, feelings, and beliefs create an energy pattern that manifests our reality. By going to a more profound forgiveness that's directly related to your trauma, you'll be less likely to attract similar emotional experiences. For instance, you won't be comfortable in relationships that ask you to give up pieces of yourself like you were forced to do with your dad."

"That's pretty heavy." Miriam could look back on her own life and see that she had jumped into her own forgiveness before she understood it.

"Why heavy?" Susie wanted to know.

"Because you think you're moving forward when your adult self forgives, but your energy pattern hasn't changed, so you're still caught in the web of your trauma. I can certainly see that for myself."

"So you think I need to do some work on this," Susie concluded.

"Not at all," Miriam said. "I think you're giving yourself a great break, so you can get going on your empowering journey with school, that new hair cut, and your marriage. Then maybe, like me, you'll get to another time when you'll want to journey with forgiveness in a new way."

Vanessa stood up and started clearing the lunch mess. "Right now, we want you to celebrate yourself for rescuing your empowerment and going out in the world to manifest your new dreams."

Jill grabbed her plate and the bowl of guacamole, joining Vanessa in the clean up. "Let's get into the studio and check the energy around what will serve you when it comes to the photos and the website list. Do you have that handy, Ivy?"

From that moment, the afternoon flew by.

The detectives set up one energy dialogue after another, letting the answers from one feed the next. In the end, three energies around the photos stood out for Susie.

Burning the photos felt like going out in the snow without a coat. It made her feel ill-prepared and not taking care of herself.

Sharing them with her husband made her feel like a bug on the sidewalk about to be stepped on. She recognized she was still wearing shame and didn't trust his response.

Putting the pictures in a safety deposit box at the bank made her feel like Clark Kent in the phone booth.

"I think that makes sense," she'd shared. "The photos might become my phone booth and, someday, help me step into my power. Who knows what might happen in the future?"

"And," Kendra pointed out, "they are something you might need to use with your dad. Over time, you might find him slipping back to the power he feels behind the camera. That pull might be stronger than his wish to remain undetected."

Vanessa's asked, "How will you really know he's given up his photography? It wouldn't take much for him to buy a new camera."

"Mom says he's canceled all his tutoring. She's assuming it's a step toward retirement. That's one reason I don't want to rock the boat. I want to keep communication open with her, so I can keep tabs on him."

"So that leaves us with the insights we got about the websites." Jill summarized what they'd found. "From the energy dialogues, we know he's still active there, but we also know that's not an emotional charge for you, Susie. It feels like a storm out at sea when you're safe on the beach."

"I suppose I might feel bothered by that storm, someday."

Through the two hours of energy work, Susie had become aware energy work wasn't about a destination. It provided road signs for her journey. She recognized what she learned and experienced as she traveled her chosen path might change her feelings about her dad, mom, the photos, and the online activity.

"And if you do start feeling bothered, you'll be ready to take new steps." Vanessa put her arm around Susie's shoulder. "Just like all of us here, you'll keep healing and growing."

Thirty-Five ~ Nora

Nora had decided to work with the energy detectives, and her drive to the barn was harrowing. It took her back to the first session with Ivy. It was right up there with daring to go into a mine shaft; golden answers might be found, but the walls shoring up her vigilance could also collapse.

She knew she would be arriving an hour before the others, but that didn't ease her grip on the steering wheel. Giving the fairy statue at the entrance of the driveway a nod, Nora wondered, once again, if she knew any of the ladies she'd be meeting.

Ivy met Nora at the door. Unlike the first session, the two greeted each other with a warm hug. Their mutual regard was strong, but, for now, Ivy was in charge, and Nora was grateful.

"Your licorice tea is ready," Ivy said as she walked toward the two facing chairs that had become so familiar to Nora. "I thought we could do a bit of guided energy to help you feel grounded and centered."

Sitting in what felt like *her* chair, Nora picked up her tea. "What's guided energy?"

"It's like deep relaxation, but you only wade into a different state of mind rather than swim. No pillows or blankets, no reclining in the chair, you just close your eyes and follow what I'm saying."

"Sounds like a good place to start." Holding her warm cup on her lap, Nora closed her eyes.

"Picture yourself in a lovely meadow filled with wildflowers. The earth is warm. The sun is a gentle friend. You can hear the soothing sound of a stream nearby.

"You've come today to get answers. You'll travel with empowering, nurturing allies. And, though you haven't met them, you can be sure the energy field has been bringing this moment to you. Beyond your conscious awareness, you've been manifesting this afternoon... or it wouldn't be happening. Your thoughts, feelings, and beliefs have created this opportunity. And, like every part of your healing journey, it is here to empower you. It's here to honor your spirit.

"You've invited these women who will travel with you to find answers. At an energetic level, you already know them.

"Look over to your right, Nora. You'll see four energies, maybe silhouettes."

Ivy watched Nora's slight smile and continued.

"Each of these energies is welcoming you to the meadow where energy is used to solve mysteries. They are waiting to be with you. I'm going to name each silhouette, starting on the left.

"As I say the name, feel yourself walking up to the energy and opening up to the connection. Read the energy of the person I've named, then raise your hand when you're done.

"Kendra."

Ivy reached for her tea. Taking a sip, she watched for Nora's raised hand, so she could call out the next name.

One-by-one Nora connected to Kendra, Jill, Miriam, and Vanessa. When she was done, Ivy continued the guided energy.

"Standing with your allies, look around the meadow. Notice there's no walls, no fences. That is how your journey will feel today. You'll always be free to move where you need to go.

"You can say, *No,* or *I don't want to go there,* or *I want more.*

"All five of us will encourage you, nudge you, even push you, but, in every moment, you will be in charge."

With Nora's head slightly bobbing up and down, Ivy told her to look to her left where she could see a path to the answers she wanted. "Feel the surging, swirling energy of your allies and step on the path knowing they are walking beside you.

"This is where you'll be finding your answers, Nora. Not in the black portal. Your answers are here in the meadow with allies that will feel like Cinderella's mice getting her ready for the ball.

"Walk on the path toward the curve ahead of you. As you get closer, you'll see a stone pillar sitting in the middle of the path.

"You know you can walk around it. That's what you were doing before you came to me. Now you want to know the secrets held within the pillar.

"Today's the day.

"You're ready.

"You have clues and allies.

"Step up to the pillar and put your hand on it. Nod if you feel comfortable."

With a quick affirmation from Nora, Ivy continued. "Notice the energy detectives on each side of you. When they place their hands on the pillar, there's no resistance. Their hands can move inside because they don't hold the fear and dread that stops your hand from searching within. With ease, they can reach inside the pillar holding your secrets and find the answers you're seeking.

"Feel their power.

"Let it feed your courage.

"Know that, when I count from 3 down to 1, you get to open your eyes and join them to find the secrets within.

"Three. Two. One. Open your eyes."

"I loved that," Nora exclaimed. Wide-eyed, wearing an I-can-do-this smile, she looked at her tea cup held in her lap and was amazed it hadn't spilled. "I feel so different than I did when I walked in here."

Ivy glanced at the clock. They still had 10 minutes. "I'm curious about what you *knew* about each of the detectives."

Nora took a sip of tea and set her cup aside. "I especially liked that part. I really do feel like I know each one of them in an elemental way. Does that make sense?"

"Definitely."

Nora recalled what she'd experienced as Ivy had named the four energies. "Okay. So with Kendra, the energy felt solid. Not like the pillar, more like an oak tree with the roots going deep into Mother Earth. I liked that. It was reassuring.

"Jill was the exact opposite. Have you ever walked into a butterfly sanctuary? You go in and hundreds of fluttering, colorful wings are filling the air around you. Jill's energy was like that. I was drawn to her because she seemed like a soft ally.

"Miriam's energy was soft too, but different. She's like Bambi. Graceful and vulnerable were the words that came to me but resilient was in there too. Her energy was comforting. I think she'll get what I'm feeling."

Scratching her palm, Nora recalled the last detective energy she'd read. "Vanessa had a best friend kind-of-feeling... like the friend you had in grade school who knew everything about you and made you feel special."

Ivy totally related to what Nora had picked up on for Kendra, Jill, and Miriam. What she said about Vanessa wasn't familiar, but it rang true. It added another dimension to the usually reticent friend.

"You nailed them," she said to Nora. "Do you find it easier to imagine today's session knowing them this way?"

"Absolutely."

"Good, because, when the five of us get together, the energy force is powerful. All wonderful, but definitely strong." Ivy smiled at Nora. "You'll fit right in."

And with that said, Miriam came through the door.

Miriam... *Bambi*... thought Nora as Ivy introduced them.

Miriam was dragging her chair and a footstool over to join Ivy and Nora when Kendra walked in. The circle was beginning to form.

Nora recognized her from the library, but they hadn't formally met. She remembered her as *oak tree-energy*. "Nora, I can't tell you how glad I am that you've given us another chance to solve a mystery," Kendra exclaimed. "There's nothing that speaks to my soul more than this work we do."

Miriam placed her chair next to Nora's. "I think that's true for all of us. This is like a play date."

Nora could see why. Her time with Ivy had revealed the incredible roller coaster ride that came with the energy work. She could imagine these women spending compelling, meaningful time traveling with every emotion and sprinkled with laughter. She wondered if it sometimes felt like a slumber party with a purpose.

As she shared that thought with Miriam, Vanessa pushed the door open with her hip and entered with an awkward box.

Ivy jumped up to help her.

Kendra pulled her chair into the circle and confided to Nora, "We always tell Vanessa she doesn't need to bring snacks, but we'd be awfully disappointed if she ever listened to us."

Nora was surprised by her own laughter. She already liked the women and remembered that Vanessa's energy had felt like a *childhood best friend.* That was good because Nora knew her in a superficial, social way. They'd met at a couple of fund-raising events for the Growing Lives children's foundation. That connection smoothed away any wrinkles of concern for her anonymity.

Kendra continued *telling on* Vanessa. "Once she knows your favorite comfort food, you can be sure it will be included at every session. I'm all about salt, chips, that kind of thing. Miriam here is a cookie monster. What's your thing?"

"Grilled cheese sandwiches," Nora laughed, surprised that this information had popped out of her mouth. "Maybe it's just cheese," she mused as the fifth detective came through the door.

Kendra jumped up and pulled the last two chairs into the circle while Miriam made the introduction. "This is Jill... the youngster of the group."

Jill settled into the nearest empty chair. "Yes, but I'm one of those old, wise souls," she declared. Her voice was feathery but easily heard. B*utterfly energy*, thought Nora.

Returning from unloading the snacks in the kitchen, Ivy and Vanessa interrupted any teasing Jill might have been experiencing. They took the last two chairs while Vanessa introduced herself. "Don't believe a thing these ladies have been telling you about me. Working with energy burns calories faster than jogging... we'd never get through an afternoon without food."

Nora agreed. "I hadn't put that together, but I am ravenous after my sessions with Ivy."

"So what did you bring?" Kendra asked Vanessa. She was ready for a snack.

Everyone laughed, but the question didn't get answered. Ivy steered them toward the purpose of the afternoon. "Nora, everyone here knows you have a mystery to solve, but they know nothing about your experience or the clues you've uncovered. Would you start us off with your story?"

Nora described the dream. The beginning.

Though she assumed it would have lost its impact with passing time, telling the attentive, supportive women brought out all the emotions. They flew through her body like homing pigeons finding their way back to the angst of her experience.

With kleenex in hand and patience flowing around the circle of chairs, Nora listed the triggers from her dream: the rolled up rug, bare walls, single light bulb, bed. She included the silence and movement, then continued listing the other clues that had come up during her journey with Ivy.

... the light from the doorway shining on the cement floor.

... the smell of the laundry soap.

... the scar on her arm.

... the profound loneliness, scalp-tightening panic

Feeling like she'd covered everything, she turned to Ivy. "Is there anything else?"

"I think it would help us if you also shared the two memories you've had. Everyone here has heard many similar stories, but your story might be connected to the answers we're seeking."

As fast as she could, Nora told them about her dad, her sexual abuse, and her uncle's awareness. "I'm not sure how much my mother knew, but I'm giving her a pass for now."

Miriam understood. "There's only so much we can assimilate."

"I think we have plenty to start with," Vanessa volunteered.

Everyone agreed.

Ivy spoke up. "Before we get started, I have a dialogue I'd like to set. Nora's especially adept when it comes to energy reading, but she's never done any group dialogues. It'll be a place to start."

"How do you want this to go?" Kendra asked.

"Let's all move out on the floor. I'm going to set the four of you and have Nora read your energy, one at a time. This isn't an interactive dialogue. You'll just feel the energy I set and report back."

Nora was fascinated by how quickly everyone knew exactly what to do. In just minutes, all four detectives were standing in a mesmerized state, their eyes closed, ready to be set with an energy.

Ivy whispered to Nora to wait where she stood, then stepped forward putting her hands on Jill's upper arms. Closing her eyes, she appeared to be in a slight trance. Nora recognized Ivy was concentrating on the energy she was setting.

Moments later, Ivy moved on to Kendra. Then Miriam and Vanessa, going into the same trance-like state each time as she set their energies.

Stepping back to Nora, she whispered. "Go ahead and read the energy of each one of them. It's the same as when you and I work together. Trust any image or sensation that comes to you. The only difference is that we often leave a key word with each person to help us remember what we experienced with them. Feel free to do that."

As Nora stepped in front of Jill, Ivy returned to her chair. Watching the dialogue unfold, she was aware that she'd never witnessed Nora's interaction because her eyes had always been closed as a participant.

Nora left a word with each detective.

Jill was strength.

Kendra was light bulb.

Miriam was close.

Vanessa was party.

When Nora stepped away from Vanessa, Ivy spoke up. "Okay everyone. Nora's done. You can sit down."

Nora noticed no one was necessarily returning to the same chair they'd occupied before. She moved directly to *her* chair, unwilling to give up the comfort it offered. She wasn't yet seated when Miriam asked Ivy to tell them about the dialogue.

"I thought that since Nora is making herself vulnerable today, she might feel more open if she felt the energy of each detective's vulnerability."

"Oh, that's good," Jill murmured.

"We get to start the afternoon with our own stuff." Kendra liked that. "Ready to share insights, Nora?"

Nora started with Jill. "I saw a bodybuilder. Does that make sense to you?"

Jill rolled her eyes. "You hit it on the head, Nora. I feel most vulnerable with strong, authoritative people. Especially men."

Nora understood. "I find that a lot with the women I work with. It makes going through divorce especially challenging."

She turned to Kendra. "With you, I saw a light bulb. I'm not sure what that means, but it was very clear."

Kendra didn't have a one-liner to dampen the strong feelings she had around this issue. "It's hard for me to share my ideas, especially suggest an idea. It's a remnant from my childhood with my despicable brother, and not the funny despicable in the movie cartoon."

"But you're learning that we love your ideas, right?" Vanessa asked.

Kendra nodded. Her sass re-emerged. "You guys depend on my ideas."

The laughter around her made Nora feel like part of a team. The companionship among these women was such a different critter than friendship. Its tendrils ran deep where spirit resided, and those tendrils had reached out to her.

Looking at Miriam, Nora wondered how the detective would feel about what she'd seen in her dialogue. "Miriam, I saw you standing inside a circle of people who were holding hands. The strong feeling I got was about *closeness*."

214

Tears appeared, flowed, and were wiped away with Miriam's fingers before the box of kleenex reached her.

The others knew her whole story, but Miriam shared the significant piece with Nora. "My family doesn't believe I was abused by my grandfather. To be a part of the family, I have to pretend my abuse didn't exist. It continues to be a very tender part of my life."

"I'm sorry," Nora responded.

It sounded so small for such a significant revelation, but Miriam leaned into it. It always felt good to have her story validated with concern. "Thank you. I think you might be surprised by how much that means to me and how seldom I've had someone feel that way."

Thinking the session was going in a completely different direction than she'd ever imagined, Nora gathered her thoughts and focused on Vanessa. "Now that I know the set was about vulnerability, I have no idea why I saw a party when I read your energy."

"It's very clear to me," Vanessa answered. "Nothing makes me more ill-at-ease than a situation that encourages unthinking, self-indulgent, spontaneity. For me, a party is a bucking bronco with me strapped to the saddle."

"I'm not a party person either," Nora acknowledged. "I'd rather clean a closet."

Kendra piped up. "Or come to a Saturday afternoon session with a group of women you've never met to uncover secrets you'd rather avoid?"

Nora laughed. Couldn't believe she was laughing. Enjoyed the shared humor. And loved being with these women.

Thirty-Six ~ Nora

Shared laughter flowed seamlessly into mystery. Its light illuminated the murky waters of Nora's past as Vanessa asked a question, "Just to be clear, would you say the significant remnants of your dream were the rug, cement floor, single light bulb, bare walls, and the bed, Nora?"

"Those were the physical clues, but the eerie movement and deathly silence were equally significant to me."

Vanessa thought about these, considering possible sets. "And, from your work with Ivy, we know the intimidating doorway is in the basement of your childhood home."

"Yes. It was the door to the laundry room."

Everyone was conjuring possible dialogues. Jill spoke up. "How old is your inner child, Nora?"

"Ten. You should also know she loves the red bike she just got for her birthday. It's her escape. Her safety."

Nora paused. Turned to Ivy. "I just realized that I've placed this memory in time. It was soon after my tenth birthday when I got that bike. So late summer, maybe?"

Nora's active participation told Ivy this session was going to be powerful. "Keep sharing anything that pops up like that, even if you have to interrupt us. It's likely to happen and will be a great help."

Vanessa stood up. "I've got a dialogue. Nora, have you done any interactive dialogues?"

Unsure, Nora looked to Ivy.

"No you haven't, but it'll be easy for you to pick up," Ivy answered. "Instead of standing still and feeling the energy, you respond to the information you get."

"It's sort of like charades," Jill explained.

Kendra added, "If you see apples being picked from a tree, you open your eyes and start picking the apples. It's still silent, but now you're letting your body express the energy."

Miriam shared another aspect of the interactive dialogue. "When everyone is set, you open your eyes and look at the other energies to see if your energy is drawn to interact with them."

Ivy reassured Nora. "You'll sense that… like you do when you're reading energy. Trust whatever comes to you. If you feel drawn to interact with the other energies in any way, let yourself express what comes to you. Keep silently interacting with whatever is going on around you."

Nora had one question. "How will I know when the dialogue is over?"

Vanessa answered. "Most often it just winds down because nothing new is being revealed. Or the person who set the dialogue might say something when they feel the insight is clear."

"Okay then, I'm glad to give it a try." Nora stood up feeling pretty confident and knowing her best effort would be enough for this group.

Following everyone out to the empty space on the floor, Nora stopped when the others stopped. She followed suit when they became quiet and began taking themselves to their clear state of mind to receive the energy set.

Vanessa gently moved Kendra to the left of everyone. In vibrant stillness she concentrated, leaving Kendra with an energy before moving on to the others. One-by-one, she randomly placed each person around the floor and set them with an energy.

Nora was last. She immediately felt darkness envelop her. Though it felt like the bottom of a deep pond, it didn't trigger panic or even fear. When she opened her eyes, she noticed Vanessa had moved away and now sat on a footstool observing.

Nora looked around. All the detectives moved toward each other and stood still.

Checking in with her own sensations, Nora wondered if she should also be moving but felt no inclination. She remained where she was and continued watching the others. No one moved.

"Okay," Vanessa announced. "We've got a good insight here."

Suddenly, the restrained silence sounded like children during recess. Nora followed the chatter toward the chairs.

"I'm pretty sure I was inanimate," Jill declared.

"Me too," agreed Miriam.

Everyone paid close attention as Vanessa explained. "I wanted to see how the elements of Nora's dream connect to the mystery we're

217

solving. In other words, is the dream calling attention to a memory or is it revealing the memory?"

Vanessa then told everyone the energy they had been holding.

"Jill, you were the rug."

Jill laughed. "That explains my state of mind."

Vanessa continued without interruption. "Miriam was the light bulb. Ivy was the bed. Kendra was the bare walls. All of you were connected."

Nora asked, "What was I?"

"That is the insightful part," enthused Vanessa. "I set you as *Nora's secret*. I saw you as the mystery we're solving today."

Nora got the revelation. The bed, light bulb, rug, and bare walls were in a different location than her mystery. Her dream had brought her attention to the mystery, but it wasn't the mystery.

Nora asked, "Why did my dream have such an effect on me if it's not directly linked?"

Ivy answered. "When we dissociate an experience, it often attaches to surrounding information… the same way a drop of water on fabric leaks into the adjacent areas. For example, you might be making a peanut butter sandwich just before something happens that you dissociate, so the smell, taste, texture, or sight of peanut butter becomes woven into your dissociated state."

Jill put her hand on Nora's knee. "That happened a lot to me. It took a while for me to realize I was more able to remember what was around the traumatizing event than the actual event."

"I have an energy set, and I'll need everyone." Miriam stood up and walked out to the floor. "It's another interactive dialogue."

Once again the women met in the open space and stood ready as they cleared their inner chatter. Like before, Miriam set each detective with an energy.

Sitting down, she watched the dialogue unfold:

Kendra stood still, remaining where she'd been placed.

Ivy went directly to Kendra. Standing right in front of her, she became still.

Vanessa also moved to stand next to Kendra, but she was clearly distraught. Chewing her nails. Looking anxious.

Wide-eyed and pulling on her hair, Jill joined the others. She kept crouching down and looking for something on the floor.

Nora moved away from the action and calmly stood several paces away.

Miriam brought the dialogue to a halt and started unraveling it. "Kendra, everyone gravitated toward you. What did you feel?"

"I just knew that I was immovable. Solid. I didn't really care about the other energies hovering around me. I needed nothing outside myself."

"That makes sense," Miriam said. "You were the laundry room."

Kendra nodded and Miriam turned to Jill. "You kept crouching down. What did that feel like?"

"My heart is still pounding. My scalp tightened until I wanted to pull out my hair. Whatever I was, major distress was in charge."

Jill shook off the energy she was holding. "I felt like I was checking on something, but I couldn't focus because I was so freaked out."

"You were the *panic* Nora's been experiencing."

Vanessa was next. "The minute I moved next to Kendra, I became a bundle of nerves, but getting away didn't seem to be an option."

"Did you notice the other energies around Kendra?" Miriam asked.

"Yes. Both Ivy and Jill/*panic*. Their energies ramped up my distress.

"I set you as Nora's *ten-year-old* in the laundry room.

Miriam moved on to Ivy who stunned everyone. "I was all about curiosity that was squeezed tight and shut down."

Ivy thought about the vivid experience and shared her impression. "I think it was all the more powerful because, for me, curiosity is a playful, creative energy."

"Wow. Like a child kidnapped, then." Miriam said it, but all of them became silent in the revelation.

Nora was the one who spoke first. "What was Ivy's energy?" she asked Miriam.

"I set her as *Nora's secret*."

Miriam explained the dialogue she'd set.

"Since Nora described having a hard time entering the laundry room doorway, I made the assumption that the memory took place in there.

"We now know that *Nora's secret* is connected to curiosity that feels dark. It feels squeezed and catapulted into a vortex where it can't escape.

"We also know the root of her *panic* is from the laundry room. And both *Nora's secret* and *ten-year-old* are present at the time of the panic."

Nora spoke up. "I moved away from Kendra, the *laundry room*. So do I assume I wasn't part of what happened in there?"

"Yes," Miriam agreed. "What did you experience?"

"I wasn't especially affected by the energy you set me with, but did experience the haunting silence from my dream."

Miriam nodded. "I set you as that *silence*. I wanted to see if the feeling originated in the laundry room. We now know it didn't."

At this point, there was a strong inclination to start talking about what had been revealed, but the detectives had learned long ago that it was best to keep gathering information. Like putting a jigsaw puzzle together without a picture to use as a reference, it made sense to keep finding pieces until a picture emerged.

"I have a two part dialogue that might help," Vanessa announced. She nodded to Jill and Ivy, and the three of them remained on the floor while the others sat down.

Very quickly Vanessa set Jill and Ivy with energies and returned to sit with the others to watch.

Feeling lifeless, Jill followed her instincts to lie on the floor.

Crouching next to Jill, Ivy was frantic. She seemed to want to touch Jill but felt blocked and unable to reach her. She wrung her hands. Kept looking at her left forearm. Kept trying to reach Jill.

"Okay." Vanessa called an end to the dialogue. "What did you experience, Jill?"

"Was I a rug again?" she asked. "I was inert and unaware."

Turning to Ivy, Vanessa asked what she experienced.

Still sitting on the floor next to Jill, Ivy looked defeated. "Frantic. Concerned. Worried... helpless. I needed to do something for the energy laying on the floor, but couldn't.

"I felt utterly powerless and at risk, which is exactly the sensation that precedes dissociation. Whatever this is, it's the root of Nora's memory."

With both women sitting on the floor and the others looking on, Vanessa described the dialogue she'd set. "Ivy, you were *Nora in the laundry room*. Just like last time, there is something on the floor connected to her distress."

"Jill, you were that *something on the floor*."

220

"We're one step closer." Kendra's encouragement wove through the different insights each person was processing.

A quiet moment descended.

Nora pictured her little girl trying to take care of something on the laundry room floor. *One step closer but still mysterious,* she mused. And feeling more comfortable than scared about that, an image flashed in her mind's eye. It came and went in half a breath, but it was startlingly vivid.

"Ivy! I think another piece fell into place."

All eyes turned to Nora.

Ivy got up from her chair and walked over to the footstool where Nora's feet were resting. Sitting down on it, she waited.

Nora shared. "It came to me like a lightning bolt. In my childhood home, there was an unfinished room across from the laundry room. The summer between fourth and fifth grade, my dad and uncle started fixing it up. That's where I saw the rolled up rug. I'd totally forgotten that part of the basement until right now."

Nora sat forward, riveted by the breakthrough. "The bare walls, cement floor. The light bulb dangling from the ceiling. They were all part of that room early in the renovation that summer.

"Oh my gosh, I just realized that there was a bed in the corner of that room, pushed against the wall. My friend, Julie, and I liked to play there that summer. We used the bed for a trampoline."

Nora covered her face with her hands. Looked through fingers spread across her eyes. Looked for more information while everyone sat silently.

She leaned back and ran her hands through her hair. "It's all there."

Looking around at the quiet, caring faces, Nora saw smiles, encouragement, and eyes that believed. "You were right when you said the dream was about taking me to my memory. I can feel myself inching closer. I can feel that to the tips of my toes."

Thirty-Seven ~ Nora

Watching Miriam take notes, Jill let her thoughts drift. Mesmerizing movement was her portal to intuitive hits. As the others discussed whether or not there was value in pursuing more dialogues around Nora's dream, a very different path flashed in her mind's eye.

She got up and walked out to the floor. "I have something I'd like to try."

Miriam was glad. She thought they did their best work when they called on their sixth sense to guide them. Each of them connected to that inner knowing differently, but it seemed to be activated when they kept the dialogues flowing.

With the grace of a swan, Miriam joined Jill and was followed by everyone else.

Jill spoke to Nora. "This kind of dialogue is like the one Ivy used when she had you read our vulnerabilities, where you felt each energy. The only difference is you'll be leaving the room while we discuss which energy each of us will hold."

Kendra whispered loudly, "This is when we use the bathroom or check out Vanessa's snacks."

Nora headed for the kitchen, leaving the detectives huddled together as she wondered what Jill might have in mind.

The revelation about the room with the rug had left her feeling free of shackles that had chained her to constant anxiety since the dream. Knowing the elements of her dream were periphery and not the focus was like turning on the lights in a Halloween haunted house. What had been frightening in the darkness of the unknown had been revealed as harmless.

Entering the kitchen, Nora saw Vanessa's box of goodies sitting on the table. Her usual reserve would never have allowed her to snoop through the box. Today, curiosity nudged, and she felt free to respond.

Leaning over the box, she pulled out a baggie filled with brownies and placed it on the table. A bag of potato chips and a covered dish with caramel-coated apple slices followed. Another baggie filled with sliced, ready-to-eat veggies was on its way out of the box when she heard Jill call her name.

Nora giggled at herself. The bold curiosity of diving into Vanessa's box was so unlike her. Curiosity had caught Nora's attention. Something was shifting here, something that felt like a sigh.

She noted the change as she walked out to the studio where the detectives where standing in a large circle. Everyone, but Jill, had their eyes closed and was standing in a trance-like state.

Jill approached Nora and quietly explained the dialogue. "I wanted to check out your state of mind in the laundry room before you panicked about the *something on the floor*. Each of us will be holding the energy of a possible feeling you had as you walked through the doorway... before the trauma that triggered your dissociation.

"After you've read the energy, notice if it felt like your experience that day. If you sense the answer is yes, have that person step forward. And remember to leave a key word with everyone, in case you lose track of energies."

Nora nodded and Jill took a place in the large, loose circle.

Choosing to start with Ivy, Nora felt her scalp tighten as soon as she stood within inches of Ivy. She stepped away, whispering, "Scalp."

Kendra's energy made Nora feel like her life force was being leeched. Her body felt airy. She quietly said, "Life force", and stepped away. Clearing that energy sensation out of her body by waving her hands like she was shooing flies away, Nora moved on to Vanessa.

Vanessa's energy made Nora feel like a soldier on a march. "Soldier," she said as she stepped away.

With Miriam, Nora saw Sherlock Holmes. Smiling, she whispered, "Holmes."

Jill's energy was like swinging in a hammock. Nora said, "Hammock" and gently pulled her forward.

Walking into the center of the circle, Nora let them know she was done.

Everyone opened their eyes and noticed Jill was the only energy Nora had asked to step forward... the only one Nora associated with entering the laundry room.

Starting with Ivy, Nora began revealing the dialogue. She didn't need the key word to remember. "Your energy made my scalp tighten."

"I was panic," Ivy said. "You entering the laundry room in a state of panic."

"Nope. That didn't ring true, at all. I got a really good read on that set, but it's not connected." Nora was surprised because going through the doorway had been so terrifying in her memory work with Ivy. *So panic came after I walked in*, she thought as she turned her attention to Kendra.

"You made me feel like my life-force was being pulled out of me. Your energy was definitely not what I was feeling when I walked through the door."

Kendra shared what she was holding. "I was the loneliness you talked about earlier. So you can assume you didn't feel lonely before your memory."

Nodding, Nora looked at Vanessa. "With you, I felt like a soldier marching off to war. Sort of powerful. Knew what I was doing."

Vanessa smiled. "I was holding the energy of you walking into the laundry room with something you needed to get done. Maybe fold the clothes or get something that was stored there."

"That's totally logical, but not what was happening that day." Nora felt confident about that conclusion.

Moving on to Miriam, she said, "I saw Sherlock Holmes when I felt your energy. His hat, pipe and cape. Ready to investigate."

"I held the energy of you feeling vigilant," Miriam responded. "We wanted to see if you felt on-guard as you stepped into the laundry room."

"All of these surprise me," Nora said to no one in particular. "They sound so reasonable. I would've guessed anyone of them could explain how I felt walking through the doorway that day." She turned her attention to the one energy that had felt like her truth when she walked into the laundry room.

"Jill, your energy made me think of lying in a hammock. Just cruising on a summer day."

Reaching out to give Nora a quick hug, Jill shared, "I was you hanging out. I focused on you being in your summer-time, play-time groove."

Nora was stunned. "I would have never guessed that." Yet, she remembered how strongly she'd felt about Jill's energy being part of her ten-year-old's experience. "So, I was coming in from the garage, feeling pretty casual, and something in the laundry room caught my attention?"

Ivy spoke up. "That fits what we know. During your last session with me, you talked about entering the doorway with the stairs in front of you."

Vanessa had a possible dialogue shaping up in her mind's eye. "Knowing everything was okay as you entered the laundry room, do you think you could walk into a dialogue that includes that room, Nora?"

A jolt of resistance caught Nora's breath, but the anticipation in Vanessa's eyes filled her with courage. "Yes. What do you want me to do?"

"Jill and I will stand a couple of feet apart. We'll be the energy of the doorway when you walked in as a ten-year-old feeling like you were just hanging out. Once you walk between us, Miriam will be holding an energy I'm going to set. I want you to go through the 'doorway' and read her energy. See if it was present when your ten-year-old walked in."

"I can do that." Nora wanted to believe she could.

She waited while Vanessa set Miriam and then aligned herself with Jill to create the energy-doorway.

It felt weird to look at Vanessa and Jill and feel scared, but Nora had to talk herself into moving forward. As she got close, she realized their energy felt neutral. She took a deep breath and walked between them.

Miriam's energy felt immediately uncomfortable, but Nora reached out and laid her hands on Miriam's shoulders. Everything shifted.

Nora *knew* she was in the barn, but she could also see the laundry room of her childhood like it was a Norman Rockwell painting. Real and vivid, the washer and dryer stood in front of her, the counter her dad had built was to the left of the dryer. Deep shelves, mounted over the counter caught her attention.

Nora's hands involuntarily jerked up in front of her as though warding off a blow, but it wasn't a fist that she was avoiding. It was the pet carrier sitting on the shelf above the counter.

She froze.

Everything was wrong about that carrier being there. Nora knew it had never been there before. Her curiosity was calling her like a siren's song.

Smooth, gentle circles moving between Nora's shoulders brought her focus back to the barn. Vanessa's voice revived Nora's lungs and her breathing returned.

"Do you want to step out of this dialogue?" Vanessa asked.

Nora nodded, stepped back, and sat on the floor.

Without hesitation, everyone joined her. They were settling in when Nora started sharing what had happened. The image felt plastered to the insides of her eyelids.

"The minute I touched Miriam, I saw the entire laundry room in stark detail. There was nothing present that would scare me, but there was something out of place.

"My mom was beyond organized. I could walk into that room and grab something off the shelf in the dark. That pet carrier did not belong there. I doubt if it was there when I left the house to ride bikes with my friend." Nora shivered. "My heart is pounding just thinking about it."

Nora kept playing that image over and over in her mind. Everything about the carrier was outside normal. Nothing made sense. Why was it there? Who put it there?

Vanessa spoke directly to Nora. "I set Miriam with the energy of *Nora's scar/Nora's wound*. That's what triggered your response."

Nora's right hand reached for the spot on her left arm.

All eyes went to her inner arm, just below Nora's elbow.

Looking down at the faint scar, Nora asked, "So, you think the pet carrier and my scar are connected?"

Vanessa nodded. Nora saw the consensus among the women.

"Should we set up a dialogue to learn more?" Jill threw out the idea.

"No!" Nora was clear, though she didn't know why. She just knew she wasn't ready to know any more about the pet carrier. Not today.

Thirty-Eight ~ Nora

It was time to bring the Saturday session to a close, but Ivy had two burning questions she hoped to explore. "I have two quick sets that have nothing to do with the pet carrier," she said to Nora. "Would you feel okay about watching?"

"Sure. Should I sit here or move out of the way?"

"Whatever feels best for you," Ivy answered.

"I'll watch from the chairs."

Kendra jumped up. "Wait a minute, while you're gathering your thoughts and getting settled, I'm going to grab Vanessa's box of goodies and bring them out."

That brought a smile to Nora.

It made Vanessa happy, though she rolled her eyes. "Bring napkins," she advised as Kendra headed for the kitchen.

A big smile on her face, Kendra came back with the box and napkins and set them on a footstool. Everyone dug in, found what most pleased them, and the next dialogue began.

Nora nibbled on a brownie while she and Miriam watched Ivy set Jill, Vanessa, and Kendra.

Having set the energies, Ivy stepped away to watch.

Kendra glared at the two energies near her and seemed to be giving them a stern lecture… shaking her finger… expressing disdain. She was in charge but not threatening. Vanessa looked away. Jill bowed her head.

When nothing more transpired, Ivy stopped the dialogue and told everyone what she'd set. "I wanted to see what happened among Nora's ten-year-old, her mom, and her dad after she experienced the pet carrier."

Focusing on Kendra, she asked her to share her experience. "Oh, I was so in charge. I was the guy with all the answers."

"You were Nora's *dad*."

Ivy asked Vanessa to share. She had looked away.

"I knew Kendra's energy was in charge, and I felt like I'd heard it all before. I had no intention of engaging. Knew any challenge would blow things up."

Ivy nodded, "You were *Nora's mom* after the trauma."

She moved on to Jill. "How about you? You bowed your head."

"I felt defeated. Kendra's ranting energy deflated me. It felt like she was letting the air out of my balloon and I was all alone."

"You were *Nora's ten-year-old.*"

Ivy looked over at Nora and shared her impression of the dialogue. "From the interaction we just saw, it seems like your ten-year-old's profound loneliness stemmed from your dad's response. Maybe your mom's non-response. Does that resonate with you?"

"Definitely. I felt the loneliness just watching Jill in the dialogue. It seemed to seep out of her. I knew she was me the minute she bowed her head."

Ivy nodded. "Do we have time for another quick one or should we call it a day?"

Everyone was game, including Nora.

Ivy chose Miriam and Jill for the final dialogue. When they were set, Ivy stood by as it unfolded.

She watched as Miriam and Jill immediately turned to each other and appeared to be in an argument. Neither was more powerful. Neither was winning the argument or backing off.

Ivy stepped forward, bringing the dialogue to a close. Turning to Nora she explained, "This is about your dad and uncle. I kept getting a feeling they were connected to your laundry room memory. I wanted to see what might happen."

Turning to Miriam, she asked for her feedback.

"I was pissed off and self-righteous. Didn't mind having a good dogfight at all."

"You were *Nora's dad.* And I placed you *soon after Nora's trauma.*"

"How about you, Jill? What did you experience?"

"Pretty much what Miriam said except I also felt like the other energy wasn't going to roll over me this time. I wasn't going to back down."

Ivy nodded. "You were *Nora's uncle*… placed in the same time frame… *soon after Nora's trauma.*"

Nora picked at the brownie crumbs on her napkin. "Looks like Uncle Neil and Dad had a fight soon after I found the pet carrier."

"Do you feel like you've answered some questions today?" Jill wanted to know.

"Definitely. I'll be going home with a much lighter load."

Nora couldn't wait to share with Luke.

She couldn't wait to fall asleep without her dream hovering like a storm cloud. Now that she knew it was only there to take her to healing, the dream didn't feel like a specter.

The carrier might keep her awake, but that felt different. She'd learned enough to see it as a challenge rather than a marauder of her peace of mind.

With a brownie nestled in a napkin on her lap, Nora reviewed how this session had felt.

"I have to admit... I resisted having this time with all of you, right up to the moment I walked through the door this afternoon. But, it turns out, you guys aren't half as scary as I thought you might be."

Everyone laughed.

"Today we discovered that I walked into the laundry room feeling comfortable, just hanging out.

"I know something was on the floor that was deeply distressing to my ten-year-old. She wanted to touch it but couldn't.

"I know my scar is connected to a pet carrier.

"We know I do not want to know anything more about that pet carrier today!

"And this is a big one: you helped me recognize that my dream came to me as a messenger, not a boogeyman. It came to insist I heal my childhood wounds."

Nora paused, realizing her time with the detectives had been a big step forward. "I've hated every step of my healing journey, but, as Ivy predicted during my first session, personal treasures keep coming to me as I look for the answer about my dream. I love the changes in my life.

"Luke and I've discovered a much deeper and joyful intimacy. I've learned how to relax and play drums. Today, another gift showed up... I was reunited with my curiosity... with laughter!

"And, oh my goodness, I don't want to forget the way my healing brought this time with you. Before now, I wouldn't have opened myself up to others. Being with you guys has taught me how to trust and lean into support from other women."

Every head nodded. Every woman knew what she meant. Life felt much different when childhood wounds were no longer calling the shots.

Nora picked up her brownie. Broke off a corner and let her taste buds have a feast. She liked what had happened today. In every way, she felt herself part of something magical.

Thirty-Nine ~ Vickie

Ivy dashed through the rain, running up the steps of the coffee shop. Sitting at the edge of town, Coffee Heaven was painted bright blue. Its yellow trim and fuchsia door clashed in a way that warmed the hearts of the locals.

Wet umbrellas littered the large front porch. Like dogs patiently waiting for their owners, they came in all sizes and colors.

Slipping inside the door, Ivy glanced around. Smiling and nodding to those she knew, she looked for Vickie, a young woman she'd never met.

Self-described as 'wearing short, red hair that never needed a comb and carrying a Road Runner backpack', she assumed Vickie would stand out.

Ivy had said she'd be in purple, and she was... all the way down to her shoes.

They spotted each other at the same moment, and Ivy weaved through tables to the far corner. The hum of the shop was as delicious as the coffee.

Vickie's smile could be used to light up a gymnasium. "I tried to pick a cozy spot. Is this good for you?"

"Perfect," Ivy said as she pulled off her wet raincoat and placed it on the back of the chair across the table from Vickie. "Thank you for snagging a spot for us. Looks like everyone's escaping the rain."

"I waited to order. What can I get you?" Vickie asked.

Ivy opened her purse. "Tell them it's for Ivy, and they'll know."

Vickie shook her head. "No, no. I've got this. I appreciate you taking the time to see if you and your detectives will work with my mystery."

"Thank you. I'm anxious to hear what's prompted you to seek us out."

Vickie navigated the clutter of tables and chairs like a lioness moving through the jungle. So far, everything about her indicated she would be a delightful client.

Sitting down with their coffees, Vickie handed Ivy her cup and kept her own in hand as she leaned forward. "I just want you to know I'm totally good with the work you do. No convincing needed here. If you guys will take me, I'll be over the moon."

Without taking a breath, Vickie added, "I wanted to meet with you because I thought you'd want to get a feel for me before you decided whether or not to open up a space in your schedule. Know what I mean?"

Ivy's smile turned into a light chuckle. She loved Vickie's voice. Her words ran together in a deep tone. *A Lucille Ball voice*, thought Ivy as she responded. "I'm sure we'd like working with you. I could tell that by our text exchange. For me, today is more about getting a feel for your mystery."

"That's the easy part." Vickie jumped in without hesitation. "It's about my grandpa. He's been my favorite person in the whole world since I can remember. Then, last February, he died unexpectedly."

Vickie's hands gripped her cup.

"I was in Bali at the time, having a great vacation, but on the day he passed, I could feel it. I think you probably know what I mean. It wasn't like he invaded my body or anything. I just felt flat that day. Uneasy, like I'd forgotten something. Then I got the call from Mom."

"Is he your mom's dad?" Ivy asked.

"Yeah, but they had a kind of on-and-off relationship. Nothing big deal, but friction that showed up sometimes. That's all history and has nothing to do with why I want your help.

"I want to work with you and the detectives because I feel like he's trying to contact me. I'm positive that he wants to tell me something.

"Do you think that's possible? Everyone tells me I'm just grieving, but I think it's more than that."

Vickie waited for a response. Relief soared through her as she listened to Ivy.

"I honor you trusting what you know. I have no doubt he's reaching out to you."

Vickie leaned in closer to Ivy, almost conspiratorially and asked, "Have you worked with people on the other side?"

"Yes, we have. When you work with energy, it feels the same whether you're working with the present or past because there's no dimension of time in the energy field."

Vickie's eyes lit up. "Oh my gosh… that's just what I hoped to hear. When can I start?"

Forty ~ Nora

The intense work on her dream, and seeing it so clearly through the dialogues with the energy detectives, had given Nora bone-deep relief. It felt over. Done.

Now she wanted that feeling around the pet carrier.

The image still made Nora feel like she was pinned to a stake while cannibals boiled the water and danced around her. She knew the key to letting go of that feeling was re-experiencing her ten-year-old's trauma. That's what would bring her dissociated memory out of the shadows and into the light.

Feeling more ready than she'd imagined possible, Nora walked into the barn for a personal session with Ivy.

Hearing the door open, Ivy turned from her view of the meadow. She walked over to greet Nora, who shared what had been on her mind during the drive to the barn. "I had thought my worst fear about working with the detectives would have been people in the community knowing my stuff, my very personal stuff. But it just occurred to me... I dreaded their sympathy. I didn't want someone feeling bad, sad, or sorry for me."

That didn't surprise Ivy. "I could have told you there would be no sympathy. But empathy? There was sure to be empathy."

"What's the difference?"

Sitting down with Nora, Ivy shared her thoughts on the two. "Sympathy is a victim energy. With all good intention, it consoles and pities. It feels diminishing.

"Empathy is a companion energy. It expresses recognition and compassion for a common experience. It honors our spirit."

"I did experience empathy," Nora realized. "Nothing was said directly, it was just there and felt bonding. That might have been as powerful as the dialogues."

Ivy pulled off her shoes and tucked her feet under her. "It does feel healing and powerful to know you're not alone. I think that's one of the tragedies of social silence and family secrets. It leaves untold numbers feeling alone with emotional wounds that are common."

"Like me not wanting anyone to know my life had veered off track." Nora saw it so clearly now.

Ivy brushed her hair off her forehead. "Are you telling me your time with the detectives was a good step in your healing… that it didn't leave you feeling exposed?"

"Absolutely. Instead of coming away feeling naked, I was given an empowering cape to wear. I became part of something bigger than my fears. Now I'm ready to find out about that pet carrier and what was on the floor. I want to know what happened that day."

Getting up from her chair, Ivy walked over to get a blanket and pillow. "I have no doubt we can make that happen."

With the pillow behind her neck, the blanket snuggled across the front of her, and the chair reclined, Nora was quickly taken to a state of deep relaxation. Her ten-year-old showed up at the retreat. She was as ready as Nora to go into the memory so it could be released.

When Nora was deeply relaxed, Ivy started in the laundry room, but didn't focus on the pet carrier or the *something on the floor* that had become such an alarming part of the dialogues.

"Nora, feel yourself leaving the laundry room, leaving the pet carrier and what's on the floor. Feel yourself escaping the panic you experienced. Tell me what happens."

Her face scrunching, her eyebrows pulling together, Nora spoke up. She sounded like she'd been running. "My arm's bleeding. Where's mom?"

"Where are you, Nora?"

Grabbing her left arm, Nora moved her head as though looking around. "Going up the stairs. Where's mom. She's always home."

She started panting. Ivy caught her attention with another question. "Tell me what's happening?"

"Up the stairs. No one's here. Why? Not in the living room. It's never this quiet."

Ivy gave Nora a moment to travel in her memory. The panting continued. She continued to hold her arm. Her facial muscles worked frantically reflecting her challenge.

She's in panic, but not stuck there, Ivy thought as she monitored Nora's body language.

"Band-aid," Nora exclaimed.

Ivy waited a few moments. Nora's expression quickly changed. She looked like a squirrel pausing as if gathering nuts checking movement or noise. "What's happening, Nora?"

Frowning, Nora answered. "My dad and uncle are downstairs. Yelling at each other."

"Down in the basement?" Ivy asked.

"No. In the living room or kitchen. Can't tell. I'm in the upstairs bathroom."

"What are they yelling about?"

Nora didn't move.

Ivy waited.

Whispering, Nora said, "Uncle Neil said dad should break up with her... not give her daughter a birthday present. Said he's had enough, and he's not going to be part of my dad's shenanigans any more. He used a naughty word. Said he's done."

Ivy waited to see if Nora recalled more of the fight.

"Dad's swearing. Told Uncle Neil to get out of the way. He sent Mom on an errand and doesn't have time for this."

"Does their yelling upset you?" Ivy prodded.

Slowly nodding her head yes, expressing a sadness that slipped into Ivy's heart, Nora started crying. "They're downstairs. I can't go down." She clasped her hands over her ears as though shutting out the sound. The tears flowed. "I need to go down."

"Why do you need to go down?"

The plaintive sound spoke of pain even more than Nora's tears. "I need to go down to the laundry room."

Sensing Nora was stuck in the high emotion of the moment, Ivy nudged her toward a different focus. "The fighting's stopped. Listen. There's no more fighting. You can go down now."

Nora took a deep breath. Letting the tears hang on her cheeks, her entire body went into tension. "Silence." The stillness was a void warning her to stay.

"Does the silence upset you?"

The intensity of Nora's expression was palpable. She would have looked the same if she'd woken up and heard her bedroom door opening when she thought she was home alone.

Assuming Nora was going downstairs to check the pet carrier, Ivy watched for any signs that she needed to intervene. Nora appeared determined, but not in panic. Ivy waited until the tension shifted. "What's happening Nora?"

"It's gone!" She tipped her head, clearly confused.

"What's gone?" Ivy asked.

"The pet carrier's gone."

Ivy nudged Nora with questions, but, once again, she was caught up in the emotion she was experiencing. Shock, disbelief, and confusion held her captive.

Remembering one of the last dialogues during the session with the detectives, Ivy moved Nora's attention to her dad and mom. "You're no longer in the laundry room. Now it's later, and you're with your mom and dad. You and your mom are listening. Your dad's talking. Tell me what's happening."

Nora's expression became flat. Withdrawn. Her voice was lifeless. "We're at the dining room table. Dinner time. I asked where the pet carrier went. My dad's mad. He's waving his fork in the air, yelling."

"Why is he mad?"

"Girls shouldn't make up stories to get attention. We don't have a pet carrier. Never did." Her face was so washed out it looked bleached.

"How does his lecture make you feel?" Ivy asked.

Nora seemed distant as she said, "I'm all alone." There were no tears just hollow energy clinging to her.

Ivy's voice was firm, "But you know different, don't you? You saw a pet carrier in the laundry room."

Ivy saw a slight nod. A brow barely raised. "Nora, I'm going to count one to three. On the count of three, go to the laundry room where you'll see the pet carrier.

"One. Two. Three."

If Nora's eyes had been open, they would have been bulging and unblinking. "It's there. On the shelf just where I saw it before."

"Move closer to it, Nora. Feel its energy. Know your truth," Ivy encouraged.

Nora shook her head. Distress was taking over. "No. I can't do it."

Ivy took another path. "Stand there and look at it. Remember the feeling of *just hanging out* as you walked through the doorway. Feel that easy curiosity. Tell me what you see when you look at the carrier."

Taking a deep breath, Nora's body relaxed. Became still. "There's a bow on it. I see a bow… and a big tag."

"Can you step a little closer and see what's on the tag?"

Nodding her head, Nora took a moment. *"Happy Birthday, Frannie.* And there's something inside."

"Step closer. Can you see what's inside?"

"No. It's up too high. Second shelf up." A moment later Nora announced, "I'm climbing up on the counter. I want to see what's inside."

Ivy waited.

Nora exclaimed, "It's a puppy! But I can't pet it. Can't get my hand inside the carrier."

Ivy watched as Nora's face transformed from joy to angst. Frantically squeezing her hands into fists, she exhaled. "I pulled it too far forward, and it came off the shelf topsy-turvy. I just wanted to look."

"What's happening, Nora?"

"I'm on the floor. My arm's bleeding. Oh no! I think the puppy's hurt or dead."

Nora started hyperventilating.

Ivy placed her hand on Nora's shoulder. "You're okay. Where's the puppy?"

"On the floor. In the carrier. I think it's dead. My arm's bleeding."

"What's making you feel most disempowered in this moment, Nora?"

There was a pause. Nora's breathing came down a notch from frantic. "I can't touch the puppy. Can't reach into the carrier and touch it… let it know I'm sorry."

Powerless grief swirled around Nora. It was thick, heavy cement that had hardened the ten-year-old's fragile need for loving touch.

Ivy lightly massaged Nora's arm. "You're still carrying grief. What does that grief feel like to your little girl?"

"Like being lost in a thick fog."

Ivy leaned in. "Nora, I want your adult-self to go into the laundry room. Go to your little girl with all the ways you feel powerful and strong. She's feeling lost in guilt and grief. I want you to lead her out of the fog. Can you see her?"

Nora nodded.

Ivy urged, "Reach out and take her hand. Talk to her. Tell her that her curiosity was natural. Her intention was good. That she gets to let her heart lead her. Nod when you're done finding the words that will release her grief and guilt."

Ivy sat up and stretched her back. Glanced at the clock, not having any idea how long they'd been traveling in Nora's inner world. They still had plenty of time.

When Nora nodded her head, Ivy asked if she and her ten-year-old felt complete.

"Yes. Can I bring the carrier back to the retreat?" she asked.

"Of course."

"We're going to get the puppy out of the cage and hold it, then bury it. My little girl wants to plant roses around it."

Ivy choked up. "What a beautiful idea. We don't have to bring the carrier. We'll leave it in the laundry room, but bring the puppy. Does that sound good?"

Nora nodded.

Ivy counted and took all three back to Nora's retreat. "One. Two. Three.

"Take your time to honor the puppy and let me know when you feel done. Be aware of the healing that's happening right now."

Five minutes passed before Nora said, "I'm ready to come out. My little girl is going to stay at the retreat and play with my other little girls."

Ivy counted down.

Nora opened her eyes.

They looked at each other, a million unspoken words coalescing into tangible fondness. They had faced the shadows together. They had shared the belief that Nora's truth would bring light into her life.

Nora pushed on the lever at the side of the reclining chair. She pulled the pillow out from behind her neck. "I don't get why the death of a puppy could have felt so big. I know it's sad, but to have it turn my life upside-down. Freak me out? How can that be?"

Ivy took the pillow from Nora and set it on her lap. "When you say that, you're looking at what happened from your adult point of view. Now that you've recovered pieces of your memory, go back to that day and tell me the story from your child's perspective."

Nora placed her deep relaxation kleenex on the end table. She looked down at her hands as she pulled together what she'd been learning that day. "I came home from a bike ride and walked into the basement from the garage, feeling like I was just hanging out.

"I noticed the area on the left where my dad and uncle were remodeling. Nothing out of the ordinary there, but when I glanced over at the laundry room entry, something on the shelves caught my eye. It made me curious.

"From the floor, I could tell it was a pet carrier with a ribbon on it and a tag… Ivy! I forgot I saw the name on the tag. How's that for a clue?

"You can bet your bottom dollar I'm going to have my receptionist check into that. There couldn't have been that many Frannies in town back then."

Nora was ignited. Sally was just the person to track that down. If anyone could find a connection, she was the bloodhound who would do it.

Nora refocused on the story. "I saw the carrier and jumped up on the counter to get a better look. When I realized it was a puppy, I wanted to pet it.

"The carrier was heavier than I thought, and it fell from the shelf onto the floor. As that happened, my arm was sliced by a metal corner and the puppy was hurt."

Nora looked into Ivy's eyes. "The puppy looked dead." Looking beyond Ivy, toward the kitchen door, Nora took a deep breath.

"I left the puppy in the carrier on the floor and went to the upstairs bathroom to get a band-aid for my bleeding arm.

"The house was eerily silent because my mom wasn't around, and she was always home. She never left without telling me. It was like it was my house, but not my home.

"While I was putting on my band-aid, I suddenly heard my dad and uncle yelling." Nora paused. "Uncle Neil was mad."

"I couldn't go downstairs. Mom says 'stay away when dad and Uncle Neil are fighting', so I waited until everything was quiet. Then I went back downstairs to the laundry room. I don't know what I thought I was going to do, but I felt compelled to go back to the puppy.

"But the carrier was gone. The laundry room looked completely normal." Her skin getting clammy, Nora felt the same chilling confusion she'd experienced in her dream when everything started moving. She took a deep breath. Rubbed her hands on her pants and continued.

"At dinner, I asked my parents where the pet carrier went. My mom seemed clueless." Nora stopped. "I think it's important to note that she didn't seem surprised by the question. I may have to ask her about that someday… knowing full well I'll never get a straight answer or know the full story.

"Anyway, that's when my dad went off on how I shouldn't make up stories to get attention."

"Do you see why you dissociated this memory?" Ivy asked and then answered. "You felt overwhelmed and helpless:

"… when you saw the blood on your arm

"… when you saw the puppy you couldn't save

"… when you felt caught upstairs and needed to be with the puppy

"… when you went to the laundry room and the puppy had disappeared

"… when your dad denied the existence of the carrier and called you a liar."

Seeing Nora was still confused, Ivy summarized. "Up until the time you went back to the laundry room and everything was back to normal, you were a little girl having a horrific experience. You were traumatized.

"When the evidence was eliminated and then your reality verbally denied, your dissociation was triggered."

Nora added, "Even when I showed him my band-aid, he told me to quit making up stories."

Ivy nodded. "You thought you'd killed a puppy and couldn't go to your parents for support. At any age, the accidental death of a puppy feels huge. At ten-years old, it's life-changing, especially when your mom and dad disregarded your feelings and essentially you.

"Dissociation came to your rescue. It took your trauma to the primitive part of your brain, so you didn't have to live the conflict. It stored the incomprehensible until you were ready to understand and release what had happened."

Nora thought about d*issociation coming to her rescue.* She recalled sitting on the floor of her shower the morning after her dream. Never could she have imagined she was about to uncover a summer afternoon held deeply within her awareness. She couldn't have comprehended the way her mind~body~spirit responded to protect her when she was a child. And, most certainly, Nora wouldn't have believed she would journey with energy detectives to find the answers that would set her free.

Forty-One ~ Nora

The full moon was leaving splashes of light throughout her living room as Ivy greeted the day just hours after midnight. It was the perfect time for catching up on emails. Her dog, Spirit, was the perfect companion.

She was refilling her thermos with more coffee when she heard a text coming in on her phone. Who, she wondered, was sharing the other side of night with her?

It was, surprisingly, Nora.

Meant to text you last night, but Luke took me out to celebrate. Sally found Frannie!!!!!

We've talked. We're both thrilled. What a connection. Lives in San Francisco. Meeting for lunch on Saturday. Seems we're half sisters! She's three years younger.

Honestly, Ivy, I'm not an exclamation point kind of woman, but can you believe it?!!!!

And this… you've got to share all of this with the other detectives. On Frannie's seventh birthday, she got a golden retriever puppy. Maybe the puppy didn't die after all. Either way, I planted a rose bush in my yard to honor it.

Got up early to check on golden retriever puppies in the area. Found them just blocks away. Guess what Luke and I are doing right after breakfast?!!!

Love to all of you!!

~ ~ ~

If you want to join a workshop and learn how to be an energy detective, go to unwindexplore.com and click on the tab:
Ignite Energy Insights
Or write to me: jeanne@gotospirit.com

You'll be my hero if you leave a review
on Amazon or Goodreads!
Help other readers find this adventure
with the energy detectives ~ Jeanne

Join the energy detectives as they unravel more mysteries
in the novel, "Beyond the Obvious".   (Spring 2020)
Share the adventure as they seek answers for Vickie and others.
Who knows…
maybe a life mystery will walk through the door at Ivy's barn,
and it will be very similar to yours.

If you want a self-help book about using energy, read my easy-to-use guide: "Ignite Changes Using Energy"

Write and tell me what you think about Ivy and the energy
detectives. I love hearing from readers!
jeanne@gotospirit.com

Check out "Insights" on GoToSpirit.com

Join me on Facebook:

Go To Spirit with Jeanne McElvaney ~ energy insights

Jeanne McElvaney ~ insights and support for survivors of
childhood abuse

BOLD Insights ~ podcasts for a different perspective on everyday
thoughts, feelings, beliefs

Appreciations

Linda McClellan is like sunshine. She's a joyful editor who is passionate about nailing down the details while celebrating my voice.

My readers felt like cinnamon rolls on Christmas morning. Absolutely essential.

Nat McElvaney was better than a foot massage… patiently empowering me through every technology pain.

Joel McElvaney saw possibilities during a conversation and ignited the magic for this novel.

Family and friends who brought heart, turquoise, and encouragement to this writing picnic.

About the Author

An author and energy guide, Jeanne has traveled many miles with those who want to explore and express their authentic selves. Her novels celebrate personal empowerment.

She lives in North Central Washington where she has one foot in the unfolding world of family and friends and the other foot in the magical realities of quantum energy. Most days, Jeanne is kidnapped by emerging characters in her novels.